The Maker's Medicine Girl

The Flintlock Sagas
Book 2

The Maker's Medicine Girl

WRITTEN BY

ALAN W. HARRIS

~ ~ ~ † ~ ~ ~

Fruitful Tree Publishing
Lexington, South Carolina 29072

This book is published by:

Fruitful Tree Publishing

509 Aspen Glade Court

Lexington, South Carolina 29072

www.StoriesChangeHearts.com

ISBN-13: 978-1-7341845-2-5

1. Harris, Alan W. 2. Christian 3. Historical 4. Adventure 5. Family 6. Teen 7. Young Adult 8. Character Development 9. Faith Building 10. Nature Tales 11. Inspirational 12. Flintlock 13.Girls Adventure

This book is lovingly dedicated to all of
the precious females in my life:

Valerie,

Lisa,

Abby,

Natalie,

Juliana,

Sonora,

Honnah,

Mia,

Adaline,

Linnaea,

Luciana,

Katherine,

and any future daughters-in-law,
granddaughters, and great-
granddaughters the Lord may bless our
family with.

CONTENTS

PREFACE

I love writing adventure stories—the more exciting the better! Because of that, it is not surprising that my books appeal mostly to boys. As I considered my own family, I realized that I have one wife, three daughters, one daughter-in-law (so far), and seven granddaughters (so far). My girls needed a story.

I was actually convicted to write this one as I was writing the first book in the *The Flintlock Sagas*: *The Young Frontiersman*. I was anxious to get to *The Maker's Medicine Girl*, but because I wanted it to be in *The Flintlock Sagas series,* I had to complete the first book before I could turn my attention to the second.

I must admit that this was a real a challenge from the start. I wasn't totally convinced that I could write a story that would appeal to girls. I was afraid too much of my 'guyness' would come out. I always pray over my writing and ask for God's direction, but I believe I prayed over this book significantly more than over the others. The end result is that I am very pleased with how it turned out. Granted, it's a guy saying that, but I think the girls who honor me by reading it will be pleased as well.

I was both surprised and excited at how Jesus chose to reveal Himself in the story, and those quickly became my favorite parts to write. As I typed, I found myself thinking more and more about being with Jesus. I'll have to admit that I now look at heaven differently after writing those chapters.

The story takes place in the Kentucky territory during the late 1770's. It follows the heartbreaking experiences of young Remember Warren as she loses her family and is enslaved by a ruthless, renegade trapper who lives with the Shawnee. At first Ember is consumed with bitterness and anger, and her life goes from bad to worse until Jesus enters the pit of darkness where she exists. Not only does the Lord have a powerful effect on her life, but Christ even begins to use the girl to bring light to others in the darkness.

Because it's me writing this, you have to know that there is a lot of adventure, as well as some very sweet and wonderful revelations of the beauty of the Lord. It will remain to be seen how you, my readers, will feel about this book, but I am more excited about this story than any one I have ever written.

I want to thank and praise the Lord, Who led me both to write the book and inspired so much of its content. I also want to thank my wife, Valerie, for all her invaluable help, both with advice, spiritual council, and with the incredible task of editing. "Once again, Sweetheart, YOU ARE AMAZING!"

Obviously, I am hoping that girls of all ages will delight in and be blessed by this story. I also hope that the overall story is exciting enough that boys will enjoy it as well.

May each of you who experience *The Maker's Medicine Girl* be drawn closer to God and fall more in love with the Lord Jesus Christ. That certainly happened to me as I wrote it. To God the Father and His wonderful Son, Jesus Christ our Lord and King, be praise and glory and honor both now and forever, amen!

In His Service,

Alan W. Harris

West Columbia, South Carolina
March 30, 2020

Chapter One

CRUSHED

She had stopped crying over an hour ago, but her cheeks still burned from the salt of dried tears. Her soul felt completely crushed from the living nightmare she was being forced to endure. In spite of the overwhelming agony in her heart, she was too emotionally spent to sob again.

Sixteen-year-old Remember Warren, or Ember, as her family and friends had called her, was being led north through the thick woods of eastern Kentucky by a war party of almost fifty Shawnee braves. The braided leather rope cinched tightly around her wrists chaffed her skin raw as her captor repeatedly yanked it to keep her moving. She had been continually subjected to this abuse for almost eight hours.

The monotony of the long march had done nothing to ease her tortured mind. All she could think about was the sight of her parents, her older brother, her friends, and her neighbors being brutally murdered. The final devastating blow had been to watch the attacking and looting Indians burn the entire village to the ground.

Apparently she wasn't walking fast enough to suit him, because suddenly the cruel captor yanked hard on the rope, and her exhausted body jerked forward once more. He was not an Indian, although the Shawnee all seemed to accept him as one, and he had certainly acted like one in the attack.

The man was tall with broad shoulders, a thick black beard, and hate-filled, steel blue eyes. She had watched him kill several of her neighbors, so she knew his savagery, and yet, when the Indian who had killed her mother had grabbed Ember, the bearded man stopped him and said that he wanted her alive.

As the daylight began to fade, the party came to a creek in the woods where they stopped for the night. The tall man led Ember over to thick brush by the creek. He tied the rope to a nearby tree and checked the knot that bound her hands to the other end. "Drink an' do what you need to do," he said roughly. "I'll be back in a few minutes."

Later, as the dark of night engulfed her, the gruff captor led Ember to a make-shift camp and tied the rope to a small tree near him. Dropping a piece of dried pemmican in her lap he said, "Eat," but Ember had no appetite. The Shawnee did not make a fire, and the night air chilled her. She drew her knees up to her chin and wrapped her arms around them, feeling crushed, as if all of the sadness in the world was on her. Everything that had meant anything had been taken away, and a cruel, harsh life awaited. Lost and alone, she had no one to care for her.

Now that's not entirely true, Ember. An inaudible voice interrupted her thoughts, sounding to the girl like her mother. She remembered the words from a conversation they had shared a few weeks before. *God will never leave you. He will never fail you or forsake you. That's a promise!*

BUT HE FAILED YOU...HE FORSOOK YOU! Ember wanted to scream.

No, He didn't, the imaginary voice answered. *He took us home. Life is wonderful for us now!*

"Well, it's not wonderful for me," Ember whispered a sad and angry reply.

Between the cold and the nightmares, she didn't sleep much. It seemed to the girl that she had just drifted off when a booted foot nudged her in the side. "Get up; we're goin'."

Stiff, sore, shivering, and tired, the young captive stood while the bearded abuser untied the rope. As they walked along, she noticed the sky to the right glowed red with early morning light, revealing that they were headed north. The heavy grey clouds directly overhead made it seem as if even the weather shared Ember's mood. Crows cawed in the limbs above, adding to her despair and loneliness.

For two more days they moved steadily north. A steep, moss-covered limestone ledge rose on their right, and they trudged several miles along its base, coming eventually to another wide forest. Ember had reached a point of emotional numbness and felt nothing except how tired she was. On the afternoon of the third day, she realized they were walking on a trail. She had no idea when they had come to it but was grateful that the walking was easier. About an hour before sunset, they arrived at a fork in the trail, and the war party called a halt.

As they stood on the path, one of the war chiefs walked back to face the bearded man. "Rayford," the young chief said in broken English, "Braves go to camp. I come with you. Must speak with sister."

"Well, come on then," the man Rayford spat back. "It'll be dark soon."

While the rest of the Indians continued on, the chief and Rayford, leading his exhausted captive, took the trail to the right. They walked in silence for almost another hour before arriving at a small clearing where a log cabin stood tucked against the side of a steep, wooded hill.

With no call of greeting, Rayford marched to the stout wooden door, threw it open, and stepped in. Immediately angry words that Ember couldn't understand were hurled in Rayford's direction.

When the young captive was drawn into the cabin, she saw a short, hostile squaw standing toe to toe with her large captor, shaking a wooden spoon in his face. She hurled words at the big man so quickly that Ember could not conceive of how anyone could make sense of them.

After a couple of minutes, Rayford had enough. With a growl he snatched the threatening spoon from the angry woman's hand and broke it in two. In fury the squaw drew back both hands to hit her opponent in the chest, but before she could, one of Rayford's large hands shoved her back into a chair. "I DON'T WANT TO HEAR IT!" he yelled fiercely. He yanked hard on the rope in his hands and jerked Ember to him. Grabbing the girl by the hair and shoving her in front of the cowering squaw, he said, "Because you cain't keep up with the work around here, I brought you a slave! Here she is! Now there ain't gonna be no more complainin' about the work. If the two of you can't keep up with it, then I'll jus' kick you out an' get me a better squaw! Now get some food on the table! We're hungry!" He repeated some of his words in Shawnee to make sure the squaw understood.

The angry Indian woman jumped up and stomped over to Ember. She grabbed the girl painfully by the hair and dragged her to the cooking pot in the fireplace. Still grumbling, the wife placed a clay bowl in the girl's bound hands and, using a large hunting knife, began stabbing hunks of cooked rabbit from the pot and dropping them into the bowl. Using her knife to point at the two men seated at the table, she snapped impatiently at Ember, who understood that she was supposed to take the food to the men. As she set the bowl down, the bearded man pushed her hands away and grabbed the largest piece of meat.

Suddenly the rope attached to Ember's hands yanked her back beside the squaw, who placed another, smaller bowl in the girl's hands. The squaw snatched up a piece of deer skin, and using it, grabbed a hot clay pot off the fire and held it over Ember's bowl. With a wooden spoon the cook dished out a steaming mixture of red beans and corn into the container. As Ember moved to place it on the table, the squaw yelled at her and slapped her on the wrist with the spoon. Startled, with tears beginning to form in her eyes, the girl turned back to her tormentor and watched her use a knife to scoop roundish pieces of flat corn bread from a hot, flat rock sitting in the coals of the fire. She dropped two large cakes on top of the beans and corn and impatiently pointed toward the men with her knife.

After placing them on the table, once again the girl was pushed away as the men ate greedily. Ember started to lick some of the bean juice off her wrist where the spoon had hit her when she was suddenly jerked again back to the squaw, who was digging something out of the coals of the fire. When the Indian stood up, she held a large, roasted sweet potato in between two sticks. She shoved it toward Ember, who without thinking, put out her hands to catch it. The captive screamed in pain and dropped the hot potato at her feet. Immediately the angry squaw began hitting her with the sticks she held. Ember fell to the floor sobbing.

Hearing the squaw yelling again, the girl raised her arms to protect herself and saw the Indian pointing at the hearth. A large patch of deer skin lay there. With an understanding nod, Ember wiped away the tears and grabbed the piece of leather. She picked up the potato from the floor, and as she stood, the squaw placed another potato in the pad and pointed impatiently toward the men.

After being shooed away from the table yet again, Ember looked back at the squaw, who had stabbed a piece of cooked rabbit from the pot and sat beside the hearth eating. The exhausted girl slumped to the floor as tears streamed down her cheeks. Her misery was interrupted when a savory-smelling piece of rabbit was stuck under her nose. Looking up, she saw the squaw extending her knife towards the girl. Ember quickly reached for the meat, slid it off the blade, and ate. As she chewed the first bite, the Indian ran the sharp knife blade between the girl's wrists and cut the leather rope binding them.

After they had eaten, the squaw made Ember help with the nightly chores. They carried all of the dirty pots and bowls outside, scoured them with sand, rinsed them in the nearby creek, and carried them back to the cabin. Then Ember was required to sweep the hearth and the floor while the squaw put the dishes in their place. When all was as clean as the Indian wife wanted, she took the tied bundle of stiff grass Ember had used as a broom and handed the slave a rough blanket. The squaw pointed the girl to a short ladder that led to a storage loft. Ember understood that was where she was to sleep. Grateful to be left alone, she climbed the ladder stiffly. Pushing sacks of dried grains and herbs out of her way, Ember found a stack of animal skins on one side. She didn't want to get another beating for ruining the hides, so she took the top skin and turned it over so that the fur side was down. Reclining on the tanned side, she covered herself with the blanket and cried again.

Below her a long conversation ensued, mostly in the Shawnee language. Occasionally Rayford or the chief said something in English. From the little she could understand, Rayford's wife was the chief's sister and was of some importance to the tribe. As the discussion continued, Rayford vented his anger because her responsibilities to the tribe took her away from the work he wanted her to do at the cabin. The meaningless conversation droned on until Ember's fatigue finally overcame her, and she dropped into a dreamless sleep.

Chapter Two

WAXING MOON

The soundly sleeping young captive was startled to wakefulness by loud, banging thumps under her head. Ember jumped up from her mat of skins and hit her head painfully on the low roof of the cabin. The squaw began yelling with a screeching, high-pitched voice. Still in pain, the girl crawled over and descended the ladder. As soon as her feet touched the floor, a wooden bucket was pushed into her hands, and she was led firmly to the door of the cabin and shoved through the opening into the early morning darkness. When she looked back at the squaw in confusion, the Indian pointed in the direction of the small creek to Ember's left and yelled something. With a sad sigh the girl made her way to the nearby water source and filled her bucket.

She was halfway back, trying to be careful not to stumble and spill the water in the dark, when the door jerked open. The squaw stuck her head out, gave an irritated screech, and waved at her to hurry. When Ember entered the cabin, her shoes were soaked with sloshed water. As soon as she had placed the bucket where her task mistress pointed, she was pushed onto her knees in front of a stone grinding trough resting by the hearth. The squaw handed Ember a large, smooth rock and dumped a bowl of dried corn into the depression. The girl looked at the corn and back up at the squaw. Suddenly the angry Indian began jumping up and down, yelling and looking for her spoon. In desperation Ember did the only thing she could think of, and that was to start grinding the hard corn kernels with the stone. That seemed to calm the squaw, and she turned in a huff to work on the fire.

Angry and upset at her miserable situation, the young captive ground the corn against the stone bottom of the trough until her arms were sore. She was still working when suddenly the spoon came down hard on her hands, followed by more yelling. Ember wasn't sure what she had done wrong this time, but she kept on with her grinding.

A few minutes later the spoon once again smacked into her knuckles. With an angry cry of pain, Ember dropped the stone and grabbed her sore hand. "WHY ARE YOU DOING THIS TO ME?" she yelled without thinking. Ember looked up at her tormentor and saw the wooden spoon drawback, but before it could descend, a child's voice called from behind.

"You too slow. She want you grind faster." The words came from a young, plump Shawnee girl who stood in the doorway and chewed on a piece of flat bread. "Hiho, Prisha!" the little girl smiled and waved her bread at the squaw.

"Tapakekesefewi!" the squaw said with a relieved tone, waving the girl into the cabin.

A very animated conversation took place between the Indian woman and the young girl. Finally the girl nodded and turned to Ember. "You grind corn faster! Rayford be mad if him food not ready when he get back from village. He hurt Aunt Prisha...Hurt you too." As a second thought she added, "He no hurt me...I run."

In response to this ominous warning, Ember put new effort into her work. She knew what the murderous Rayford was capable of.

As soon as the corn meal was fine enough, the squaw scooped it into a bowl and mixed it with water and liquid marrow melted out of fresh deer bones. She kneaded the mixture into dough, rolled it into balls, flattened it into cakes, and dropped them onto a hot stone resting in the fire. As they sizzled on the makeshift griddle, the squaw grabbed a clay bowl, shoved it into Ember's hands, and spouted a slew of words at her niece.

"Take bowl and fill from big pot with skin tied around top over by wall," the young girl ordered.

"It full of nuts and dried berries. Good, good...ummumm!" The girl closed her eyes, rubbed her stomach, and smiled as she spoke.

Ember obediently untied the skin from the pot and immediately was struck with the strong, pungent scent of hickory nuts. Filling the bowl, she took it back to the squaw, who was placing a stack of flat bread on the table. Suddenly the door burst open and in walked Rayford.

Snatching the bowl from the girl and shoving her away, the squaw quickly placed the nuts and dried fruit beside the bread. There was a crash as Ember lost her balance and fell into the pots and covered bowls beside the hearth. She wished she could hide when everyone stared at her.

Rayford's stern gaze dropped to the table. His eyes grew hard as he stared at the bread and berry mix set for him. "Is this all you have for me?" he growled threateningly.

The small plump niece began to inch for the door.

"IS THIS IT?" he yelled angrily.

The squaw cowered beneath the hate-filled eyes.

Looking down at her side, Ember noticed that one of the pots she had knocked over held left-over rabbit meat from last night's supper. Quickly snatching it up, she stood and handed the bowl to the squaw. "Uh, no...sir," she stammered fearfully.

The squaw saw the girl's discovery and quickly placed it on the table, saying something in

Shawnee. When Rayford spotted the meat, the tension in his face relaxed, and he sat down and ate. As soon as Prisha's husband was distracted by his food, she turned and looked at the captive girl. Ember observed the relief in the squaw's eyes as she gave the girl a faint nod before turning to the hearth to cook more flat bread.

"Good thing you find meat," the niece told Ember after Rayford had finished eating and left the cabin. "Wekano! Big trapper hurt all of us if he no happy!"

"So who are you?," the captive asked the niece as they cleaned the hearth., "And how did you learn to speak English?"

"I am Tapakekesefewi," the girl said proudly, "niece to great medicine woman, Prishanese of the Maykujay clan." As she spoke, the girl beamed at her aunt, who smiled back at the mention of her name and gave her niece a dismissing wave of her hand.

"Your name is...uh...impressive," Ember returned, trying not to offend. "It's going to be hard for me to say it correctly."

"Yes," the girl answered, "ver' 'pressive. It okay you use my Englitch name, *Waxing Moon.*"

Ember took a moment to study the young girl before her. Guessing her age to be somewhere between ten and eleven, she had straight black hair that flew wildly around her face and roundish cheeks that matched her shape.

"Nice to meet you, Waxing Moon," Ember returned politely, as her mother had taught her. Ember held her anger in check. It really wasn't nice to meet any of them.

"Yes," the young girl answered, "nice to meet me. What you name?"

"My name is Remember Warren, but you can call me Ember."

Waxing Moon began to giggle. "That silly name. You name no good. You no worry. Tapakekesefewi find you better name."

"NOW WAIT A MINUTE!" Ember snapped. "I DON'T NEED A BETTER..."

Just then the squaw began speaking as she dropped a load of dirty pots and bowls into Ember's arms and pointed toward the door.

"Aunt Prisha say you go clean pots," Waxing Moon interpreted her aunt's words as she chewed on another piece of flat bread. "She also say you be quick."

"UGH...FINE!" the captive exclaimed and walked to the door with her load. The eating girl followed her out to the creek beside the cabin.

Ember furiously scrubbed the pots and bowls with creek sand, venting her anger. After several minutes she calmed and noticed that Waxing Moon stood behind her, still chewing on her bread.

"So how did you learn to speak English?" Ember asked curiously.

"My Englitch good!" Waxing Moon announced proudly. "I go to Englitchman school when Shawnee camp in Canada. Learn much Englitch ways. That why Auntie Prisha want Waxing Moon to tell you what she say. Prisha no speak much Englitch."

Ember gave a sigh and an annoyed snort as she continued to clean the dishes. Not only was she a slave, but she was to be bossed around by an annoying eleven year old.

All that day Ember worked on one miserable chore after another, but never fast enough to suit Prisha. The slave put away the dishes, shook out the bedding, and scooped and carried out ash from the fireplace. Then she was ordered to sweep the hard packed dirt floor and the hearth. Grinding corn until her arms got too tired, Ember was then given the task of cracking hickory nuts on a smooth rock by hitting them with another stone. Her work wasn't finished until she had picked the nut meats out with the sharpened end of a thin deer bone. All the while Ember was shadowed by her talkative companion and interpreter, Waxing Moon.

"It no wonder Auntie Prisha mad. You slow...like turtle. You look like turtle too, with you head down. Maybe Turtle Girl good name for you."

I've got a good name for you, Ember grumbled under her breath.

"Tapakekesefewi not like Turtle Girl. She no hold her head down. She hold her head high cuz' she Shawnee...she niece of great medicine woman, Prishanese of the Maykujay clan. I be great medicine woman like her someday. Whole tribe come to Tapakekesefewi for to be helped. She march proudly among all Shawnee..."

As the one-sided conversation droned on and on, Ember eventually tuned out the longwinded girl while continuing to pick out the nut meats, letting her mind drift back to the happy times with her family.

Oh Mother, this is so awful! the captive girl said in her heart. *I so wish I were with you, Father, and Jesse. My life is nothing but misery and sadness. I hate all this! I wish I had died with all of you.*

REMEMBER WARREN, a strong rebuke seemed to shout from within her. It was a reproof she had heard many times before. *How can you say such things? The Almighty spared your life for a reason.*

What possible reason could God have for putting me through THIS? Ember questioned in her mind as tears formed in the corners of her large brown eyes. *He must hate me, and...and...I hate Him too!*

A few days later Ember was awakened earlier than usual. Prisha was yelling by the time she started down the ladder. The squaw furiously tried to fan the coals into a flame. As Ember reached the floor of the cabin, Prisha screeched some orders over her shoulder and pointed to the bucket. Ember thought she recognized the word for water in the woman's tirade, so she angrily snatched the bucket and hurried out the door.

She ran to the creek, figuring that Rayford must have demanded an early breakfast for some reason. With her full pail she hurried back as quickly as she could, knowing that as bad as her life was, an angry Rayford would make it infinitely worse. She decided that she must have made good time in completing the chore because, when she stepped back inside, the look Prisha gave her was not one of anger but of panic.

It must be really bad if she looks that scared, Ember concluded with a sense of dread. The slave girl noticed the squaw mixing dough for corn cakes from the meal that had been ground the day before. Ember had seen these made several times and thought she could do it. Anxious to spare all of them from Rayford's wrath, she hastily knelt beside her mistress and extended her hands toward the bowl of dough. With a furious nod of relief, Prisha pushed the bowl to the girl and jumped to her feet, wiping her hands on her dress.

Ember worked as quickly as possible to shape the flat cakes and lay them on the thin, hot stone in the fire. Using the wide-bladed hunting knife on the hearth, the captive girl flipped the cakes. Just as she was wondering if they might be ready to be taken up, she heard Prisha's screeching voice behind her. The squaw's long, boney finger shot past the girl's shoulder and pointed anxiously at the browning bread. Quickly Ember used the knife to scoop them up and stack them on the deerskin pad on the hearth.

When she placed them on the table, the door of the cabin flew open and Rayford walked in. A bowl of nut-berry mix and a large slab of deer steak from the night before were already on the table to make the trapper's breakfast. The fierce-looking man surveyed the spread critically for a moment. When he saw the big slab of meat, he gave a slight nod of approval and sat to eat.

A few minutes later a blast of frosty autumn air shot through the cabin as two Shawnee warriors threw open the door and walked in. At the intrusion Rayford shoved the last of the deer meat into his mouth and stood up to leave. "We're goin' to check the traps," he announced gruffly as he pulled on his deerskin coat. Grabbing his rifle and powder horn and throwing the strap of his leather pouch over his head and shoulder, he strode toward the door. "We'll be back late this afternoon, an' I'll be hungry when I get here."

The squaw and girl were just finishing a breakfast of leftover corncakes and nut-berry mix when the door opened again, and in walked Waxing Moon eating a corn cake. "Hiho, Prisha," the girl called. A very involved discussion between the aunt and her niece interpreter began as the squaw pointed to various places around the cabin and explained the work she wanted done.

Just then they heard a rifle shot nearby. A look of concern came across the squaw's face, and she grabbed the ax by the door and went outside to look around. Waxing Moon and Ember quickly joined her as they strained their ears to identify what might have happened. Soon they heard talking in the woods as men approached. There was enough light to see Rayford and one of the Indians carrying a very large buck. They walked to the cabin and tossed the huge beast at Prisha's feet, turning to retrieve their rifles from a second warrior who had followed them.

"We came up on this buck just a short ways into the woods," Rayford announced. "I killed him with one shot!"

Ember let her eyes drop to the massive carcass lying at her feet. She saw a wound in the top of the deer's forehead.

"Skin 'im out an' have a big piece of that loin ready for me when I gets home," he ordered as he turned and led the two warriors back into the brightening autumn woods.

Ember heard the squaw grumbling something under her breath as she stared down at the large buck. Obviously she was not happy about the sudden change in the day's plans. Finally she turned and spoke quickly to her niece.

"Auntie Prisha say you go get big knife from hearth an' bring to her...an' she say..."

"I know, I know," Ember growled as she hurried back into the cabin, "'I be quick.'"

When the captive returned, she handed the blade to her mistress and stepped back to give her room to work. Still grumbling, Prisha lifted the buck's front leg and stabbed the knife through the thick skin. Suddenly, with a trumpeting squeal, the massive deer leaped to his feet, knocking the squaw into the two girls behind her. Dancing in pain, the injured creature was furious to identify who or what had hurt him. Prisha and the girls were scrambling to their feet when they heard powerful snorts from the angry beast. He had his head down and shook his massive rack of antlers. Blood from his head wound ran down his face. The angry animal swayed back and forth as the unsteady buck stared at Prisha and pawed the dirt.

The Indian woman yelled something, and Ember heard Waxing Moon cry, "Run!"

The three dashed in different directions as the buck charged at the space where they had been and crash into the side of the cabin. When they turned to look back, the crazed beast staggered around the yard, tearing up everything he bumped into. Prisha screamed angrily and threw rocks. When the second stone bounced off his antlers, he spun around and charged drunkenly at the squaw. With more yelling from Prisha, the three of them once again zig-zagged around the angry creature. Ember and Waxing Moon hid behind the trunk of a large oak growing nearby. Prisha ran in circles because the injured, dizzy buck staggered badly when he tried to turn too quickly. Finally the squaw yelled again.

"Auntie Prisha say, 'run to cabin'!"

As soon as the buck looked the other way, the two girls rushed for the open door with the squaw right behind them.

Hearing Waxing Moon's squeals as she ran, the large deer spun quickly around and spotted his escaping enemies. Lowering his head and bellowing his anger, he threw himself at the retreating squaw. Prisha had just crossed the threshold when the buck arrived. There was a loud *thunk* that shook the entire cabin, followed by more bellowing. Turning around, Prisha and the girls saw that the deer's antlers, too broad to get through the cabin door, had impaled themselves into each side of the wooden frame.

The squaw pulled herself off the floor where the buck's head had shoved her, her eyes glaring fiercely at the stuck animal as it bellowed and thrashed in a futile effort to free itself. She yelled passionately as she picked up the ax and slowly approached the creature.

"What's she saying?" Ember asked anxiously.

"Well...uh...Auntie Presha angry," Waxing Moon answered, never taking her eyes off the squaw.

"She's always angry," Ember shot back.

"This different than with you," the younger girl answered. "She ver' angry...ver'much, BIG angry! She tell mean buck him come from bad place, an' she gonna' send him back!"

"Should we help her?" Ember asked with concern.

"No-o-o-o," the confident response came from the wide-eyed girl. "We stay here. Auntie Prisha, she no need our help. If we get in way, she so mad, maybe she send us to bad place too."

Uttering a bloodcurdling scream, the angry squaw charged forward. One swing of her ax ended the huge buck's struggle. Even though the deer was dead, his antlers were still embedded in the door frame. The beast's massive head, shoulders, and front legs were suspended lifelessly in the entryway.

Waxing Moon called to her aunt.

"How are we going to get through the door?" Ember asked.

"Tapakekesefewi jus' ask Auntie Prisha same thing."

The squaw stared at the huge, dead creature hanging in front of her. With an angry snort Prisha stepped over and swung her ax hard at the base of one set of antlers, severing it from the head of the buck. She then quickly chopped through the other side. Instantly the deer collapsed on the threshold. Prisha turned and said something to her niece.

"Auntie Prisha say it gonna' take all of us to drag big buck out where she can skin him."

That afternoon, an hour before sunset, Rayford and his two companions came back to the cabin, dragging a makeshift travois loaded with a stack of freshly skinned beaver pelts. They noticed that the front yard was all torn up. As they approached the cabin, Rayford stopped and looked with surprise at the two large antler racks embedded deeply in each door post. All the men took turns trying to pull them out but were unable. Suddenly the door flew open, and Prisha came storming out with her cooking knife in her hand. She angrily began hurling Shawnee words at her husband and shaking the knife in his face. Rayford and the other Indians began laughing as the big trapper held his hands up and backed away from his very angry wife.

"What's going on?" Ember asked as she and Waxing Moon stood in the doorway watching.

"Auntie Prisha, she still big angry," the plump girl returned, giggling. "She say, 'You crazy man, next time you bring game home, you be sure it dead first!'"

Chapter Three

ASSISTING

One of the benefits of the hard work that Ember was forced to do was that it left very little time for her to think about her sad situation. But every night before she let her exhausted body fall asleep, she took time to remember her family. She actually tried to say prayers like they had done when her mother, father, and brother were alive, but now the words seemed empty and useless, so eventually she gave it up.

Though every day was difficult, a few interesting things did happen. Quite regularly people came to the cabin looking for Prisha. When the captive girl asked Waxing Moon what it was all about, she learned that most of the people were sick or were coming on behalf of a sick or injured relative or friend.

"Auntie Prisha give them medicine to fix them," the Indian girl answered. "Everyone in whole tribe who gets hurt or sick come to Auntie Prisha. She great medicine woman!"

"I knew your aunt was a medicine woman," Ember returned with interest, "but I thought that meant she spoke to the spirits and had visions."

"Only vision Auntie Prisha have is vision of you being lazy when she see you working too slow."

"So what kind of medicine does she give them?" Ember asked with an irritated growl as she pounded dirty clothing on broad, flat rocks in the creek.

"She give good medicine," Waxing Moon shot back, "all kind of plants and herbs to make people better. She great medicine woman! Someday Tapakekesefewi be great medicine woman too. You see...everyone will see..." Once again the plump Shawnee girl lapsed into a dreamy monologue of her future.

Ember stopped listening. *Well,* the slave girl thought to herself, *at least that battleax of a squaw is doing something worthwhile. I thought the old witch was a caster of spells.*

Later as Ember spread the freshly laundered clothing on the limbs of nearby trees, a Shawnee woman ran to the cabin and hurried inside. It was no more than a minute before the door burst open, and the woman and Prisha, with a large leather bag slung on her shoulder, came out. She spotted Ember hanging the last of the wash and shouted some anxious words. When the squaw finished speaking, Ember looked expectantly at Waxing Moon sitting on a nearby stump.

"Auntie Prisha say you go with her," Waxing Moon translated. "She need you help with ver' sick woman. You carry Auntie Prisha's herbs she put in basket on table. Go get basket. Follow Auntie Prisha. You go quick."

"Are you coming too?" Ember asked.

"No, Auntie Prisha say woman you go help is ver', ver' sick. She no want Tapakekesefewi to get sick."

"But it's okay if I get sick?" the captive girl shot back angrily.

Waxing Moon simply shrugged her shoulders and said, "You slave."

The squaw began yelling angrily and shaking her finger impatiently at them.

"All right! All right!" Ember grumbled as she rushed toward the open cabin door. She grabbed the basket from the table and hurried after the two squaws as they moved rapidly up the path. Following the well-used Indian trail, they crossed a creek and eventually came to the Shawnee village in a large, open area. The woman led them to a particular stick hut, the outside walls of which were covered with dried red clay. Entering through the low doorway, she motioned towards an older squaw lying on a pile of animal skins, covered in sweat and moaning.

Prisha squatted beside the sick woman, feeling her cheeks and forehead. She looked into her eyes for several minutes and smelled her breath. Then she put her hand on the sick woman's chest and held it there. She finished her exam by placing her ear on the invalid's chest and listening to her heart and breathing sounds. Finally she turned to the one who had led them there. For several minutes they talked. The medicine woman apparently asked many questions about the sick person. When finished, Prisha squatted in thoughtful silence for several minutes before turning to Ember. Pointing to a clay pot, she spoke more words and pointed to the fire pit.

Ember picked up the pot with a look of confusion and said, "I know you want me to boil some water, but this pot is empty, and I don't know where to get the water."

Both Prisha and the other woman just looked at her with a blank look. Prisha then scowled and began firing words at her that the girl couldn't understand.

When Ember just stared at her, the other woman began saying some of the same words at her, only louder and slower.

"UGH! This is so frustrating!" Ember snapped. "I need water...WATER! What's that Indian word for water?" she muttered to herself. "Think, Ember, think! It's...*nepi*...NEPI, NEPI!"

A look of understanding came over both of the Indian women, and the first one quickly pointed to a pile of skins in the corner of the hut. When Ember lifted them, she saw a large clay jar containing the water. Filling the pot, she quickly placed it on the hot coals in the fire pit.

She heard Prisha speak again, and when the girl glanced up, the medicine woman was looking at her. She pointed to the jar of water in the corner. "Nepi," Prisha said, then pointed from the jar to a spot beside her.

Ember understood and quickly went to get the pot. It was a struggle, but she managed to carry the heavy container and set it beside the sick woman. Prisha said some words to the other woman, and the medicine woman and the squaw dipped water from the jar and rubbed the cool liquid over the sick one's hot arms and legs.

Several minutes later Prisha turned to Ember and said something that sounded like a question. When she saw the confused look on Ember's face, the squaw said *nepi* and pointed to the jar on the fire.

The girl looked at the pot of water and back at the squaw. "What is it?" she asked. "Do you want me to bring you the pot?"

At first an angry look crossed Prisha's face, then she thought of something. She held up her left hand like she was holding something. Then she began to wiggle the fingers of her right hand inside her open left hand, after which she pointed again at the pot.

She wants to know if the water is boiling, the captive girl realized. Looking in the pot and seeing no evidence, Ember imitated the squaws hand gesture and said *no* while shaking her head. Turning back to her task, Prisha and the other woman continued to bathe the hot limbs of the sick one with cool water from the jar.

Before long Ember spotted the first bubbles forming in the steaming pot. When the water was at a steady boil, she called to her mistress.

"Ahh," Prisha said with a satisfied look when she walked over and saw the churning contents. She reached into the basket Ember had carried and pulled out three separate bunches of dried herbs. Grinding them vigorously between her palms, she allowed the bits to drop into the boiling water. Almost immediately a pungent smell began to fill the hut. Prisha picked up a cooking stick lying beside the fire and stirred the brew. When she seemed satisfied, the medicine woman pointed to a deerskin pad lying nearby and talked to Ember as she walked back over to her patient and waved for the girl to follow.

Hoping that she understood correctly, Ember grabbed the pad, lifted the hot pot from the fire, and carried it over to Prisha kneeling beside the sick woman. The medicine woman pointed where she wanted the steaming pot set so that it was close to the face of the invalid. Prisha then grabbed the deerskin pad from Ember and fanned the strong, pungent steam from the pot so that it drifted across the face of the sick woman. The patient's breathing slowed and grew easier after inhaling the steaming herbs.

That's amazing! The girl said to herself. *That stuff really works!*

Over the next two hours, Ember had to reheat the pot of herbs several times to keep it steaming. When Prisha felt that her patient was breathing normally and that her fever was down, the medicine woman handed Ember a second pot.

"Nepi," she said, then pointed to the fire and wiggled her fingers palm upward as she had done before.

Sakes alive! the captive girl growled to herself as she received the second pot irritably. *How much boiled water does she need?*

When the second pot was steaming, Prisha once again searched through her basket and found the needed herbs. Measuring out the correct amount into the palm of her hand, she dropped them into the water, stirring them gently. When ready, she poured some into a shallow wooden bowl and gave the sick woman small sips of the tea. After the bowl was empty, the medicine woman handed the small bowl to the other woman and gave her instructions on how she was to continue treating the invalid. Then she stood up, said something to Ember, pointed to the basket, and walked out of the hut. The slave girl, not quite sure what she was supposed to do, grabbed the basket and hurried after her mistress.

Stepping outside into the cool fall air, Ember spotted Prisha quite a ways ahead, traveling toward the cabin. The girl had to run to catch up with the squaw, who immediately yelled at her angrily, continuing her rant for most of the trip back. When they arrived, Waxing Moon sat by the fireplace eating a corn cake with some of Prisha's nut and berry mix heaped on it. The medicine woman immediately began a discourse with her plump niece.

"Auntie Prisha say you too slow," the girl began as the squaw continued to vent her anger. "You walk slow, you think slow, you carry pots slow, you boil water slow..."

"I can't make water boil faster!" Ember shot back.

"You too slow!" the girl continued. "Must work faster. Because Auntie Prisha had to help sick woman, now whole day's work must be done in half day. Rayford home soon, and he not be happy! Auntie want you sweep floor quick, quick...then she have more for you to do."

"Okay, okay!" Ember shot back as she picked up the grass broom.

"You need work fast, Turtle Girl," her miniature slave driver barked at her. "If you don't,

Auntie may beat you, but Rayford, he kill you...or worse."

Suddenly the seriousness of what could happen struck Ember, and she pushed herself like never before. She swept, dealt with the bedding, ground corn, cut up squash, and shelled beans. When she finished, Prisha had her take over cooking the flat bread while she heated a pot of squash and beans, all the while barking at Ember to hurry and finish. As soon as the girl scooped up the last piece from the griddle stone, Prisha shoved her out of the way and dropped a large deer steak on the hot cooking surface and barked more orders to Ember.

"Auntie Prisha say you put food on table," Waxing Moon reported with a mouth full of corn bread. "She say you be quick...Rayford be here soon. He be mad if him food not ready."

As Ember put the bread, squash, and beans on the table, the squaw shouted, and her niece said, "Turtle Girl, you grab platter and take to Auntie quick, quick!"

Just as the slave girl did so, the door to the cabin flew open, and in strode the trapper while Waxing Moon shot out the door. Rayford looked around at the cabin, inspecting the interior with a hard look. Then his eyes dropped to the food on the table and anger flashed across his face.

"IS THIS..." But he stopped his question short when Ember quickly turned, holding the wooden platter of deer steak. As the large hunk of cooked meat was set before him, the look of anger left, and a stony hardness took its place. The trapper greedily consumed his food, and Prisha and Ember squatted beside the hearth, taking turns dipping flat corn bread into a shared dish of squash and beans.

Over an hour later, when the mess from the hastily cooked supper had been cleaned and all of the pots and bowls put away, Ember made the weary climb to her bed. She lay on her deer skin too tired to sleep. As she replayed the day in her mind, all the misery and pent up frustration overwhelmed her. Tears of despair streamed down her cheeks. She fought to stifle her sobs so she didn't get in trouble with Rayford or the squaw.

Just let me die, God! Ember cried in her heart. *What have I done to make You hate me so?*

Now hush that, Sweetheart! The voice in her heart was her mother's from another remembered conversation. *Your father and I have always taught you that God loves you with an everlasting love. His word says that clearly. You are worth...*

Yes, Mother, I know. I am worth the life of His Son Jesus.

That's right. Because you are loved so much, Jesus came to earth and died on a cross to pay the price of your sins for you and to save you. That's the greatest expression of love that anyone could ever give, and you should never forget it.

Ember answered the voice, *But, Mother, if He loves me so much, why is this happening to me? Is*

He punishing me for something? I've asked Him over and over what I've done to deserve this, and I can't think of anything. More tears streamed down her cheeks.

Your loving Heavenly Father would let you know if there was something between you and Him. Since He hasn't, you can be at peace knowing that you are right where He wants you.

BUT MOTHER...

Ember, God knows everything, He sees the end from the beginning, and He never makes mistakes...He never makes mistakes...

The last words seemed to echo over and over in the young girl's mind. The more she thought on them, the more comfort she felt. She could not see any good purpose that God could have in her being a slave, but as she reflected on her mother's words, one thing did take root in her mind. The only reason that made any sense for Jesus to suffer so much for her on the cross was His love. *He must love me to go through all of that,* she told herself. *It just doesn't look like it right now.*

Remember, dear, she heard her mother's voice again, *as much as God loves His Son, He let Jesus go through really hard times too.*

Oh, Mother, Ember thought as tears once again began to stream down her cheeks, *I miss you so much!*

As the tired and sad girl began to drift off to sleep, the last thing she told herself was that she would try to look for God's love for her in the hard times.

Chapter Four

NUT GATHERING

For the last two days, life had been much more bearable. Rayford had gone off with the warriors and wasn't expected back for a week. Ember hoped that he would never come back, but at least for now, her life wasn't in jeopardy every time they prepared a meal. One particular morning while Ember cooked the flat bread for breakfast, Prisha bustled around the cabin emptying and collecting hand-woven grass baskets and stacking them by the door.

After Ember placed a small stack of bread on the table, Prisha handed her a bowl and waved her over to the pot of nut and berry mix. Joining her, the squaw removed the covering, turned the large pot on its side, and scraped out the bottom with a carved spoon. Removing the entire contents, she deposited them into Ember's bowl. The slave was surprised at how little there was left. They both covered their bread with what remained of the sweet topping and ate in silence.

After a few moments the girl's curiosity got the better of her, and she asked the squaw, "Don't you have more berry mix?"

The squaw gave the girl a questioning look.

"The berry mix," Ember said again, walking over to the now empty pot and pointing inside. "Do you have more?"

With an understanding nod Prisha got up and stepped beside another covered pot by the wall. Lifting the lid, she pointed inside at quantities of blueberries and blackberries soaking in honey.

"Yes," the girl nodded, "I remember when we collected those. But what about the nuts?"

The squaw again gave the girl a questioning look.

"The nuts...the nuts," she repeated, thinking that if she said it enough times, the Indian would understand. Taking her bread, she picked off a piece of hickory nut and held it before the squaw.

"Ahh," Prisha said with a knowing smile. Then she went over to where the baskets were stacked by the door and pointed to them. She began sewing together a string of words that Ember did not know.

As she continued to talk, the door suddenly flew open, and in walked Waxing Moon with two Indian women. "Hiho, Prisha," they all said as they entered. When the two squaws looked at Ember, the slave girl gave them a polite, nervous smile and nodded. In response the two women lifted their heads, gave Ember a look of disdain, and quickly turned to face the medicine woman. An animated discussion began between the three adults.

"Who are these women?" Ember asked Waxing Moon as the conversation continued.

"They are Auntie Prisha's sisters. The closest one is my mother. Her name is...well, her name too hard for you, but it means Moon Beam. I named for her...kind of. The one on other side is younger sister. Her name mean Graceful Deer. She got wrong name. She not graceful...not gentle like deer. She hard woman...always angry. Her name should be War Club."

Suddenly the conversation stopped, and Prisha barked orders at Ember. "Auntie Prisha say we go get nuts. That's what she was telling you when we walked in. Now she say you pick up and carry baskets, Turtle Girl."

"This is not going to be a good day," the slave girl muttered under her breath as she slid the handles of the three large baskets over her arms and followed the women and Waxing Moon out the door. Once outside, the others handed her six more baskets to carry.

"Can't they carry their own baskets?" Ember growled at the plump girl.

"You slave," Waxing Moon smiled back with a mouth full of bread. "Now you follow, and Auntie Prisha say you keep up."

Walking quickly in the crisp air, they traveled along the bank of the nearby creek to the west for almost half a mile. Ember struggled to get the large baskets through the brush. When they arrived at an outcropping of rocks, they turned to the north, away from the creek, until they came to a small meadow. On the far side was a cluster of hickory trees that blended into a rocky, forested hillside.

Ember saw at once that the ground was covered with fallen hickory nuts. The women came and snatched baskets from the slave girl.

"Auntie Prisha say you fill baskets with nuts...and you be quick. She also say you only pick up good nuts...no bad ones."

As Ember began collecting, a depressing thought came to her. *All of these baskets of nuts will have to be cracked and picked out, and since I'm the slave, it's going to be my job to do it. My fingers are hurting just thinking about it.* She sighed to herself.

By late morning the sun was high, the air was warming, and most of the baskets were filled. Ember started to hope that they might head back to the cabin in another hour. Suddenly she heard a sound in the distance. Immediately all of the women stood upright and looked at one another. They heard the noise again, only closer. A look of fear crossed each face, and they began talking rapidly. It looked to the girl like two were for making a run for the cabin. Finally War Club took charge and moved everyone further up the wooded slope to the base of a limestone ledge.

"What's going on?" Ember asked Waxing Moon.

"Wolves come! They eat you, Turtle Girl."

As the five of them struggled up the forested hill, the three squaws snatched dead branches lying on the ground around them.

The wolves drew nearer, and their howls turned into fierce growls and barks. Looking behind her, Ember could see the terrifying creatures leaping through the woods, their mouths open and anxious for the feast to come.

When the fugitives reached the base of the bluff, they could go no further. War Club yelled and directed them to their right where there was a small grotto. It wasn't large, but if they all crowded into it together, it would protect their backs as they faced the foe.

Prisha shoved a long tree branch into Ember's hands and directed her to stand at the end of their line of defense. The slave didn't understand the words Prisha yelled at her as the wolves raced towards them, but it didn't matter. The girl knew they were fighting for their lives. Waxing Moon was shoved behind as the killers arrived.

Ember took courage from the three squaws who stood resolutely beside her. With fierce yells and screams, they jabbed the ends of their long branches at the attacking wolves. Fortunately they stood on the high ground, giving them an advantage over their assailants, who had to leap to get at them. There were seven large beasts in the pack, but due to the women's location in the small grotto, only three or four could attack at one time.

When a wolf threw itself at Ember, she screamed and in fear jabbed the branch she was holding at its head and chest. The smaller stems and twigs on the end of her makeshift weapon splintered into pieces as the beast crashed into it. The creature lost its footing and slipped back down the hill, but another jumped over it and continued the attack. Once again the determined girl jammed her weapon forward. The broken ends were jagged and sharp, and when they found their mark in the mouth, lips, and tender nostrils of the terrible animal, it let out a squeal of pain as it too tumbled back down the slope.

Ember heard Waxing Moon's mother yelling at the other end of their short line of defense. Glancing over, the girl saw that two wolves had locked their jaws on Moon Beam's branch and were trying to pull it out of her hands. Standing beside her, War Club made a violent jab at the beast in front of her, rolling it down the hill. Immediately she sent her now free weapon into the face of one of two wolves gripping Moon Beam's limb. With a scream the injured creature released its bite and retreated. Reaching quickly across, War Club rammed the sharp end of her branch into the face of the second attacker, causing it to turn loose as well. But there was no time to rejoice, as three more of the relentless beasts took their place.

The slave girl felt her arms tiring as the battle raged on. They were forced to jab and stab fiercely at their assailants to keep them back. Suddenly the largest of the wolves threw itself at the tired girl and crashed hard into her weapon, its heavy, muscular body pinning the branch to the ground and knocking her down. Prisha, who was fighting beside her, saw the danger and jerked her own fighting stick hard to her left, hitting the wolf she was fighting painfully across its head and sending the branch into the face of the wolf that was attacking Ember. Prisha also stabbed at the beast to drive it back, but the maddened creature only snapped at the limb, gripping it with its powerful jaws. Just then the first wolf Prisha had been fighting bounded back to charge at her again. She jerked her stick from the large animal's mouth, which caused the wolf to lose its balance and slip down the hill. The medicine woman swung her weapon at the new threat with all of her might, slamming it painfully against the side of the head of her attacker. With a painful yelp the injured wolf retreated rapidly back down the wooded slope. But Ember's enemy clawed back up the hill, moving forward with undeterred anger. Prisha took a quick look at her slave scrambling up from where she had fallen, and the medicine woman stabbed hard at the big wolf once again, screaming at the girl to fight back.

Ember hurried painfully forward and grabbed the end of her weapon as Prisha rammed her sharp branch into the side of the creature's head. As the rage-filled beast twisted to escape the stabbing limb, the girl stabbed hard with her weapon, causing the wolf to tumble down the hill. When the others saw their leader roll away, they stopped attacking and fell back to regroup.

The four defenders stood with their weapons at the ready, panting fiercely. All the wolves, bleeding from multiple wounds to their heads and necks, paced back and forth about fifteen feet below them, never taking their savage eyes off their intended victims.

Attacking us is a lot harder than they thought it would be, the captive thought to herself, immediately taking courage and gripping her stick even tighter. As if he had suddenly made up his mind, the largest wolf bared his teeth and launched himself back up the hill straight at Ember.

"OH NO, OH NO!" the girl yelled as she saw the great beast's eyes locked on her as he charged. She screamed and shoved her stick at the creature as he slammed into her. The rage-filled animal hit her weapon so hard that he impaled himself through the chest on the sharp end of the stick. As he did so, the limb snapped in two, and the dying beast crashed into the terrified girl, knocking her back into the grotto and slamming her against the back wall. The three squaws fought off the half-hearted attack of four other wolves, but when the beasts saw that their leader had fallen and was not getting up, they turned and fled.

The squaws watched with satisfied relief as the remainder of the pack raced off into the woods. The celebration for their survival was suddenly interrupted by an agonizing scream of pain. Turning quickly, they saw the slave girl writhing in terror and torment.

The three squaws looked with disgust at the emotional girl and vented their loathing at her lack of courage. "What wrong with you, Turtle Girl?" Waxing Moon barked at her. "Big fight over. No need to cry now."

"MY...MY LEG!" the girl yelled through clenched teeth.

The Indian girl translated the words, and it was then that they noticed that one of Ember's legs had slid into a dark crevice in the rock. As the slave girl painfully drew her leg out of the hole, they all gasped when they saw a copperhead snake affixed to the girl's calf.

Quickly Prisha dropped beside Ember and grasped the serpent behind its head. Squeezing the creature's jaws from both sides, she loosened its grip and pulled it off. The furious copperhead thrashed its long body around Prisha's arm in an attempt to get free. Standing upright, the medicine woman grabbed the serpent's tail with her free hand and whirled the snake around her head, slamming it hard into the rock wall and crushing its skull.

The slave girl was still in intense pain as Prisha knelt to examine the bite marks. The medicine woman turned, made some kind of demand of the other two, and a lively argument began.

"What are...they...doing?" Ember gasped at Waxing Moon.

"Auntie Prisha want to help you, but War Club say she should let you die since you just slave. Too bad for you, Turtle Girl. War Club always wins."

Just when it looked like Waxing Moon's prediction was about to be proven correct, Prisha gave an angry yell and grabbed her sister fiercely. Taken aback by Prisha's livid response, War Club pulled out a knife from a sheath at her side and handed it to the medicine woman. Still angry, Prisha snatched the blade and hurried to Ember's side.

Before the slave girl realized what was happening, the squaw made two deep slashes over the bite wounds. Lifting Ember's leg to her mouth, the medicine woman sucked at the gashes and spit out as much of the poison as she could draw. She repeated the action five times, then used the knife to chop branches off two large, fallen limbs that lay nearby. When they had been fully prepared, she cut vines and wove them hurriedly back and forth between the two limbs. Once the woven mat was secured to the poles, she laid the travois near Ember and motioned the girl to drag herself onto it.

Still angry, Prisha approached her two sisters and apparently let them both know what she expected them to do. The two sisters didn't say a word as they each obediently took an end of one of the limbs of the travois. Prisha stood in between her sisters, and at her direction, the three of them lifted and dragged Ember down the wooded slope of the hill.

Chapter Five

A LIFE CHANGING EXPERIENCE

Dizziness suddenly struck Ember as she drug herself over to Prisha's travois. She had hoped that the medicine woman had been able to suck out most of the venom, but it was now uncomfortably clear that plenty remained. The effects of the snake's poison on her system rushed upon her, and she had never been so sick in all her short life. Moving to the mat became almost more than she could handle, and she vomited twice before finally rolling onto the hand-made frame. She gripped the sides and tried to hold herself as still as she could, but it didn't help.

As the three squaws pulled the travois down the wooded hill, every bounce and jar made the dizziness increase. She wretched several more times, but her stomach was empty, and nothing came up. Suddenly she also began to feel really hot and light-headed.

The pain in her leg, the severe vertigo, the nausea, and the fever were too much for the girl, and she lost consciousness. To Ember it was a relief. Everything that was causing her distress seemed to drift away, or did it? Maybe she was the one drifting away.

It was like she was floating aimlessly, but not on water. She was in the air. At one point she looked down and saw the squaws dragging her through the woods far below. It was so strange to see her body lying on the travois with Waxing Moon walking behind. Remembering that she had been snake bit and that it had really hurt, it surprised her that the injury didn't hurt now. Examining her leg, the slashed and bleeding wounds were not visible. Neither was it bruised, red, or swollen. Instead, a bright light covered the place where the bite marks had been. But other than that, her leg seemed normal.

Then she noticed that fog or smoke began to drift across her legs. Glancing around, she realized that she was engulfed in a thick cloud. When she reached toward it, she felt it as her fingers passed through. It was soft and velvety. She also observed something else.

That's funny, she reflected as she inhaled the vapors, *I never thought clouds smelled.* She breathed in the wonderful fragrance again and again, trying to identify it. *It's like my grandmother's rose garden when I was a little girl! I had forgotten that smell! It's so wonderful!*

Both the fragrance and the memory gave Ember a deep, satisfying sense of peace. "I must be dying," she said matter-of-factly, "but it's nothing like what I thought. I've always been afraid of dying, but this...this is really nice!"

After a few minutes the fragrant clouds began to drift away, and Ember discovered that she wasn't floating any more. She felt something underneath her and realized she was resting on solid surface.

When the last of the mist slipped past, she discovered she was sitting on a path—a very smooth path that felt both warm and soft. She had no difficulty standing up because her leg felt strong and well. In fact, everything seemed wonderful to her. She hadn't felt this good in quite some time.

Without thinking, she began jumping and twirling. Was it her imagination, or did she actually float a little in the air as she spun? The joy of the moment overcame her, and she delighted in it. How long had it been since she had actually been happy? She felt so good as she skipped along that she wanted to sing, but she couldn't think of a song. Instead, she simply began humming wordless notes and was immediately shocked at the sound of her voice.

"Sakes alive! My voice is amazing! I've never been able to sound like this!" She sang whatever notes came to mind and was stunned at the beautiful, unique melody. It wasn't long before she heard other voices around her harmonizing with her.

When she tried to identify the source of the other notes, she discovered they faded away when she quit. She repeated the cycle: singing, then stopping, then singing again and stopping. Finally she realized that the sounds came from the trees, the rocks, and even the ground.

"This is wonderful!" she exclaimed as she walked over to the trunk of a tree and began singing to it. Almost immediately a deep base tone rumbled from the trunk, harmonizing with her melody as the leaves and branches above began to sway. A thick vine grew up the side of the tree, and Ember heard a higher, lively, springy sound coming from it that blended wonderfully with the song that she and the tree sang. It made the happiest sounds that she had ever heard, and she couldn't help but laugh.

Sighing contentedly as she finished, she looked in wonder at her surroundings and saw that the path ran through a grove of beautiful trees and shrubs. They weren't very thick, so light from above shone down through the canopy, making warm, golden sunbeams, illuminating everything with a distinctly golden hue. It reminded her of special, clear autumn afternoons at home when bright yellow sunlight made the colors stand out.

"But this doesn't feel like autumn," she said out loud. "It's warm here, and the grass is green—greener and healthier than I've ever seen. A cow could make a meal out of just a few blades of this."

She leaned down to study the plants a little closer. Suddenly a look of amazement appeared on her face. "I've never been able to smell grass before! I've smelled it when it was cut and as it dries, but I've never smelled growing grass. It's pungent...and earthy, like the smell of tea leaves when my mother brewed them."

"There's more to see here than just grass," said a friendly voice to her left.

"Oh!" Ember replied, startled by the voice. "I thought I was alone."

"Dear one, you are *never* alone."

As she looked at the tall figure who spoke to her, she saw a kind face that seemed familiar. He reminded her of the preacher in her old village before it was destroyed.

"Parson Roberts? Is that you?"

"No, my little one," the Stranger chuckled, "but I thought you would remember him. He is a good servant of Mine, and he was always kind to you children."

"But you look so much like him," Ember returned.

The Stranger smiled even bigger when she said this. "I wanted you to see the face of a friend so you wouldn't be afraid," He responded genuinely.

"How can you make your face look like someone else?" the girl asked, dumbfounded. "Are you an angel?"

"No, I'm not an angel, although some who have seen Me have mistaken Me for one."

"So who are you?" the girl persisted.

The Stranger smiled and placed His hand tenderly on the head of the confused girl. "I am someone Who loves you very much."

"Do I know you?" the girl asked.

"Yes, you know Me, Ember," the kind Stranger continued. "Your parents and Parson Roberts told you a great deal about Me, but you have forgotten. You have let the difficulties and hardships of your life distract you from thinking about Me, but I have not forgotten you. I think of you every day.

"Do you remember the Sunday service three Easters ago?" the Stranger asked with a bright look in his eyes. "You were playing with the folds of your dress when I prompted your mother to correct you and make you listen. Parson Roberts was at the part of his sermon I especially wanted you to hear. He described how much I loved you, and you *did* hear it. He told of the beatings, the scourging, and My sacrifice on the cross for you, and it finally touched your heart. You began to believe in Me."

Ember gasped and fell to her knees. "YOU'RE HIM!"

"Yes, dear one, I AM."

Tears streamed down her face as she said, "Lord, I am so sorry! I hardly even remember that day."

"But I do," He responded lovingly, reaching down and lifting up her bowed head. "In fact, it is one of my most precious memories."

"I don't deserve Your love, Lord. I have been a terrible follower of Yours."

"None of that matters, dear one," the Lord returned, smiling into her tear-filled eyes. "As long as you want Me, you have Me.

"So, Ember," He said firmly, lifting the crying girl to her feet, "Do you want Me?"

The eager girl grabbed His hand with both of hers and looked straight into His beautiful eyes and cried, "YES, LORD, YES! I WANT YOU! I WANT YOU!"

"Then you have Me," He answered, a big smile spreading across His face, "and I AM enough. I AM all you need, and I AM greater than all your mistakes. Do you believe that?"

"I want to, Lord," she responded honestly.

"Spoken like a true follower of mine," He said with a chuckle. "That's good enough. I will help you believe. Now, walk with Me."

58

Chapter Six

ELIZA

It took the squaws a little over an hour to drag the travois with the injured girl back to the cabin. When they arrived, Prisha threw two buffalo robes on the floor near the fireplace.

The medicine woman's sisters helped carry Ember in and placed her on the pallet. As Prisha hurried to treat the girl, the two squaws and Waxing Moon walked out. Just before she closed the door to the cabin, War Club looked at Prisha and the very sick girl. She curled her nose and shook her head back and forth to pronounce her opinion of the worthless venture.

Immediately stirring up the coals of the fire, the medicine woman put a pot of water on to boil. She also filled a shallow dish and very carefully began to pour small amounts past the girl's lips, waiting until she saw that the patient swallowed before serving more.

In between sips, Prisha cracked several hickory nuts, picked out the larger chunks of nut meat, and quickly crushed them, collecting several drops of oil on a flat stone. Using her grinding stone, she crushed a piece of wild ginger root and wild onion into the oil. She heated the mixture on the flat stone resting on the hot coals.

Stepping over to her shelf of pots, the squaw lifted the covering on one and pulled out a hardened chunk of blue clay. Breaking off a few pieces, she put them on her stone and crushed the material into powder. Adding water, she soon had a pliable ball. She quickly flattened it and scraped the warm ginger, onion, and oil onto it. The last thing she did was to take a little charred wood and crush it into powdered charcoal that she spread liberally on top of the poultice. She placed it all face down onto the open wounds of the girl's leg and wrapped a wide length of deer skin around it.

The water in the pot boiled, and the medicine woman added handfuls of several dried herbs from her shelf. After the mix simmered for several minutes, she removed the pot from the fire and allowed it to steep.

While waiting for the brew to cool, Prisha examined her patient again. Ember was very pale, and her skin felt cool to the touch. With a cry of alarm, the squaw jumped to her feet and yanked the buffalo robe off her own bed, spreading it over the slave girl. Using a couple of sticks, the squaw took hot stones from beside the fire and placed them under the buffalo blanket, careful not to let them touch Ember's skin. The tea had cooled enough to drink, and she poured small sips down the girl's throat.

After half an hour Ember moaned and moved uncomfortably under the robe. Prisha put her hand to the girl's cheek and could tell that she was warmer. With a nod of satisfaction, the squaw quickly put another pot of water on the fire. By the time it was steaming, Ember groaned more and was in obvious discomfort. The medicine woman stepped over to another jar on her shelf and lifted out a leather wallet. From it she drew a long, thick leaf. Pulling the robe off the girl, Prisha studied the thrashing slave's size for several long moments. She started to tear the leaf in half but stopped herself. She thought again and tore a third off the top of the leaf, dropping it in the steaming pot, mumbling to herself as she did so.

After it had steeped for several minutes, Prisha poured the brew into a shallow dish to cool faster. It took a lot of patience and persistence to get the liquid into the struggling girl, but ten minutes after she did so, Ember settled down and slept.

The medicine woman was exhausted. She reached over and pulled a piece of cold flat bread from a covered pot near the fire and ate. When her meager meal was finished, she pulled a deer skin from a peg on the wall and wrapped it around her shoulders. She was thankful that Rayford was off with the warriors, because he would probably have killed the girl rather than allow Prisha to try to treat her. The squaw sighed, squatted down on the floor beside her patient, and closed her eyes.

The medicine woman knew it would require several long, hard days of work to treat the young woman, and there was a very real chance that she would die anyway. She was only a slave, and not a very good one, so the squaw wondered why she was even trying to save her. Prisha didn't know the answer to that question, but she did know that something inside her demanded that she do what she could for the poor girl, and she was determined to do her best.

"I thought there would be other people around," Ember asked as she curiously scanned the empty path ahead.

"There are," Jesus responded, "but I wanted to spend some time alone with you first." He led them along until they came to the top of a small hill. Ember gasped when she saw the view.

"I knew you'd like it," the Lord said as he smiled at his companion. "Flowers are your favorite."

The small meadow in front of them was aflame with brilliant colors. There were the most eye-popping crimsons and rich yellows, plus blues so deep that they seemed to glow.

"I've never seen flowers like these before!" Ember blurted out. "And the colors...the colors are...are..."

"Breath-taking?" Jesus suggested with a smile. All Ember could do was nod her head in open-mouth amazement.

"Come, let's walk in them." As the Lord said this, He took Ember by the hand and led her into the gorgeous, floral field. The waist-high flowers actually moved to the side and created a small path for them. Each bloom had its own lovely fragrance, but the mixture of all of them made Ember want to dance as she breathed in the delightful perfume.

"I noticed that you were singing with the trees earlier," Jesus said. "Now listen to the flowers." Suddenly the Lord sang out in a full, rich, baritone voice praise to His Holy Father.

By the time Jesus had sung the second word, a majestic chorus of sopranos, altos, and high tenors joined Him in a magnificent, harmonious choir that sent chills up Ember's spine. The pure worship brought her to tears.

When He finished His song, Ember looked at her Friend. "I wish I could worship You and the Father like that."

"But you can, dear one. Whenever any of the Father's creation does what it was created to do, *that* is worship. He made you to be His daughter, and when you show Him a daughter's love and devotion, that is the purest form of worship, and We love it!"

As she was absorbing those thoughts, the Lord spoke again. "Before we leave the flowers, I want you to try the nectars." Jesus held out His hand, and in it appeared a shallow white dish with a gold rim. He placed it under a crimson bloom that resembled a bird with its wings outspread. Tipping the blossom, a clear red liquid poured into the dish. He handed it to Ember, and she eagerly tasted it.

Suddenly her eyes flew wide, and she drained the bowl.

"It's good, isn't it?" Jesus asked as a big grin spread across His face.

"Glory!" the girl exclaimed and was immediately surprised at her choice of words.

"Exactly!" Jesus laughed. "Well said! You also need to be sure to try the peach-colored flowers that look like ladies dancing. Those are especially tasty."

After sampling more delicious nectars, Jesus led them through the meadow along a path through another lovely forest. A rushing creek bordered the walkway, and Ember loved the sound the splashing water made.

"It sounds like a song," she said.

"It is."

"What is it singing?" the girl asked again.

"What do you think, since it is doing what it was created to do?" Jesus asked with a faint smile.

"It's a song of worship!" Ember answered enthusiastically.

"Very good!" the Lord returned, giving the girl a look of delight.

"Lord Jesus, I love that You are so open with Your love and genuineness," Ember said with admiration. "When You smile at me, I know you mean it."

"And what I love the most about you, Ember, is your courage and wisdom."

"But, Lord," the girl returned solemnly, "I'm not brave, and I'm certainly not wise."

"Not yet," the Lord smiled, "but you will be. I can see what you're going to be for Me and the Father, and I love it!"

"But Lord, I'm so scared, foolish, and selfish. How will I ever learn to be wise and brave?"

"That's the easy part, dear one," Jesus answered. "I will make you wise and brave. All you have to do is to say *yes* when I make a request of you. The fruit that I will bear in your life will be wisdom and courage as well as peace, compassion, and love. Just remain with Me, Ember. Always stay with Me, and I will do the rest.

"Now, would you like to meet some of the others who live here with me?"

"Oh yes, Lord!" Ember answered excitedly. "I really would!"

"Then come with me."

The Lord and Ember walked across the small meadow of flowers, and as they entered a fragrant woods, Ember asked curiously, "So who are we going to meet?"

"I am going to introduce you to two sweet and precious daughters of the Father that I have asked to join us. You will find that you have a lot in common with both of them, but I will let them tell you their stories."

Ember heard the water before she saw it. As they exited the narrow strip of woods, she saw a powerful river splashing over and around scattered boulders that rose above the surface of the rich, greenish blue water. Standing on the bank were two beautiful women.

When Ember saw their gorgeous dresses, she thought they were princesses. One's skin was very dark. The other had a tanned complexion. As both ladies saw Jesus and Ember walk out of the forest, they gave the newcomers smiles that could only be described as radiant.

"Ah, my sweet ones!" Jesus exclaimed with genuine delight when He saw the ladies. "I'm glad you are here. This is Remember Warren. She is visiting me from the shadow world.

"Ember, I want you to meet Eliza and Zoe. Both of them are now citizens of the City of Light, but when they lived in the land of shadows where you are from, they were slaves like you. Both endured many sufferings for My name and were welcomed with great honor into My home.

"Let's all sit here by the river," Jesus said to His three guests as he pointed to His right. "Eliza and Zoe, I want you to tell Ember about your lives before you came here."

Jesus led them to two ornately carved, stone benches that faced each other. Placed close to the river, they were shaded by tall trees. Ember sat beside Jesus while He directed his friends to the opposite bench. Nodding to the woman with the dark skin, once again Ember saw her give the most beautiful smile.

"It's a genu-wine pleasure to meet you, Ember, I'm Eliza. My folks' names was John and Weesie. Dey was slaves on a plantation in Virginie. I grew up dere, an' as a child I worked as a house servant wif my momma. Da work was hard an' long, but my folks loved each other, an' dey loved me.

"I first learned about da Lord from my folks an' Preacher Westbrook, who would travel around to the different plantations an' give sermons. He'd stand up on da porch where da family sat, an' us slaves would stand in the yard an' listen. Dose sermons meant a lot to my daddy an' my momma, but dey didn't mean much to me." As she said this, Eliza looked sheepishly at Jesus, Who only smiled back at her.

"The really bad times began shortly after I turned seventeen," Eliza began again. "Massa Robert got the plantation into money trouble. I reckon he figured one way to get mo' money was to sell some of us slaves. When he sold me, it broke my mamma's an' my daddy's hearts, and it crushed mine.

"Oooh, Lord! I was so mad at You!" the speaker said, looking at Jesus.

"I remember," the Master returned. "But you know now why I let it happen."

"Yes, Lord, I do. It took a while an' a lot of pain an' heartache, but eventually I realized that gettin' sold away from my family was a really good thing.

"Why?" Ember asked with interest.

"Like I said, I gots angry. I was mad at God an' ever'body! I was first sold to a plantation in South Carolina. Dey wasn't mean to me, but I was so worked up dat I decided to run away. A couple of weeks of steady walkin' could bring me back to my folks. But dey caught me the day after I left. Dey gave me a bad beatin' and tol' me not to run away no mo', but dat jus' made me madder. As soon as I healed up enough to get around, I stole some food an' took off again.

"I was smarter dis time. I kept to the woods and traveled mostly at night. I found some slaves workin' in a field in North Carolina an got dem to hide me for a few days till I rested up. Da slave hunters who was lookin' for me came by an offered a ham to anyone who knew where I was. Can you believe it? Dose slaves who was hidin' me turned me in for a ham!

"As soon as da hunters brought me back, my massa in South Carolina figured I was too much trouble, so he sells me to a plantation in Florida. Ember, when dey sends you dat far south, dere ain't no goin' back home. Dems was da blackest days of my life. Dey put me in a slave hut wif a lady named Ol' Sukie. She must have been close to ninety years old then."

"She's not old anymore," Jesus said with a smile.

"That's true, Lord," Eliza agreed. "She's beautiful now."

"Yes, she is," agreed Zoe, "and when she sings her praises to Jesus, her voice is so wonderful that even the angels stop to listen."

"Well, as you can tell," Eliza continued, "Ol' Sukie loved the Lord, and Jesus used her to show me His love.

"I wasn't havin' any of that at first," Eliza confessed. "The more niceness and kindness she showed me, the uglier I got. At one point when she was trying to tell me how much Jesus loved me, I got so angry that I hit her with a piece of stove wood. It made a gash on the side of her head. All she had to do was to turn me in, an' the foreman would a beat me to within a' inch of my life. But sweet Ol' Sukie bandaged up her head an' never said a word. When anybody asked about her injury, she jus' said that she had gotten careless.

"Later on, when the foreman tried to put me in my place, I fought back and wound up getting' that beatin' that I deserved for hurtin' Ol' Sukie. Whoo wee! Dat man tore my back up wif his whip! But guess who come got me and took care of me?"

"Was it Sukie?" Ember asked.

"You know it was!" Eliza shot back. "Bandage on her head an' all, dat woman was da Lord's hands and feet to me! I hadn't been loved like dat since I got torn from my momma's arms. Sukie made sure I knew that it was the Lord Jesus Who was lovin' me. Da Lord never gave up on me, even though I gave up on Him. When I finally understood what Jesus did for me on the cross, that absolutely won my heart. I gave my life to Him.

"From den on I was His girl," Eliza said with a smile directed at Jesus. "Everything I did, I did for Him. All of my plans an' wishes jus' didn't seem important anymore. When I finally gave myself to that sweet love of Jesus, the whole purpose of my life changed. Once I was His, the only thing that mattered to me was doin' what pleased Him, because that was the only way that I could express my love for Him. Over time da Lord gave me opportunities to show His love to others. Some of 'em even became followers of His."

"Did you ever get your freedom?" Ember asked.

"What chu talkin' about?" Eliza exclaimed. "Jesus freed my spirit da first moment I put my trust in Him. Den a few years later, after da yellow fever come, He freed me from dat life in the shadow world to live with Him in dis beautiful place forever. Now I'm back wif my momma, my daddy, an' Lady Sukie."

"*Lady* Sukie?" Ember asked with surprise

"Dat's right," Eliza returned proudly. "She's a princess of high standin' here!"

Chapter Seven

"YES, LORD."

As Eliza finished speaking, Jesus looked at the other lady and nodded.

"Hello, Ember," the olive-skinned woman began. "I am Zoe of Pamphylia. I am very glad to meet you.

"My husband, Exuperius, as well as our son Cyriacus, were slaves to a man named Catulus. We lived a hundred years after Jesus Christ was born in the shadow world. My husband, my son, and I were faithful followers of the Lord Jesus. Though we had tried to share with our master the truth about Jesus Christ, he remained a committed pagan.

"Our family faithfully served Catulus for many years, but in spite of that, our master hated our faith in Jesus and tried regularly to discredit the Lord and us. When I became pregnant with our second child, Catulus pressured us repeatedly to perform the pagan rituals that were supposed to protect my life and the life of the baby."

"But you were slaves," Ember spoke up, "why would he care if you did that or not?"

"Ember, many women died giving birth at that time, and over half of the children died before they were three years old. It was important to Catulus at first because we were his slaves, and when I gave birth, he would have another slave. We were worth some money to him, and he wanted us all to live. But later it became something totally different...something very wicked."

"What happened?" Ember asked with concern.

"Because my husband and I refused to practice the pagan rituals, the word got out, and many of Catulus's friends, neighbors, and even some of the pagan priests spoke curses on us and our baby. They said that, because we had rejected the Roman gods, my baby and I were doomed to die."

"Were you afraid?" the girl asked.

"I was at first, until my husband reminded us of the words of David in the Psalms... *When I am afraid, I will put my trust in You, in God Whose word I praise. In God I have put my trust, how can I be afraid? What can mere man do to me?*

"So we trusted in God and prayed. The result was that I gave birth to a healthy baby boy who we named Theodolus. When everyone saw that, in spite of their curses, the baby and I were healthy, it showed that our God was greater than all of theirs, and they were very angry. All of the pagans put great pressure on our master to do something about it. Catulus was furious when he confronted my husband and me. He had the four of us arrested, and ordered us to perform pagan rituals over Theodolus to show that we honored the pagan gods. If we didn't, he intended to have our whole family burned in the ovens. We prayed to God, and He gave us the grace to refuse the pagan demands."

"So what happened?" Ember asked, mesmerized by the story.

Zoe smiled as she answered. "They burned us. The Lord was with us, and the pain was brief. We were all welcomed into the City of Light with such joy and celebration that it embarrassed us. Jesus Himself gave us crowns and places of honor at His table for being faithful even to death."

"Wow!" Ember exclaimed. "I don't know if I could do that."

"At the time, I didn't know if I could either, Ember," Zoe answered. "But Jesus was with us and gave us all we needed to follow Him even to death. And, Ember, the joy of heaven and the glory of being with the Lord is worth it! I would be willing to be burned a thousand times to be with Jesus."

"Thank you, dear ladies, for sharing your stories with My friend," Jesus said as he rose to His feet. Ember and the others stood with him and followed as the Lord led them back into the forest.

Not much was said as they walked along, but Ember was in awe of her two new friends. As they emerged from the opposite side of the narrow woods, the flowers and grasses of the meadow moved to the side to make a path for the Lord and His guests.

They began to hear singing that grew louder as they traveled. Eventually they came to an ivy-covered wall, and in it was an ornately carved, wooden door. Beautiful harmonies could be heard from the other side. The door opened of its own accord, and Eliza and Zoe stepped to the opening.

"Don't forget, Ember," Zoe said as they both stopped and looked back at their new friend, "Jesus is always faithful...always! It's been such a joy to meet you."

"Indeed it has," Eliza agreed. "I look forward to our next meeting. Zoe and I will be here to welcome you when you finally join us. Until then, be strong in the Lord, sister!"

With those words both ladies walked through the door.

Eagerly Ember moved to follow them, but a hand on her shoulder restrained her.

"Aren't we going in?" Ember asked with concern as the door closed.

"No," the Lord answered.

"Please, Lord, I want to join them," the girl begged.

"It's not time for you to join them."

"Please, Lord, PLEASE!" Ember pleaded. "It's not just them. I can hear my mother's voice singing! I beg you at least let me go to her! I miss her so much!"

"Dear one, I have not yet finished preparing a place for you, but I hope you know that it will be beautiful! For now I need you to go back. There is work I have to do, and I want to use you to do it."

"Lord, this place is wonderful...YOU are wonderful! If You send me away, how will I ever find my way back here? "

"You know the way."

"No, Lord, I don't!" the girl shot back, almost in a panic.

"Ember," Jesus returned, looking deeply into her eyes, "I AM the way. Trust in Me, dear one. I brought you here this time, and I will do what it takes to get you here again."

"But won't I have to do something? How will I know what to do? What if I mess up?"

Jesus smiled at her before He responded. "The only thing that you will need to do is stay close to Me. I will take care of the rest, and I will *not* mess up."

"Oh, please, Lord," the desperate girl begged once more, "don't make me go back to that horrible life. I want to stay with You, my family, and my new friends!"

"Dear one," Jesus said, looking deeply into the distraught girl's sad eyes, "will you go back for Me?"

Ember could read all the feelings in the eyes of the One Whom she knew loved her the most.

"Yes, Lord," she finally said as tears streamed down her face, "I will."

"And that, My sweet one, is true love and true worship." Jesus wrapped His arms around her and gave the girl a big hug.

Chapter Eight

A NEW LIFE

Ember felt her head lifted and warm liquid flowing into her mouth. She opened her eyes and saw the squaw holding a shallow bowl of brown tea to her lips. Taking a second swallow of the soothing drink, the slave looked into the eyes of her mistress.

Ember remembered the snake bite in the woods and Prisha arguing with her sisters as she tried to save the slave's life. Now Ember was back in the cabin, still alive, with the medicine woman treating her. The girl knew that the squaw, as mean as she was, had worked hard to save her, and she smiled at the woman.

The Shawnee woman was relieved when she saw that her patient was finally awake, but the smile surprised her, and she didn't know what to do with it. Eventually she snorted and turned away. A moment later she faced the girl again and handed her a warm piece of flat bread.

Taking the food with another smile of thanks, Ember consumed it hungrily. As she ate, the girl thought through all that had happened to her. The people she loved the most had been killed, everything she held dear was torn from her, and she was now the slave of cruel people. She had been attacked by wolves and had been bitten by a snake. Life could not have been any worse for her...but then she met Jesus.

Maybe it had been a dream or some kind of a vision, but it was too real and too fresh for her not to believe it had happened. He was so loving, so precious, and so wonderful. Now that she knew He was looking over her and was using her slavery for His purposes, none of the rest of it seemed as bad. In fact, she was more than willing to go through it for Him.

Wait! the girl thought to herself. *That's exactly what Eliza said. Once she understood the depth of Christ's love for her, nothing mattered but wanting to love Him back. And what had Jesus said to her as she left? He said that saying* yes *to doing His will was true love and worship.*

Ember's old life before slavery had been easier and much more pleasant. But now she could see that even that nicer existence would have eventually become miserable and hopeless if it had been lived without Jesus. It was His love for her and His vision and purpose that made her life worth living, no matter the circumstances. With her loving Lord guiding and working in her as He had in Zoe and Eliza, Ember realized that life, even as a slave, had true meaning. Jesus intended to accomplish things of eternal significance. All she had to do was to trust Him enough to say *yes, Lord.*

Tears streamed down her cheeks as she remembered the sweetness of Christ's love for her. A wonderful resolve began to flood her soul. She was determined to trust in the One Who loved her with an everlasting love. *God did have a purpose for all of this,* she told herself, and she would wait for Him to show her what it was.

Suddenly she felt a great burden lifted from her shoulders. By trusting that Jesus and His Father loved her and were with her in captivity, she had hope and was anxious to discover what Jesus had planned for her. She would be God's handmaid, like Mary the mother of Jesus, and always be ready to do His will. As she had these thoughts, a smile began to creep across her face.

"What you doing?" Waxing Moon said as she looked at Ember. The slave girl had been so lost in her thoughts that she had not noticed that her translator had walked into the cabin. "You crazy girl! You crying and smiling. Are you happy that you sad or are you sad that you happy? You all mixed up...crazy girl."

Over the next few days, Ember made a rapid recovery, and Prisha was pleasantly surprised to find the girl more self-motivated and even eager to do the many necessary chores. The squaw began to wish that the girl had been snake bitten sooner.

Ember found her thoughts constantly on Jesus and her future home. Even as she cracked thousands of hickory nuts and picked out the meats, she kept a running conversation going with the Lord. No longer was her life hopeless drudgery. The Lord had said that He had work that He desired to do through her. She believed that He had a purpose for her, but she needed to figure out what it is. What had Jesus said to her? *Just remain with Me, Ember. Always stay with me, and I will do the rest.*

"Good!" Ember said as she smiled in the Lord's presence. "I don't have to figure it out. I will trust You to show me when the time is right. You are so sweet to me, Lord. That's just one less thing that I have to concern myself with."

Jesus began revealing the answer that very afternoon as Prisha changed the dressing on her injured leg. Ember was amazed at how quickly the deep gashes were healing. She had expected the snake bite to get infected, but it did not. As Ember watched the medicine woman prepare the herbs, oil, and charcoal for the poultice, she suddenly became aware of how much good a person with Prisha's knowledge and skill could do to help others. It inspired the girl. *Waxing Moon says that Prisha is the greatest medicine woman the Shawnee have ever had,* Ember thought to herself. *Maybe that's why I'm her slave. If the Lord wants me to be a medicine woman, then He has certainly put me where I can learn from the best!*

All through that winter, Ember spent a lot of time thinking and talking to Jesus about what it would mean for her to learn how to heal others. She got the sense that the Lord was pleased with the idea, and she became excited about it.

One day as Ember mixed the nut meats, berries, and honey together, she interrupted Waxing Moon during one of the young Indian girl's boring monologues. "I need you to do something for me, Waxing Moon."

"Tapakekesefewi no do your work," the young girl snapped back as she chewed on her flat bread. "*You* slave, not Waxing Moon."

"I don't want you to do my work," Ember returned with a smile. "I want you to be my teacher."

"What you want Tapakekesefewi to teach?"

"Well, sometimes you are not here," the slave girl began shrewdly, "and I would be a better help to your Auntie Prisha if I understood her and could speak to her. Since you speak English so well, I was wondering if you could teach me to speak Shawnee."

"Yes," the Indian girl agreed with pride, "my speak Englich much well. Tapakekesefewi teach you Shawnee...teach you good."

From then on, whenever Waxing Moon was around, whatever Ember was doing became language class. A fire was lit in the slave girl to learn Shawnee. She told herself that she was doing it for Jesus and that it would help her become the Great Maker's medicine girl.

At first her questions about medicine seemed to annoy Prisha, but as the medicine woman saw the great interest Ember took in learning, the squaw slowly began to share her knowledge with the girl.

Fortunately for all of them, Rayford spent much of the next spring and summer on raids with the Shawnee warriors. As far as Ember was concerned, the less he was around, the better. But all good things must come to an end, and the trapper and the raiding party returned one cool, crisp autumn afternoon from their most recent raid.

Rayford announced his return with a shout as he arrived at the cabin. The squaw and Ember saw him and Prisha's brother walk up with a strange horse loaded with plunder and two large deer. When they got to the front of the cabin, Rayford dragged one deer from the back of the horse.

"We shot these two back up the valley," he announced gruffly. "This one's mine. You brother's takin' the other one. Cut me a thick steak from this one's loin," he continued as he pulled the dead deer closer to the cabin. "I'll eat it tonight."

While Prisha went inside to grab a knife to skin the beast, Rayford unloaded the horse. After laying a strange rifle, a powder horn, and an ammunition pouch on the ground, he pulled two sacks from the pack. He held the heavy one in his right hand but tossed the one in his left hand at Ember's feet. "There's some dresses in there," he barked at her. "Find one that'll fit ya."

The trapper turned and gave his friend a farewell as the chief took the reins of the horse with the rest of the load and walked down the trail to the village.

Prisha returned with the knife, and seeing the squaw, Rayford barked more orders. "Get this rifle, horn, and pouch into the cabin. I got somethin' to do." He took the heavy bag and walked toward the creek.

On hearing the demand, Prisha growled something as she stood preparing to skin the deer. She looked angrily at Ember and jerked the knife toward the rifle. Quickly the girl nodded her understanding and hurried to haul the weapon and other things into the cabin.

Later, as the steaks were cooking and the trapper cleaned his newly acquired rifle, Prisha noticed that the water bucket was almost empty. She snapped an order to Ember to get more water, which was exciting to the girl because she understood.

The air had a frosty bite as, with bucket in hand, she hurried to the nearby creek. She suddenly realized that, because of the lack of rain the last two weeks, there was little water trickling through the nearly dry streambed. Ember moved hurriedly upstream, looking for a pool deep enough for the bucket. Walking for nearly seventy-five yards, she came to a place where the brook disappeared into some thick brush and trees. Pushing through them, she was surprised to find a cave opening that was a little taller than she was. The stream actually flowed out of the cave, and the two-foot drop from the lip of the cave to the streambed made a perfect place to set the bucket and let it fill. As she stood holding the brush back from the opening, she felt a strong push of warm air from the cave mouth and realized that it must go back a ways. When the bucket was almost full, she snatched it up, let the limbs snap back into place, and hurried back to the cabin.

Chapter Nine

A DANGEROUS SITUATION

After the trapper was served his supper, Prisha and Ember chewed on pieces of deer steak and flat bread by the hearth. Rayford said little and seemed in a hurry as he greedily wolfed down his food. When finished, he pushed back his bowl and reached for the sack resting at his feet. Ember recognized it as the heavy bag he had carried to the creek, but it didn't seem as heavy as before.

Opening the cloth poke, the trapper pulled out a brown ceramic jug with a corn cob stopper. Yanking the plug with his teeth and spitting it on the dirt floor, Rayford took long drinks from the jug. He finally pulled it away from his mouth and let out a long, contented sigh. As he did so, the strong smell of alcohol filled the small cabin.

Uh oh, Ember said to herself with concern as she watched the large trapper, *this can't be good.* At the same time she noticed that Prisha gave a disgusted snort.

Being around the savage frontiersman was bad enough anytime, but if he was drinking liquor, Ember wanted to be out of sight when the alcohol took effect. She quickly collected the cooking pots and utensils and carried them to the creek to scrub.

When the girl walked back into the cabin, she felt uncomfortable when the brooding trapper did not take his eyes off her as she moved around the room. While she was helping Prisha put everything away, the girl noticed the squaw secretly motioning her to go up to the loft. Ember gave a subtle nod and escaped to the ladder. Once in her safe place, Ember dug into the sack that had been tossed at her feet when Rayford arrived. She found several dresses and skirts. Suddenly it occurred to her that they must have belonged to the people the raiding party had attacked. When Ember realized that the previous owners had probably been killed, she stopped and prayed for direction.

Just as she finished, she sensed the presence of the Lord. "Jesus," she whispered, "I don't want to be a part of any of the wicked things Rayford or the Indians have been doing. How can I wear the clothing of people who were murdered?"

She heard no voice, but it was like Jesus was speaking to her heart. *Don't think about that, dear one. The contents of this sack are things I have provided for you.*

A feeling of peace swept over the troubled girl, and she continued to search through the bag. As she drew out more clothing, she realized there was something heavier in the bottom. The last thing she pulled out was a worn, gingham work dress wrapped around something. As she uncovered the object, she suddenly gasped. "It's a Bible!" she whispered excitedly to herself. "Oh, Jesus, thank you! Thank you!"

She ran her fingers lovingly over the leather cover and slowly turned the pages. Using the flickering light of the fireplace as it reflected off the low cabin roof, she read the precious words, looking for familiar scriptures. Ember cried when she came to Psalm 23 and saw her mother's favorite verses: *Yea tho I walk through the valley of the shadow of death I will fear no evil...*

This verse inspired Ember to think of Zoe of Pamphylia and the "valley of the shadow of death" that she and her family had walked through for Christ. *Faith in Jesus is a powerful thing,* Ember reasoned.

Suddenly angry shouts erupted in the cabin below. Prisha yelled heatedly at her husband, and the trapper bellowed back, "YOU KEEP YER STINKIN' HANDS OFF MY JUG, YA HEAR!" Rayford stood up from the table suddenly, knocking his chair back against the wall. "I'LL DRINK AS MUCH AS I WANT!"

Ember heard the squaw yelling again, then there was a loud *smack.* With a cry of pain, Prisha crashed into the wall. Ember crept to the edge of the loft and saw the drunken form of the trapper over the injured squaw, shaking his fist at her.

"I'M DONE WIF' YOU AN' ALL YER SQUAWKIN'!" he yelled as he staggered and fell into the shelves with Prisha's medicines, breaking several pots and spilling the contents onto the floor. He pushed himself back up and slurred, "...DONE WIF YOU! DAT GIRL'L MAKE A BETTER SQUAW DAN YOU, AN' I'M TAKIN' 'ER!" He staggered over to the ladder and began to climb.

In a terrified panic Ember looked for a way of escape, but there was none. She searched for a weapon, but again she found nothing. *JESUS!* she prayed desperately, *PLEASE SAVE ME! DON'T LET HIM DO THIS TO ME!*

She looked over the edge of the ladder and saw the drunken face just below her. He saw her too and, with an evil leer, reached up to grab her.

Just then there was a heavy *thunk,* and Rayford's eyes rolled back into his head. He dropped from the ladder, falling heavily onto the dirt floor. Ember saw Prisha standing at the bottom with a large piece of firewood in her hands.

Prisha looked up at the girl and said in Shawnee, "You hurt?"

Ember shook her head and returned, "Scared."

The squaw tossed the stick of wood back onto the pile and picked up Rayford's liquor jug, pouring it all into the fire, which roared up as the alcohol hit. When the jug was empty, she placed it on its side next to the unconscious man's hand. Finally she threw a buffalo robe over her husband and began cleaning up the broken and spilled pots and jars.

Ember climbed down to help her mistress with the mess. The slave noticed a bruised knot forming under the squaw's right eye. Placing her hand on Prisha's shoulder, Ember pointed to her injured eye and said in Shawnee, "You hurt!"

The squaw waved off the girl's concerns and said a long string of Shawnee words, only a few of which Ember recognized. "...much hurt...not. He...do worse."

After everything was straightened and with her heart still pounding, Ember crawled back up the ladder and over to the open Bible. She continued reading, *Thy rod and Thy staff, they comfort me.* "And Thy stick of firewood!" the girl chuckled thankfully.

The next day Ember was afraid to be near the trapper, but as it turned out, there was no reason for her concern. Rayford was too hung over to bother with her or anything else. In fact, it seemed to the girl that Rayford couldn't remember anything of the night before. When he first stirred under the robe, he growled and sat up and wanted to know why his head hurt.

After calling him a few choice names and letting him have an earful of what she thought of his drinking, Prisha told him that he had tried to climb up the ladder and had fallen.

Just then he noticed the jug. Snatching it up, he quickly put it to his lips. When nothing came out, he snarled angrily, "What happened to my liquor?"

Prisha gave him a disgusted look and just pointed at him. The miserable trapper pushed himself off the floor, staggered over to the bed, and dropped onto it. The moaning and groaning lasted for almost half an hour, but eventually the only noise was heavy snoring. Rayford got out of bed in the middle of the afternoon, but still felt so bad that he refused any food.

Prisha put a pot of water on the fire to boil and shaved some roasted chicory root into it. It wasn't long before the small cabin was filled with the delicious smell.

Rayford was sitting at the table holding his painful head when he breathed in the fragrant aroma of the brewing chicory. "Give me some of that," he demanded, pointing toward the streaming pot.

Prisha used her deerskin pad to pour a portion of the brew from the hot pot into a bowl. She handed it to her husband, who snatched it and slurped the hot liquid.

He finished the first bowl and demanded another. As he drained it, he stood up with a groan, placed the empty bowl on the table, and staggered out the door to check his traps.

Prisha watched her husband leave. When the door shut behind him, she gave a snort of satisfaction at his miserable state. She lectured Ember in Shawnee, but the only thing the girl could make out was, "...drink bad...foolish...kill himself."

The squaw then set out two more bowls and poured the chicory brew into both. One she shoved toward Ember. The squaw took a long sip of the fragrant drink and gave a long hum of approval.

The slave girl sniffed the steam coming from her bowl and took a sip. "Good," the girl said in Shawnee.

The squaw nodded and gave a faint smile in return. After several more long sips from her bowl, Prisha looked at the girl and said, "Hot chicory...make all better."

Chapter Ten

A PRICE WORTH PAYING

In order to become a medicine woman, Ember knew she must be able to communicate directly with Prisha. Waxing Moon was a big help, but the Indian girl was somewhat lazy, and Ember couldn't trust that she was interpreting all that Prisha said.

To help her remember the new words she learned, all that winter, whenever Ember had opportunity, she wrote them on an old, worn hide that she had found under her bed of deerskins. Making a writing stylus from a carved stick, she used a large pottery shard from the trash pit behind the cabin for an ink well and crushed poke berries for ink. By keeping the point of the stylus sharp, she was able to write in small letters. Every night before the light of the fire got too low for her to be able to see, Ember studied her notes and practiced her words.

You're working hard, dear one.

"Thank you, Lord," the girl whispered her response. "Shawnee is not an easy language to learn."

I want you to know that I appreciate what you're doing because I know that you are doing it for Me.

"That really encourages me, Lord!" the girl whispered with a smile.

I also want you to know that I will bless you, and I will always be with you. Do you believe that?

"Yes, Lord, I do, and I know that You love me. I love You too, and I can't wait to be with You forever. I miss walking with You."

I still walk with you, dear one.

"I know, Lord, but it is so much more fun to walk with You at Your place."

Have you noticed that your mistress is being nicer to you?

"Yes, I have," Ember responded. "Is that You?"

Actually, it is both of us. You have been letting Me do more in you, and Prisha is seeing My love starting to show through you.

"I'm just glad she stopped hitting me with her spoon. She can really be a hard woman, Lord."

I know, dear one, but she doesn't know Me. You would be just like her if you had lived her life without Me. I want you to understand that, as difficult as she has made your time with her, I care for her and love her very much. I died for her, Ember, just like I did for you. Stop looking at

Prisha through your eyes and begin seeing her through Mine. She needs to know Me.

"Yes, Lord," the girl returned sincerely.

Ah, My sweet one, the Father and I love it when you say that!

Now Ember was doubly motivated to learn Shawnee, both to learn medicine from her mistress and to teach her about One Who loved her more than anyone.

The next morning, as soon as Ember heard Prisha crawl out of her bed, the girl hurriedly dressed and descended the ladder to help with breakfast. The squaw had picked up a stick of fire wood and was about to thump the floor of the loft to wake her slave when she was suddenly startled to see the girl standing beside her, dressed, and ready to work. Prisha looked at her with a dumbfounded expression, and Ember smiled at her in return.

Now that she clearly understood the morning routine, the slave girl eagerly jumped to her tasks. Because she felt that it would please Jesus the most, she pushed herself to be as quick and as efficient as possible. She sensed Him smiling at her as she worked, and it gave her a deep feeling of joy.

Prisha watched out of the corner of her eye as her slave did her chores. The medicine woman was amazed the captive kept up the hard work while the smile never left her face. *I've never seen a snake bite do this,* the squaw thought to herself.

One late spring morning, just after Rayford left to check his traps, Waxing Moon showed up, munching on the ever-present piece of flatbread. As soon as she entered the cabin, the squaw began giving orders. It was exciting to Ember that she understood most of what Prisha said. They were to finish cleaning up the cabin, then go replenish the medicine woman's supplies of medicinal herbs.

As they searched through the woods, Prisha and Ember carried two baskets on their arms, and Waxing Moon carried one. The squaw led them up the tree-covered, rocky hill to the east of the cabin. About half way up, they came to a mossy outcropping of limestone that was wet from water dripping through cracks in the rocks. Prisha searched the shaded areas below the damp ledge, looking for a particular herb. When she found it, she lifted a large knife from her basket to dig it up, roots and all. As she harvested each plant, she would hand it to Ember and say something.

"You wash roots ver' good," the plump Indian girl interpreted, "an' be quick!"

But Ember was already rinsing off the dirt in the water trickling from the rocks. She had understood her mistress's words.

"Hohweesah?" the slave girl asked and showed the squaw the cleaned roots.

"Heenee," the squaw returned with a satisfied nod.

Waxing Moon stood with wide eyes and an open mouth. "Turtle Girl speak Shawnee now? How you learn so fast?"

"Because you're such a good teacher, Waxing Moon," Ember answered with a smile.

"Ah yes, Tapakekesefewi ver' good teacher," the girl said proudly. "Teach Turtle Girl much good Shawnee."

By late afternoon Prisha had filled the baskets with twelve different plants. Ember recognized one as feverfew, but she was unsure of the rest. When they got back to the cabin and prepared the harvest for storage, the girl asked Prisha their names. The slave girl wrote them onto her deer skin, as well as making drawings or writing descriptions so she could recognize them again. If she remembered where they found each plant, she recorded that too.

As on most days, different ones from the tribe arrived at the cabin to get help from Prisha for illnesses and injuries. One youth with a dislocated finger came by with his mother. Prisha had him bite a piece of leather as she painfully popped the finger back in place, then used small leather strips to bind the injured digit to the next one for support.

Another brave came in with a lower leg wound that had gotten infected. After cleaning it, the medicine woman mixed several herbs together for a poultice and bandaged it to the leg. Sending him a leather pouch with the same herbs, Prisha instructed the warrior to repeat the poultice daily.

An elderly squaw came with a large wound on her back that she had tried to treat, but weeks had gone by, and the injury refused to heal. Prisha sat her on a stump in the yard, and after an examination, gently scraped the tissue until it was fresh and bleeding. Pouring a thick coating of honey on the site and covering it with a pad made from compressed thistle down, the medicine woman took a leather strap and bound it around the woman's chest to hold the pad in place.

Every time Prisha worked on a patient, Ember stayed close by and watched everything. The studious youth recorded how each injury or illness was treated.

One day Prisha's brother, the chief, came in with Rayford. They had killed a wild hog in the woods, but not before the beast had charged at them and slashed her brother's leg with its sharp tusk. Prisha led him to a chair and propped his leg on the table. After thoroughly cleaning the wound, she opened a leather pouch and pulled out a very sharp bone needle that was split in the pointed end, as well as an awl with a narrow tip. She reached into another jar and pulled out a long horse hair. As her brother sat as still as a statue, Prisha used her awl to punch holes in the skin on either side of the wound. Then she took the horse hair and wedged it into the tiny split in the end of the needle.

Carefully, the medicine woman pushed the end with the hair through the holes first. After removing the hair from the split, she withdrew the needle and was able to tie the wound closed. Repeating the process fifteen times, she sutured the entire gash shut. Her brother never flinched or changed his stoic expression for the entire procedure.

When finished, the chief looked at the closed wound and stood to his feet. He stepped on his injured leg a couple of times, placed his hand on his sister's shoulder, gave her a nod of approval, then walked out.

Ember, continuing her study, examined the needle and punch used to sew the skin. Later, when they were cooking Rayford's supper, Ember asked how Prisha had made the suturing needle and punch. Ember decided they would be very useful tools for a medicine woman. So whenever she had a few minutes between chores, she pulled out deer bone fragments and, using a piece of sharp flint, carved and shaved the bone pieces into her own needle and punch. Prisha saw what the girl was doing and tried to help her. In response, Ember gave her a big smile and thanked her.

Prisha stared at the slave in amazement. "What happen to you?" Prisha asked in Shawnee. "Why...you so different?"

"I need...tell you...story," Ember smiled and stumblingly answered in the Indian tongue, quickly climbing the ladder and grabbing her Bible. When she arrived back at the table, she set the book down and put her hand on it. "This...tell about...Moneto."

"The Great Spirit?" asked Prisha as she stared at the book.

"Heenee," Ember said nodding her head. "This say the Moneto, the Great Spirit, love us much. After snake bite, I choose to follow Moneto. He love me and give me peace. He love you too, Prisha. He want you to know Him."

At that moment the cabin door flew open, and Rayford stepped in. "HEY!" he roared when he spotted the Bible on the table. Like a flash he drew his long hunting knife and stabbed through the Holy Book and into the wooden table. "WHERE'D YOU GET THAT THING?"

Ember was confused. "What? The Bible? It was in the clothes you gave me."

"THERE AIN'T NO BIBLES COMIN' IN HERE!" he roared again. "YA HEAR ME! NO BIBLES IN HERE—EVER!

Jerking his knife out of the table, he lifted it with the Bible still on it. He started to reach up and pull it off, but hesitated instead and drew his trembling hand back as he stared at it with a terrified look.

He's afraid of your book, Lord, Ember said in her heart.

Yes, he is, an answer seemed to come back to the girl, *and well he should be.*

For a very long moment, Rayford gaped fearfully at the book impaled on his knife. Finally, in a panic, he stepped over to the fireplace and, using a stick of wood, slid the Holy Book off the knife and into the fire.

"DON'T!" screamed Ember, but at that instant she saw the bully's knife pointed at her throat.

"NO BIBLES IN MY CABIN!"

Tears streamed down the girl's face as she watched Jesus's special gift to her begin to burn.

Suddenly a voice outside the cabin called out in English, "Hello, the cabin. Rayford, are you home?"

The trapper cracked the door open and called. "Yeah, be right there!"

Rayford stepped back to confront the girl and again held his knife in front of her face. "I'm goin' out there to talk with them men, an' if while they're here, you say one word or let yourself be seen by 'em, I'm shovin' this knife into your heart! Do you understand me?"

Still staring at the burning book, the crying girl nodded her head. As soon as the trapper walked out, Ember dashed for the fire. She reached in and grabbed a fistful of burning pages and tossed them onto the hearth, throwing the deer skin pad on top of them to put out the flames. When she looked back, the open part of the book was engulfed in flames. Grabbing the knife, the girl reached into the flames and flipped some of the pages over, revealing a part the flames had not yet ignited. Reaching in, she grabbed another fistful of pages that were starting to burn on the edges. She did this twice more before the flames completely consumed what was left of the book. She beat the pages on the hearth with her palms, trying to put out the flames.

Prisha knelt beside her and grabbed her hands. Both had bad burns, some extending up her arms. As the medicine woman cleaned and treated her slave's injured hands, she looked into her eyes and asked, "Book worth this?"

Ember tried to smile through the tears and the pain. "Yes!" she answered with feeling. "Oh, yes!"

Chapter Eleven

THE DOUBLE-CROSS

While Ember was frantically trying to save some of the burning pages of the Bible, Rayford walked out to meet the newcomers. It was a group of seven frontiersmen. Most were dressed in buckskins with wide-brimmed hats, but a couple had caps made of animal skins. The man standing in front wore an American military jacket over buckskin pants.

"Rayford!" the leader barked when he saw the trapper approaching.

"Cap'n Parks!" Rayford returned with a wide, toothy grin. "It's been a while. What brings you this far north?"

"You!" Parks shot back. "I need your help. In a few weeks General Clark is gonna be sending troops into Kentucky. The plan is to start attacks on Indian tribes that have been sidin' with the British. Over the last several months, a number of settlements have been attacked by Shawnee war parties. It's been real bad. They killed the settlers and burned down their homes. General Clark has had enough, and he's bound and determined to drive all the Indian tribes out of Kentucky and send 'em north of the Ohio River."

"That'll take some doin'," Rayford responded thoughtfully. "How's the genr'l figure on getting' that done?"

"Let's go inside your cabin, and I'll explain it all," Parks returned.

Rayford looked back at his cabin and rubbed his chin. "Well...I don't think that's gonna work," the trapper finally answered. "My squaw's got a bunch of chores she's doin' in there, an' she's got the inside of that little cabin plumb full of mess. We better do our talkin' out here."

With an irritated growl Parks pulled a map from his jacket pocket and squatted down to spread it out on the ground. He laid his knife and his tomahawk on each end to hold the paper down. "Eventually General Clark will be bringing an army into the territory, but he doesn't have the men together yet. Right now he's in Virginia tryin' to assemble all the troops he can get. He sent our militia ahead of the main body to attack some of the smaller Indian villages an' give 'em a taste of their own medicine.

"I told the general that, since you are an American trapper, we had a friend in this territory. I knew you'd be willing to help us out."

"What do you want me to do?" Rayford asked.

"Well, I figure since you live and trap these parts, you could tell us where to find some smaller Shawnee villages we could ambush."

The trapper thought for a moment before he responded. "It's about time the genr'l did something about all the raidin' the Indians have been doin'!" Rayford said with pretend anger. "Why, all the poor settlers are at the mercy of them thievin' cut-throats. You boys are doin' a mighty fine work! Kill 'em all, I say!"

"I told the general that you could be counted on," Captain Parks said with satisfaction. "Take a look at this map an' show us where we can best hit 'em. Just give us a target, an' we'll hurry back to camp an' gather the troops."

"How many men you got?" the trapper asked innocently.

"All total there's thirty-six of us," Parks admitted. "That's plenty to ambush a small village."

Rayford nodded thoughtfully.

"So where's the best place to start our counter attacks?" Parks asked again as he impatiently pointed to the map.

The trapper pretended to study the map as he rubbed his chin. "Hmmm...How about showin' me where we are on your map?"

The captain placed his finger on a spot, and Rayford continued his studious examination of the drawings. Finally he placed his finger on the map to the south and east of Park's finger.

"Right there's your best bet," the trapper announced. "I was in that area trappin' beaver a few months ago an' spotted a Shawnee raidin' party movin' through. I hid till they passed, then went on settin' my traps. Then another group of 'em marched through. My curiosity got the better of me, an' I followed 'em at a distance. That's when I found their village. If they're still there, you an' your men should be able to handle 'em."

Parks studied the spot Rayford indicated until he was sure he could find it again. "You're sure, right?" Parks asked.

"As sure as I can be," the trapper returned. "All I can say is that they were there the last time I was in the area."

"I knew you'd come through for me, Rayford," the captain said with a smile as he folded his map and placed it in his pocket. "We'll head back to camp to get the rest of our men. I think we can be in position to attack that village at dawn day after tomorrow."

"Well, good luck to you!" Rayford said, sticking out his hand as the wide, toothy grin spread across his face again. "Give 'em what for!"

Parks shook the offered hand, then ordered his men to head south as quickly as possible.

Watching the troops disappear into the southern forest, the trapper remained in the same spot for several minutes. Rayford knew the Shawnee would have been keeping an eye on the frontiersmen, so he gave a call that sounded like a whippoorwill. As expected, a Shawnee warrior appeared out of the nearby woods north of the cabin. With Indian sign language, so as to make no noise, Rayford told the brave to get the chief and bring him quickly.

Almost an hour later, Prisha's brother, the war chief, and two of the elders entered the cabin. They stood around the table as they talked.

As the meeting began, the squaw knelt in front of the fire preparing their evening meal. Ember's burned hands were so painful that Prisha had sent her into the loft before Rayford and the Shawnee leaders came in.

"What soldiers want?" the chief demanded.

"They want to kill you," the trapper answered just as bluntly. "They want revenge for our raids on the settlements, so they asked me to tell them where a Shawnee village was that they could attack."

"What you say?" the chief asked again.

"I sent them to the southeast. Let me show you."

Rayford shoved Prisha away from the hearth. Ember heard the squaw yell and leaned over to look through a crack in the loft floor to see what had happened. She saw the trapper reach down and lift a large, flat stone in the center of the hearth. He drew out a bundle of deerskin and carried it to the table. Ember quietly turned onto her other side to find another crack that would let her view what he did next.

When Rayford unwrapped the skin, Ember saw that it contained a compass, and a detailed map of the eastern territory was drawn on the leather. Observing the compass needle, the trapper oriented the map north.

"Okay," Rayford began, pointing to a spot on the drawing. "We are right here. Over this way, along the river to the east, is a meadow that the tribe used a few years ago as a winter camp—right where I'm pointing. That's where I sent 'em." He put his figure on the map.

"Good," the Indian leader said with a nod of satisfaction. "That long ways from our camp. How many warriors do they have?"

"Thirty-six, and they should be arriving at the old camp grounds in two days. Their plan is to attack at dawn."

The chief conferred with the elders for several minutes, then turned back to the trapper. "We will send a hundred warriors to meet them and take their scalps."

"You could do that, Kolapeka, but this is just a small group of 'em," the trapper said thoughtfully. "The cap'n made it clear that their big chief, Genr'l

Clark, is gonna be comin' with an army to kill the Shawnee in a few weeks. Killing these men won't stop that."

"Let them come," the Indian responded confidently. "We will take their hair to decorate our lodge poles."

"I know the Shawnee are great fighters. I have fought beside my Shawnee brothers many times. But if the gen'rl brings enough soldiers with him, they may be more than the braves can handle... unless we trick them."

"What is your plan?" the chief asked.

Rayford carefully laid out his idea for using the small party of soldiers to help them defeat the larger army when it came. As he spoke, it disgusted Ember to hear the trapper's shrewd scheme, but she kept quiet.

When Rayford finished, Kolapeka, the chief, explained it all to the elders. With grunts of approval, the leaders quickly decided to adopt the trapper's plan.

"I will gather the warriors, and we will leave this evening," the chief announced to the trapper.

"I'll grab my stuff and join you at your camp," Rayford called to his friend as the chief walked out the door. "Just don't leave 'til I get there."

Rayford once again rolled the compass in the deerskin map and placed it back in its hiding place, carefully replacing the hearth stone on top. Throwing on his buckskin coat, he belted it around his waist. He dashed around the cabin grabbing his traveling pack, rifle, powder horn, and ammunition pouch. The trapper shoved his long hunting knife into its sheath. Lastly he yanked his steel-headed tomahawk from where he had stuck it in the wood of the door frame, shoving the handle into his belt.

"Give me one of them deer steaks," he demanded, pointing at the meat roasting on the fire.

"Not ready," Prisha shot back.

With an angry growl the trapper jerked out his knife, stabbed the biggest of the raw, hot hunks of meat, and bit into it as he walked out the door.

Chapter Twelve

THE SCHEME

All night Captain Parks had his small company of troops creep quietly through the woods, approaching the Shawnee camp that Rayford had identified. They had come from the west and had traveled along the wooded bank of a wide river for the last several miles. The captain checked the landmarks in the light of a half moon and realized that the village should be located in a meadow through the woods to their left.

Calling a halt, he gathered his men around him. "This should be it," he whispered loud enough for them all to hear. "Spread out and keep quiet. We'll move to attack in half an hour.

"Bannon," Parks called quietly to his best scout, "I need you to check out that village. See if you can spot their lookouts, then come back and report to me."

"We're downwind from 'em," Bannon returned. "I'm a little surprised we cain't smell their camp fires from here."

"Yeah," Parks returned suspiciously, "I noticed that too."

"It could be that trapper gave us bad information," Bannon suggested.

"Maybe," the captain answered. "Just go check it out, and don't take too long."

With a nod the scout moved quietly into the woods to the north. Fifteen minutes later they heard someone approaching. In an instant over thirty rifles were pointed into the darkness.

"It's me," called a voice. "Don't shoot!"

"That's Bannon!" Captain Parks quietly announced, and everyone relaxed.

"What'd you find?" Parks asked as soon as the scout appeared.

"They ain't there," Bannon announced, "an' it looks like they ain't been there for a while. That trapper was wrong."

"Well, he did say that it's been a few months since he's been in this area," Parks answered defensively.

"He lives here," Bannon growled. "It sure seems like he could have given us better information than this!"

"Somebody's comin'!" called one of the troopers.

From the west they could hear rapid footfalls running through the woods. As every rifle anxiously waited for a target to appear, suddenly a voice called out of the darkness, "CAP'N PARKS! CAP'N PARKS! IT'S ME, RAYFORD!"

"Let him come," the captain ordered.

As the trapper ran up, Parks met him. "What are you doin' here, Rayford?"

"It's a trap, Cap'n!"

"What do you mean?" Parks asked. "The Indian village ain't here!"

"They knew you was coming," Rayford answered. "They've had scouts trailin' you the whole time."

"How do you know that?"

"My squaw was visitin' some of her family, and they told her that the Shawnee were watchin' you and had planned an ambush. They're here now, Cap'n!"

"There ain't no Indians around here!" the scout Bannon announced firmly.

Just then scores of muzzle blasts fired out of the dark woods from the west, and the bullets flew through the leaves and branches around the small company of troops.

"HOW MANY DO YOU FIGURE THERE ARE?" Parks demanded excitedly as his men began to return fire.

"There's over a hundred of 'em," Rayford returned confidently. "Way too many to fight! We got to run! Follow me!"

The trapper turned and raced to the east along the shore of the river. Captain Parks hesitated for a moment as he looked into the dark woods to the west. Just then another blast of rifle fire erupted. Quickly turning, he gave the order to his men. "CEASE FIRE, MEN, AND RUN TO THE EAST! ON THE DOUBLE! FOLLOW THE TRAPPER!"

Trusting the predawn darkness to hide their movements, the militia rushed to escape. Behind them a loud chorus of deafening Shawnee war cries filled the forest.

Rayford led them rapidly along the bank until they came to a large creek of swift water that emptied into the river. "This way!" the trapper ordered as he turned north and followed the creek. They hadn't run a hundred yards when they came to a powerful waterfall cascading over a ledge above them.

"Quick, all of you, behind the waterfall!" Rayford called, ducking behind the wide wall of rushing water. Thirty-six troopers rapidly followed their guide into the place of concealment.

"They'll find us here!" one of the men called out. "They can follow our tracks!"

"Not in the dark, they cain't!" Rayford called back. "Now everyone keep quiet! They'll think we crossed the creek an' kept runnin'."

"Pipe down, all of you!" the captain ordered. "This is all we got, so keep your yaps shut an' your powder dry...an' pray!

At one point several of the men thought they heard yelling in the distance, but the waterfall's roar drowned out all the noise around them.

After half an hour the sky in the east began to glow. It was then that Rayford volunteered to slip out of their place of concealment and locate the Indians. He was only gone for a few minutes, but as the sun began to peek over the tree tops to the east, the trapper returned.

"What'd you see?" Parks asked anxiously.

"It's like I said," Rayford returned. "In the dark they thought we kept runnin', so they crossed the creek and headed east."

"But they'll soon figure out that mistake now that it's light enough to see," the scout Bannon pointed out.

"You're right," Rayford agreed, "so before they do, we need to get out of here and head back west."

"Lead the way," the captain ordered, addressing the trapper.

Slipping from behind the wide wall of water, Rayford guided the soldiers in a rapid run back the way they had come. After almost thirty minutes, the trapper called a halt.

"What are you stoppin' for?" Parks demanded.

"This is where I leave you," Rayford answered. "I need to get back to my cabin before any of their scouts figure out that I helped you."

"Where do we go from here?" the captain asked, looking around them.

"I think your best bet is to get across the river as quick as you can," Rayford returned confidently. "I don't think they'll come after you over there. They've prob'ly already figured out that they missed us, so if I were you, I'd swim it rather than hunt for a place to ford."

"Yeah," the captain agreed, "I see your point."

Turning to his men, the captain issued orders. "We're gonna swim the river, men. Any of you who don't swim so well, grab a log, hang onto it, and kick to the other side...an' try to keep your powder dry!"

The captain turned to shake Rayford's hand. "You saved our bacon this time, my friend," Parks said with feeling.

"Glad to do it," the trapper returned, smiling broadly. "Now listen here, Cap'n. You said the gen'rl is bringin' his army down the river soon."

"Yep," Parks returned. "Could be as soon as a few weeks, or it could take a few months. You know how stuff like that goes. It depends on how quickly he can muster his troops. But when he does, they'll load up in canoes and boats and come down the river.

"Listen, Rayford, when the army comes, we'll need targets...real targets. Not like this one, where the Indians have already moved out. I need you to find where their big villages actually are."

"Now that I have the time to do the scoutin'," Rayford answered, "I can locate their villages and figure out the best way to get to 'em. All I need to know from you, Cap'n Parks, is when the gen'rl is comin' and when and where I can meet him."

"As soon as I have that information, I will absolutely let you know," the captain promised.

"Good," the trapper smiled back. "I'll be there with everything he needs. You can count on it."

With a nod the captain turned and, lifting his rifle and powder horn above his head, waded into the river to join his men in the cold swim to the other side.

After all the troopers had entered the water, Rayford disappeared into the forest. Traveling two hundred yards, he then gave the call of a crow. The second time he did it, he heard an answering *caw* to his north. He walked in that direction until Kolapeka, the chief, stepped from some brush.

"My braves were not happy to let so many scalps get away."

"We talked about this, Kolapeka," Rayford shot back. "We let these go so that I can gain their confidence. Their captain promised to let me know when the army comes. When he tells me, I will tell you, then we will defeat them once and for all, and your braves will have all of the scalps they can want."

Chapter Thirteen

A MESSAGE FROM MONETO

Over the next several weeks, Ember's Shawnee improved. She was able to understand and speak more as she and Prisha were constantly busy with various medical concerns for members of the Shawnee tribe. There were wounds to treat, some of which were infected, fevers, coughs, upset stomachs, ear aches, boils to lance, infected teeth, and the occasional baby to deliver. The more proficient Ember became in understanding and speaking Shawnee, the more help she was to the medicine woman.

Not a day went by that the slave girl did not find some time to write on her deer skin all that she had learned from Prisha. She wrote so much that, even though her print was as small as she could make it, she filled up one side of the skin. To make more room, she very carefully scrapped the hair off the other side and continued writing.

Prisha observed with interest the work the girl put into recording what she learned. One day the squaw's curiosity got the better of her. "Why you do this?" she asked, pointing at the tiny writing on the deer skin.

"I'm learning so much from you, Prisha," the girl answered with a smile, "and I don't want to forget any of it."

"You want to be medicine woman?" the squaw asked again.

"I believe Jesus wants me to be a medicine woman," Ember returned, "and I want to be a good one for Him."

"Jesus," Prisha returned, a little confused. "Who is Jesus?"

"Jesus is the Son of the Great Spirit, Moneto," the girl answered.

"I have never heard about Moneto's Son," the squaw returned suspiciously. "How you know Moneto has a Son?"

"Many years ago," Ember began, "Moneto spoke to men and told them many things. Those men wrote down the signs so that we can read the Great Spirit's Words."

"What did He say?" the medicine woman asked with interest.

"The book that Rayford threw into the fire were the Great Spirit's Words."

"Ah!" Prisha said as realization struck her. "That is why you stuck your hands in the fire to save it!"

"Yes," the girl answered, looking down at the scars. "Moneto's words are very precious to me. Would you like for me to try to explain some of what He says?"

"Yes, I would," Prisha nodded, "but we must not let Rayford catch us. He hate Moneto...Get crazy mad."

Ember quickly climbed the ladder and returned with a single page of the Bible. She decided not to bring down any more in case Rayford caught them. That way she would only lose one page rather than all of them.

As a precaution, Ember sat with her back to the cabin door. Lovingly she read the scorched page in her hands. She could just make out that it was from Isaiah chapter fifty-five.

"This is from the book of Isaiah," Ember announced.

"Ay-say?" Presha tried to imitate the name.

"I-sa-iah," the girl repeated.

"Ay-say-yah," the squaw spoke again.

"Good! Isaiah was a man who lived many years ago and loved Moneto. The Great Spirit spoke to him, and Isaiah wrote down Moneto's words in his book."

Ember read the words to herself. *Seek ye the LORD while He may be found, call ye upon Him while He is near:*

Let the wicked forsake his way, and the unrighteous man his thoughts: and let him return unto the LORD, and He will have mercy upon him; and to our God, for He will abundantly pardon.

"What does Moneto say?" Prisha prompted impatiently.

"He tell Isaiah He want people to look for Him and find Him. Moneto want us to call to Him because He is near."

"He is near?" Prisha asked with a concerned look.

"Yes," Ember answered.

"He is here?" the squaw asked again, looking around the cabin.

"His Son, Great Chief Jesus, told His followers *I am with you always.* So, yes, He is here...right now."

"You see Him?"

"No," Ember returned with a smile, "I no see Him, but I feel His love, and I believe Him when He say He with me."

"What more Moneto say?" Prisha asked, nodding toward the burned page in the girl's hand.

"He want bad people to be bad no more and come to Moneto. He promises to show mercy and make them right with Him."

"NEHIWE!" Prisha exclaimed. "Moneto *want* bad people?"

"Prisha, we all bad people," the girl responded. "That's why the Great Spirit sent His Son to us. Moneto and Great Chief Jesus love us so much that Jesus came to take our punishment for the bad we do."

With both words and actions, Ember tried to explain how Jesus died on the cross for everyone's sins. She also talked about how each person makes a choice, either to receive or reject Him. To receive the gift of salvation, people must believe that Jesus is God's Son and that His death paid the price for their sin.

"One more thing," Ember added. "You must trust Jesus enough to make Him your Great Chief."

"You do this?" the squaw asked.

"Yes," Ember said with a smile. "Jesus loves me more than anyone, and I proud for Him to be my Chief. Knowing Jesus and having Him as my chief has changed everything for me."

"That why you different now?" Prisha asked.

"Yes," the girl answered with a smile. "When Rayford first brought me here, I was sad, bitter, and angry. But while I was sick from the snake's poison, the Son of Moneto come to me and show me how much He and the Great Spirit love me. Now all I want to do is love Him back. He say He want me to serve you and learn from you, so I do that because I love Him."

Suddenly in her heart Ember heard a very sweet voice say, *Tell her how much I love her.*

"He loves you too, Prisha," the girl said, looking the squaw in the eye. "He asked me to tell you that He loves you very much."

The squaw sat there in silence for several long minutes. Finally she gave a snort and quickly busied herself with chores.

She didn't believe me, Lord, Ember prayed as she watched Prisha moving around the cabin. *How do I make her believe that You are real and that You love her?*

That's not your job, dear one, Jesus seemed to respond. *Your work is to respond in faith to what I ask of you. It is MY job to author faith in the unbelieving heart just as I did in you.*

Now, I want you to show My love to Prisha by helping her with the chores. After supper this evening you will have time to go over your notes again. As you do this for me, I will join you.

"Yes, Lord," the girl said humbly and rose to help her mistress with the work.

Chapter Fourteen

AN EMERGENCY

About midday on a beautiful, late summer day, Ember swept the cabin as Prisha stored roots of medicinal herbs. Suddenly there was a shout from the woods in front of the cabin. The slave girl stuck her head out of the already open door and saw Rayford, the chief, and several warriors hurrying out of the woods carrying two of their comrades.

Ember called to her mistress, who quickly put down her herbs and rushed out. "WHAT IS WRONG?" she screamed as she ran toward the group of warriors.

"RED FEATHER AND CROW FOOT HAVE BEEN SHOT!" Prisha's brother called back to her. "YOU MUST HELP THEM!"

Immediately the medicine woman slid to a stop and turned to sprint back to the cabin. "MOVE TABLE!" she shouted at Ember. "PUT BUFFALO ROBES ON FLOOR!"

As the girl quickly rushed to obey, the squaw ran to the fire and put a large pot on the coals. The bucket beside the hearth was only half full of water, but she poured most of it into the pot and set the bucket with the remainder on the floor near the two robes Ember had laid out.

As the Indians brought in the two injured warriors, Prisha directed them to lay the braves on the robes. When Ember saw their terrible wounds, she prayed out loud, "Oh Lord, please help them!"

HEY!" shouted the trapper angrily. "NO PRAYIN', YOU HEAR ME...I'LL KNOCK YER TEETH OUT!"

The squaw quickly examined the first. He grimaced in pain as she carefully studied the wound in his right thigh. After checking, she found no wound on the back of the leg. She snatched up the leather pad on the hearth, folded it, and placed it on the wound.

"Bullet still in leg," she informed Ember. "Press this to stop bleeding while I look at other warrior." Prisha noticed that the girl's lips were moving, but she wasn't saying anything. The medicine woman also noticed with relief that Ember had her back toward Rayford.

As the slave girl put pressure on the leg wound, Prisha examined the second warrior. The brave was very pale and had a difficult time breathing. Cutting away his buckskin hunting shirt, she realized that he had been shot through the chest.

"Can you help him, Prisha?" her brother asked urgently.

The medicine woman leaned down and listened carefully to his chest as he struggled to breathe. Finally she looked up and sadly shook her head.

With a snarl of frustrated anger, the chief turned away. "He is a brave warrior, Prisha," he said again with his back still turned, "can you ease his pain?"

"Heeni," Prisha acknowledged, moving quickly to the herbs on her shelf. Pulling several rhododendron leaves from a pot, she picked the largest one and hurried back to her patient.

"Red Feather," she said as she knelt beside the injured warrior.

"H-help...me," the warrior whispered as he gasped for breath.

"Chew this leaf. It will help you rest." Before he could respond, the squaw folded the leaf and placed the whole thing in his mouth. Obediently the desperate brave began to chew.

Prisha quickly stepped over beside Ember. Again she pulled out a rhododendron leaf and carefully studied the injured warrior. She selected the particular leaf she wanted. After evaluating his size again so she would not overdose him, she sliced a small piece off the end of the leaf and placed the remainder in the warrior's mouth. The medicine woman told him to chew the leaf but not to swallow.

As he did so, the medicine woman, using a shallow bowl, drew steaming water out the pot on the fire. She dropped in a handful of crushed spotted alder leaves as well as some ground squawroot, covered the mixture with one of the deer skin pads, and set it aside to steep.

When Prisha turned back to her original patient, she found that the potent juice from the chewed leaf had done its work. Red Feather was unconscious, and his breathing was less labored. It wasn't long after that the brave with the bullet in his thigh also slept soundly.

Prisha removed the remnant of the chewed leaf from his mouth. Checking the leg, she determined that the bone was not broken. Breathing a sigh of relief, she retrieved a long leather pouch from her shelf and withdrew two instruments made of bone. The first was a long, sharp piece that resembled a knitting needle that she used to probe the wound and locate the bullet. The second piece had a narrow, flat, spoon-like end that was used to remove the lead slug.

"How do we stop the bleeding?" Ember asked.

"Spotted alder tea," Prisha answered as she picked up the bowl and its steeping contents. "Squawroot also help wound not go bad." She carefully dribbled the hot contents of the bowl into the open leg wound. The sleeping warrior felt nothing as the squaw repeated the process many times. Eventually Ember noticed that the flow of blood from the wound diminished markedly.

"Now put pressure on wound again," Prisha ordered. "When bleeding fully stopped, we bandage."

A loud cry of anger erupted behind them. Turning back to Red Feather, Prisha discovered that he had died. Her brother, who had been Red Feather's friend, was furious.

"Kolapeka," the squaw said, addressing her brother, "I told you that with such a wound he could not be saved."

"We were at the Shawnee hunting grounds south of here," Rayford volunteered. "A party of settlers was also there. They had already killed several deer when Red Feather and Crow Foot found them. We heard the gun fight from where we were some distance away. By the time we arrived, the braves had been shot, and the settlers had run off with their kill. I followed them until I could tell which settlement they came from.

"Now they will all die!" snarled the chief. "Rayford, we will get all the warriors, and you will lead us to their village. For what they did to Red Feather, we will kill them and burn their houses to the ground."

Kolapeka looked at his sister.

"Crow Foot will be fine," she answered his unspoken question.

"I will send his people to come get him and care for him," the chief returned.

"We go to war!" Kolapeka announced as he rushed out the door, followed by Rayford and the others.

The medicine woman sat back and gave a long sigh. She directed the girl to lift Crow Foot's injured leg as Prisha wrapped a poultice of crushed herbs around it with a band of leather, tying it in place with thin strips of deer skin. When all was finished, she covered her sleeping patient with an elk skin.

As they both worked to set the cabin in order, Prisha spoke. "You say the Son of Moneto is with us...Jesa."

"Yes," the girl responded. "Jesus is here with us."

"You talk to Him even after Rayford threaten you," Prisha observed.

"The men were hurt and in trouble," Ember answered. "I was asking Moneto's Son to help them."

Prisha thought on this for a moment and spoke again, "You say Chief Jesus love me?" the squaw asked suspiciously. "What Chief Jesus want from me?"

"He wants you to believe that He is the Son of Moneto and that He loves you," Ember responded cheerfully. "He wants you to love Him and trust Him so much that you will let Him be your chief."

"Rayford will be gone to fight for several days," Prisha said again. "You tell me more of what Moneto say in His book."

Chapter Fifteen

SUSANNA AND REBECCA

For the next three days, Ember looked for opportunities to pull out pages of scripture and explain to Prisha what they said. The girl sensed that Jesus was very pleased with their talks and was even eager for them to progress.

Once when she was trying to decide what to read to her mistress next, she felt a very strong suggestion in her spirit. *Tell her about Psalm twenty-three.* Ember found the scorched page and began to read. *The Lord is my shepherd I shall not want...*

It took some creativity to explain to the squaw what a shepherd was. Prisha had never seen a sheep. It became a little easier when Ember found out that the braves brought back a goat once from one of their raids.

"If you had goats," Ember asked the squaw, "what you do to care for them?"

"Find food and water," the medicine woman answered. "Protect them from wolves and hungry neighbors. Care for them when they are sick or injured."

"Hohwisa!" Ember nodded her agreement. "You are right. All of those things that you do for goats, Moneto does for those who love Him and follow His Son Jesus. I remember that Jesus said to His followers once, *I will never fail you or forsake you.*

"I believe Him, Prisha. Even though my family is dead and I am slave, Jesus has come to me and made me know that He love and care for me. When I was so sick from the snake bite, I went to visit Him in His beautiful place, and it was wonderful! I begged Him to let me stay with Him, but He said He wanted me to come back to tell you how much He love you."

"The Son of Moneto sent you back to *me?*"

"Yes, Prisha, yes!" the girl exclaimed in her limited Shawnee, excited that her mistress understood. "I know it wasn't dream. Jesus say to me every day I am to tell you He love you. He really love you very much, and He want you to be with Him forever."

"I don't know Him," the squaw said firmly.

"But He know you," the girl returned, "and He loves you enough to die for you."

"You say Jesus coming back to take His followers to live forever with Him," Prisha began again. "If He take me, I be lonely. I not know anyone there."

"You will be with the One Who love you the best and the most," Ember countered, "and you will know me."

Prisha looked imploringly at the girl and said, "At Chief Jesus's table, will you sit beside me?"

"Oh yes, Prisha!" Ember exclaimed and reached over to hug the squaw. "I will sit with you, and you will sit with me and my family... and we will all love you!"

"How can you do this?" the medicine woman asked in disbelief, tears starting to form in her eyes.

"Because Jesus loves us, and He is making us like Him."

The next day as the squaw and Ember walked to the Shawnee village to treat several patients, Prisha announced, "I believe in Jesus, and I have decided to make Him my chief."

"Prisha, that is wonderful!" Ember exclaimed.

What does Chief Jesus want me to do for Him?" Prisha asked.

"I know He love that you heal people," the girl responded. "He told me He want me to be a healer. I also know that Jesus want you show people how much He love them. I think He want you to keep healing, but do it for Jesus. That way you show your people how much Chief Jesus loves them. And if you get chance to tell people about Jesus, do that.

"Prisha, I know Jesus have much for you to do, but He will tell you when it time."

"But I no hear Him like you do," Prisha argued.

"That because you no listen for Him," the girl returned. "Talk to Him. Ask Him to speak to your heart, then listen for Him. Jesus is Moneto's son! Trust Him. He speaks all languages and understands what you say. If you ask Him, He will reveal His will. Chief Jesus told His followers that, if we stay close to Him, He will stay close to us. He said that we are like branches attached to a vine, and He is the vine. We are to get everything we need from Him. When we trust Him to be everything for us, He show us what to do, what to say, even what to pray. When we make Him our life, He free to do all that Moneto want to do through us. Jesus calls this bearing fruit. When we let Him bear Moneto's fruit through us, it make Moneto very happy and honors Him."

"Chief Jesus bear fruit through you when you tell me about Him," the squaw observed.

"Hohwisa!" Ember agreed excitedly.

Three days later Prisha and Ember were preparing their evening meal when they heard someone approaching the cabin. Prisha quickly snatched up the ax, but just as she turned, the door flew open and in walked Rayford and Prisha's brother dragging two captive girls.

"Put that ax down an' get us some food," the trapper demanded.

"Who these?" the squaw shot back as she looked at the terrified girls.

"The older one is to be one of my squaws," Prisha's brother announced. "I will keep the younger one as a slave until she is older. Then I will make her a squaw or sell her."

"Why bring them here?" Prisha asked firmly.

"BECAUSE WE'RE GOIN' OUT AGAIN," Rayford screamed at her, "AND HE NEEDS SOMEPLACE TO KEEP 'EM TILL WE GET BACK. NOW QUIT YAPPIN' AND FIX US SOME FOOD!"

"The settlement we attacked was too small," Kolapeka told his sister as she angrily turned back to her cooking. "I want to destroy a bigger village for Red Feather's revenge. We came back to look at the map and find a larger settlement."

Ember took all of this in, realizing that neither Rayford nor Prisha's brother knew she understood Shawnee.

"Rayford," the chief snapped, "bring out the map!"

With a growl the trapper glanced at the girls and at Prisha, who was looking at him. He gave a quick nod at the door, causing the squaw to spring to her feet. She grabbed the bucket, shoved it into

Ember's hands, and ordered her to take the girls out and show them where to get water.

"Come on," Ember said, trying to hurry the new captives through the door. "They want us out of here."

"Don't push me!" the older girl protested as she slapped at Ember's hand on her arm.

"Just get out!" Ember urged. After they were outside, she turned to shut the door behind them and saw Rayford headed for the large, flat stone on the hearth.

Ember studied the two girls. The older one was taller than Ember and seemed about two years older. She was actually rather pretty with blond hair and blue eyes. The younger one was plain featured with brown hair and green eyes.

"I'm sorry about that," Ember said, trying to be pleasant, "but it's much better if we do what they say. If we upset either of those men in there, they will kill us."

"I don't care about them," the younger girl snapped as Ember hefted the bucket and led them toward the creek. "I want to go home!"

"BECCA!" the older girl barked, "DO YOU HAVE MUD FOR BRAINS? THERE IS NO HOME TO GO BACK TO. THEY BURNED IT AND KILLED MOTHER AND FATHER!"

"Listen," Ember tried again, "I know you've had a rough time..."

"YOU HAVE NO IDEA HOW WE'VE HAD IT!"

"Oh, I think I do," Ember returned calmly. "They did the same thing to my parents and village about two years ago. My name is Remember Warren, but you can call me Ember. What are your names?"

The older girl ignored her, but the younger one answered, "I'm Rebecca Norris, and this my sister Susanna."

"They sent us out to get water," Ember said, bucket in hand. "Follow me, and I'll show you the creek where we get it."

"What are they going to do with us, Ember?"

"Right now we are all slaves. The chief said that, when he and Rayford get back from their next raid, he is going to make your sister his squaw."

"I will not be any one's squaw!" Susanna huffed. "I am the daughter of the leader of our village, and I will not be treated like this!"

"Listen to me, both of you!" Ember said firmly as she stopped and turned to face the two girls. "It's terrible what you both have had to endure, but that life for you is over! The sooner you figure out how to survive the one you are stuck in now, the better things will be for you. I will try to help you all I can, but if you try to resist these people, your life is going to get much, much worse. The only thing left for us is to do what they tell us to do and to pray."

"That's fine for you, but we are getting out of here!" Susanna shot back. "There's no way I'm staying here to be a squaw to that murdering savage!"

With a sigh Ember shook her head and walked to the creek. After filling the bucket, the three of them returned to the cabin, but Ember was afraid to enter. After a few more minutes, the door opened, and Prisha waved them in.

Ember and the squaw hurried through the routine of cooking a meal while the two girls stood nearby. Ember handed Rebecca the bowl of nut and berry mix and told her to place it on the table between the two men, which she quickly did. Ember was finishing the flat bread as the squaw dug a large sweet potato out of the coals and said something to the older girl.

To help her, Ember grabbed the patch of deer skin on the hearth and put it in Susanna's hands. Prisha then placed the hot potato on the pad. "She said to take the potato to the men," Ember translated.

Suddenly the older girl threw the potato and the pad onto the floor. "I WILL NOT!" she yelled and stamped her foot.

An instant later Prisha's wooden spoon came down hard on the girl's knuckles. Susanna screamed and drew back to hit the squaw. She was stopped instantly by the point of a knife against her throat. The terrifying form of Rayford towered over her as he glared at the rebellious girl with hate-filled eyes.

"Pick it up," he growled threateningly.

Just then a hand was placed firmly on the trapper's arm, and Kolapeka stepped between them. The Shawnee war chief gave Susanna a long, hard look, then suddenly slapped her hard across the face.

With a shriek of pain, the girl doubled over and grabbed her face. Strong hands gripped the crying girl's shoulders and stood her up. Kolapeka forced her to look him in the eyes. The stare he gave the girl was just as threatening as the trapper's. The chief pointed to the dropped potato, then very firmly, he jabbed his finger at the table. The spoiled girl shook uncontrollably, both from pain and terror.

"He wants you to pick up the potato and serve it to him," Ember said to motivate the girl. "If you want to live, you should do it."

Still shaking, Susanna slowly bent down, picked up the pad, and used it to set the potato on the table. With a nod of approval, Kolapeka turned and resumed his seat.

The squaw spoke again, and when Susanna turned, another potato was placed onto the pad in her hands. This too she set with the other food. Ember then put her flat bread before the men, and Prisha carried over two freshly cooked deer steaks.

When the men were fed, Prisha cut a piece of steak for each of the girls, and Ember gave them both a piece of flat bread. After supper, since both girls were emotionally and physically exhausted, they were told where to bed down for the night. Susanna was sent up into the loft to sleep on the deer skins with Ember. A buffalo robe was spread near the hearth for Rebecca.

As Ember and Prisha cleaned the kitchen area, Rayford and the chief finished their meal. Kolapeka pushed back and said "Let's go! The warriors are to meet us at Falling Waters."

"I have to do something first," Rayford returned.

The trapper then opened a large sack he had brought in with the girls. He rummaged through it, looking for something. Pulling out a knife in its sheath, he placed it on the table and kept searching. Finally he tugged out a smaller bag that was tied around the top. Without opening it, he stood and moved over to the fireplace. Grabbing an empty clay bowl, he scooped hot coals from the fire and walked quickly out the door. "I'll be right back," he called to the chief over his shoulder.

Prisha handed Ember a pile of dirty dishes, and the girl carried them to the creek for washing. The sun had set, and the light was fading when she dipped the dishes in the water. A flash of light to her left caught her eye, and she noticed a flame flickering in the distance. Her curiosity peaked, she hopped up and cautiously made her way upstream toward the illumination.

Drawing near, she peered around a tree and saw Rayford at the cave entrance. He had used the coals he had gathered in the bowl to start a small fire. Reaching into the cave, he drew a torch down from a rocky shelf and lit it. Immediately the flame was drawn almost sideways into the cave by the draft. He picked up his sack and disappeared into the dark opening.

Retracing her steps, Ember hurriedly cleaned the dishes. She didn't know what the trapper was doing, but she wanted to be back in the cabin before he returned.

Chapter Sixteen

BECCA

As soon as Rayford returned from his errand, he grabbed what he needed and left with Kolapeka to meet the warriors. As they stepped out the door, the trapper looked back at the squaw and announced, "This raid's gonna take some time. The village is a good ways off. We may be gone a month or more." He walked out, shutting the door behind them.

Ember and Prisha, grateful to be left to themselves, took their time cleaning up after the meal. The squaw put a pot of water on the fire to heat when they finished their work. Grabbing some chicory root from her shelf, Prisha trimmed shavings of the roasted root into the steaming water. In a few minutes the rich, savory smell of the brew began to fill the cabin. After placing two shallow bowls on the table, the squaw poured a serving for both of them. Calling to Ember, Prisha pointed toward the bowls. "Sit. Drink. Rest."

"Thank you, Prisha," Ember returned with a smile. "That smells so good!"

After sipping contentedly for several minutes, the medicine woman turned and looked at the younger sister sleeping heavily beside the hearth.

"These girls," Prisha began as she set her bowl on the table, "they not like you. They not let Chief Jesus work on their hearts. Older girl is very angry. It will not go well with her."

"They've been through a lot," Ember returned.

"You have been through a lot as well," Prisha countered.

"Give them time," Ember answered.

"What Chief Jesus want us to do?" the squaw finally asked.

"We should pray for them."

The squaw nodded but then said, "Older girl need more than prayer."

"I will look for a chance to talk with each of them," Ember said.

The next morning Prisha woke them all early to do their work. Since she spoke Shawnee reasonably well, Ember replaced Waxing Moon as the official interpreter. There was a lot of grumbling and huffing, and twice Prisha had to use her wooden spoon, but the cabin chores eventually were finished.

Later all the captives were sent to the creek to wash the dirty clothing. As they pounded and scrubbed the laundry on the large, smooth rocks, the sisters vented their anger and frustration at Ember. "I hate this! I HATE THIS!" Rebecca fumed as she slapped a dirty pair of pants on her rock.

"This is unacceptable!" Susanna agreed fiercely as she swatted away a string of blond hair that had fallen into her eyes. "We should not be treated in this way!

"Can't you do something to stop this?" The last question was directed angrily at Ember.

"No, I can't," Ember answered, trying to be patient. "But I know from experience that, if you do your work with a good attitude, Prisha will treat you much better."

"A GOOD ATTITUDE?" the younger sister yelled at her. "How ridiculous! WE'RE SLAVES, DUMMY! HOW CAN WE HAVE A GOOD ATTITUDE ABOUT BEING SLAVES?"

"Prisha?" Susanna cross-examined. "Why in the world are you using that Indian's name? Are you friends with her?"

"That must be it, Susanna," Becca chimed in, "Ember's an Indian lover. No wonder she's telling us to be happy that we're slaves."

"Instead of siding with that squaw," the older sister added, "you should be helping us plan an escape."

"And how do you think you're going to do that?" Ember asked, getting annoyed. "The closest settlement is over a week's hard march from here through the wilderness. Do you know which direction it is?" She stared at the clueless look on both of the girls' faces. "Neither do I!

"How are you going to get food for a long trip like that?" Ember continued. "Plus the Shawnee are the best trackers in the world. Can you walk through the woods without leaving tracks? If you can't, they'll find you in no time. Can you defend yourselves from bears, wolves, or rattlesnakes?" As she said this last word, she turned the back of her left leg toward the girls so they could see scar forming that was caused by the snake bite.

"You're just trying to scare us, squaw lover!" Becca sneered angrily.

"Just stop it!" Susanna said sharply. "We've heard enough from you. We are going to escape from this terrible place, and if you help us, we may take you with us."

Shaking her head in disbelief at the two angry, foolish girls, Ember scooped up the wet clothing she had finished and walked back to the cabin to drape them in the branches to dry.

Just as Ember completed hanging the last shirt, Susanna arrived with her pile.

"Susanna!" Becca cried from the creek. "Help me! I've still got all these clothes to wash!"

"You had the same amount as us," the heartless sister called back. "Wash them yourself!"

"But it's going to take forever!" the younger girl moaned.

"That's your fault!" the older sister responded. "You spent the whole time whining and crying about having to wash them and never did it."

About this time Prisha walked out to see how the work was coming. She was pleased to see the two older girls nearly finished, but when she spotted how little Rebecca had done, she got angry and started yelling at the young girl.

"What did she say?" Becca whimpered in dread.

"She said," Ember translated, "that she has made a midday meal for us, but because you are lazy, you will not eat anything until you are through."

A moaning wail came from the girl when she heard this.

"THAT'S NOT FAIR! I'M HUNGRY! I'LL NEVER GET ALL OF THIS WASHED!"

"You got the same amount of clothes to wash as the rest of us," her sister shot back. "Just do your work and quit whining."

"BUT I CAN'T DO ALL THIS! IT'S TOO MUCH! I'LL NEVER GET IT ALL DONE!"

As she bemoaned her miserable lot in life, the others walked into the cabin to eat. A few minutes later Ember came back out and walked to Becca beside the creek.

"I'll never get this done!" the young girl complained when she noticed Ember standing beside her.

"You're looking at it the wrong way," Ember said. "Instead of worrying about how much you have yet to do, just concentrate on the next thing. Take one piece of clothing and focus on that." Ember handed the girl a dirty shirt, and she took a dress from the girl's pile.

"Now, all we are going to do is wash this piece of laundry," the older girl announced as she dipped the dress in the creek. "That's right. Get it wet, then slap it on the rocks a few times to loosen the dirt. The slapping is actually my favorite part." The younger girl began to imitate the older girl's actions.

"You know what," Becca giggled, "the slapping is kind of fun."

"Good job, Becca! That's the way!" Ember said encouragingly.

After another especially vigorous smack, the younger girl announced, *"Hee hee,* I think I'm going to name my slapping rock *Susanna.*"

"Now start rubbing the wet clothing across the smooth rock. After you've done ten good scrubs, flip it over and look at your work. Can you still see dirt? If so, we slap it a few more times and give it ten more scrubs. When you have gotten it as clean as you can, then we dunk it in the water again and do the same thing on the other side.”

When each girl had cleaned their garment, Ember directed her to pile the finished clothes on a smooth rock nearby.

“Alright, Becca, this next part is really important. Don’t look at the pile of clothing still to be washed. Only look at the piece on top. Ignore all of the others. Take the top one and wash it the same way you did before.”

After Becca picked up the next article, Ember also took another and washed it beside her, giving the girl cheerful encouragement the whole time. With both girls working steadily, Rebecca was amazed at how quickly the task got done.

“All right!” Ember announced as they laid the last clean pieces in the washed pile, “Good job, Becca! You did it!”

“That’s because you helped me,” the younger girl said humbly.

“I was just teaching you the secret of getting a big job done,” Ember said with a smile. “Now that you know, you will be able to do hard tasks much more easily.”

“Why did you come back to help me, Ember, when my own sister wouldn’t?” Rebecca asked sincerely. “I said some really mean things to you.”

“I’d be lying if I said that I wasn’t angry at you,” the older girl returned, “but Jesus wanted me to help you. So I did.”

"Well...thank you," the younger girl returned meekly.

"Thank Jesus," Ember responded. "He cares for you a lot."

Chapter Seventeen

SUSANNA

Ember and Becca walked into the cabin to eat, and they told the squaw that all the laundry was done. With a nod of approval, Prisha set another bowl on the table for the younger sister, scooping hot beans and corn in it.

As they finished their meal, the cabin door opened, and in walked a middle-aged squaw helping an older woman. Prisha quickly found a place for elderly squaw to sit. As Ember listened to the conversation, she understood that the feeble woman suffered greatly from arthritis in her back. As Prisha gathered herbs to help ease the sufferer's discomfort, it gave Ember a sense of satisfaction to see the medicine woman choosing the same plants that her apprentice thought she should use.

As the squaw put water on to boil for her medications, she realized that the wood pile was getting low. "Take girls," Prisha ordered. "Get more wood."

"And be quick," Ember added with a smile.

In spite of herself, the hard medicine woman's face cracked into a faint smile before she snorted and nodded toward the cabin door.

"We need to get wood," Ember announced to the other girls and immediately walked out of the cabin.

Grateful to be away from their Indian captors, both sisters quickly followed. Once outside Ember led them east of the cabin and into the thick woods at the base of the steep hill near the trapper's home. There were plenty of fallen limbs to gather.

As they picked up arm loads of firewood, Ember heard Susanna speaking to her sister. "We need to escape today or tomorrow," the older girl announced. "There are a few pieces of uneaten flatbread in the basket beside the hearth. I will try to grab them, and you look for a chance to steal the squaw's knife."

Through all of this Rebecca did not stop picking up limbs, nor did she even look at her sister.

Susanna noticed and was annoyed. "Did you hear what I said to you?" the older girl snapped angrily.

"I heard you," Becca snapped back, then turned a glanced at Ember.

"How can you possibly succeed?" Ember called out. "You're only going to create more problems for yourself."

"YOU STAY OUT OF THIS!" the older girl yelled. "THIS IS BETWEEN ME AND MY SISTER. WE'VE HAD ENOUGH OF THESE INDIANS *AND* YOU...AND WE'RE LEAVING!"

"I'm not going with you, Susanna," Rebecca announced firmly.

"WHAT? ARE YOU AS DUMB AS SHE IS? WE'VE GOT TO GET AWAY FROM HERE!"

"Ember is not dumb!" the younger sister growled, looking her older sibling hard in the eyes. "She is smart and kind, and she's trying to help us. Since we've been here, she's done a whole lot more for me than you have, and I'm staying with her."

"THEN YOU CAN HAVE HER!" Susanna screamed back. "I'M DONE WITH BOTH OF YOU! I'M LOOKING OUT FOR ME NOW!"

"That *is* what you do best," Becca shot back.

When their arms were loaded, the girls returned to the cabin. Prisha had the two sisters break the collected branches into usable lengths, and Ember assisted in preparing the herbal treatments for the arthritic patient. Later, as she reviewed all that they had done for the patient, the slave girl was able to add some new information to her medical notes.

"What are you writing?" Rebecca asked her as she looked over Ember's shoulder. The girl explained that Jesus had made it clear to her that part of the reason she was Prisha's slave was to learn medicine from her.

"You're telling me that Jesus actually speaks to you?" Becca asked suspiciously.

Susanna, who was busy grinding corn into meal, openly laughed at hearing Rebecca's question.

"Well, it's not like I actually hear a voice," Ember answered, "but I do talk to Him a lot, and...uh...I get answers."

Rebecca stared at her with a blank look.

"Okay," Ember tried again. "There are times when I can sense the Lord's nearness, and at those times I seem to understand what He's saying to me. Like when you were having trouble washing the clothes. After we came inside, I sensed Him telling me that He wanted me to go back out and help you."

"Wow!" the girl said in amazement. "I want to hear Him like that!"

"That's dumb, Rebecca!" Susanna called over her shoulder.

"I'm not talking to you!" Becca shot back.

"The first thing you have to do is believe in Him. Believe that He is the Son of God and that He died on the cross to pay the full price for your sins."

"Then what?" the younger girl asked.

"Well, if you truly believe in Him, you will want to do what He says."

"So what does He say?"

"In His word He says a lot of things," Ember answered. "He wants His followers to repent of their sins, confess their faith in Him, and be baptized. I've repented, and I've confessed my faith in Jesus to Prisha and to you. I haven't found the opportunity to be baptized yet, but that's on my list."

"Since we're talking about this, I want to say that I do believe in Jesus too, and I am very sorry for my sins. I've actually sinned a lot in my life, and I want Jesus to forgive me," Rebecca said sincerely.

"Have you asked Him?" Ember questioned.

"I guess I haven't," the younger girl returned humbly, "at least, not formally."

"Then why don't you ask Him now?"

"You mean right here?" Becca asked.

"No time like the present," Ember smiled back. "I'll even pray with you."

"Oh, please," they heard Susanna grumble under her breath.

After Rebecca spent several minutes humbling herself before God, confessing her sins, and asking for His forgiveness, Ember thanked God for the work that He was doing in Rebecca's heart and for giving the younger girl to Ember as a sister in faith.

When the prayers were finished, Rebecca was ecstatic about her new life with Jesus. Glancing over at her sister, who was still grinding corn, the younger girl asked, "Susanna, I've said some really mean things to you in the past. I want you to know that I'm sorry for all of them. Would you please forgive me?"

When the older girl heard these words, she stopped grinding but didn't turn to look at her sister. Finally, with a cynical snort, she simply said, "Whatever."

Disappointed at Susanna's response, Rebecca turned back to Ember. "I want to be close to Jesus like you are, Ember, so how do I do that?"

"Start spending time with Him," Ember coached. "I pray to Him all the time."

"Is there anything else?" Becca wanted to know.

"You need to believe what He says. Like when He says, *I will never fail you or forsake you,* believe it! Trust in His promises."

"It sure looks like He's forsaken us," Rebecca observed.

"That's when you have to decide that you're going to believe what Jesus says instead of how things appear. Truth is not determined by our circumstances, but by what God says. Remind yourself of His promises and start eagerly looking for how He will fulfill them."

"You really believe Jesus will deliver us from being slaves?" Becca asked.

"I don't know yet if He wants to deliver us or not," Ember answered with a smile, "but I have no doubts that He can."

"How could He possibly do that?"

"I don't know," Ember answered matter-of-factly. "That's not my job. That's His job. My job is to be faithful to Him and be ready for whatever He wants me to do."

As the afternoon progressed, two sick Shawnee and a girl with a leg wound showed up for treatment. Prisha put Susanna to work making flat bread dough out of the meal she had ground and had Rebecca cut up deer meat for a soup. Ember was allowed to assist the medicine woman in her treatments.

It was late in the afternoon when the last patient was treated and sent home. Prisha checked the water bucket and found it almost empty.

"Need water in big pot for soup," the squaw explained to Ember. "Fill bucket too."

Setting the water bucket beside the older sister, the slave girl picked up the soup pot and directed the grumbling Susanna to follow her to the creek. Ember placed the pot beside the stream and, taking the bucket from the older girl, dipped it into the deepest spot and drew out an almost full bucket of water. She carefully poured it into her pot, then handed the bucket to Susanna to refill.

"Jesus really does love you, Susanna," Ember said as she turned to pick up the full pot. "If you would just trust Him, your life would be so much better."

"I DON'T WANT YOUR ADVICE!" the older girl screamed.

Suddenly the wooden bucket smashed into the back of Ember's head, and everything went black.

Ember felt like she was swimming through light. Everything was so bright that she couldn't see clearly, but she could hear a voice. She remembered later that it was the sweetest voice she had ever heard, and it was calling her name.

The light never dimmed, but her eyes began to clear. The first thing she saw was a face...His face, and it thrilled her to see Him again.

"Welcome back, dear one."

"Oh, Lord, it is wonderful to see You again," the girl said excitedly. "But what am I doing here?"

"You've been hurt in your world, and I brought you here."

"Do I get to stay this time?" she asked eagerly.

"Not yet," the Lord answered with a smile. "I just wanted us to spend more time together."

"If I've been injured, then that means when you send me back, it's just going to hurt. So it's okay with me if you let me stay as long as you can."

"It will hurt," Jesus said with tenderness, "but I will be with you, and I will use it for good."

"That's enough for me, Lord," the girl answered with a smile.

"Since you're here," Jesus said, the smile spreading across his face, "let me show you more of my home."

"YES!" Ember responded excitedly as she clasped her hands to her chest, hardly able to stand still.

Chapter Eighteen

THE KING'S FRIENDS

Ember had remembered that it was beautiful in Jesus's home, but she had forgotten how much more beautiful than her world. The colors were just as amazing as last time. Some of them she had no name for and were beyond imagination. The fragrances from the flowers and plants were delightful. She could see further and so much more than she could on Earth.

"It looks different than when I was here last," she said as she looked around.

"I brought you to a different part this time," Jesus answered. "The West Gate is through those woods to our right."

"Is that where we're going?" Ember asked excitedly, remembering that her family and Zoe and Eliza would be there.

"No, I want you to meet some other friends of mine. Let's go this way." As they walked, Jesus pointed out flowers and plants that Ember had never seen before. The blossom that amazed her the most was tall, upright, and looked like a person wearing a gorgeous gold and burgundy robe. The center of the flower had a prominent pistol with a rounded top that was crowned with a circle of yellow stamens.

"What would you call that one?" Jesus asked as Ember studied the impressive bloom.

"It really looks like a princess or a queen in her royal robe and crown," Ember observed. "I think I'd name it the queen flower!"

"Hmmm," Jesus said thoughtfully. "If we call it that, do you think the other flowers will be jealous?"

"Lord," Ember said, giving Jesus a sideways glance, "You know there's no jealousy here." The girl's quick response and the mischievous look she gave prompted a laugh from Jesus.

While they stood beside the flower, suddenly a bee flew over and landed on the bloom. Ember was stunned. "I have never in my life seen a bee that big!"

"That's because these are *MY* bees," the Lord said proudly. "Here, let me show you something." As he spoke, He wiggled His fingers in front of the huge insect and turned His palm upward.

The bee quickly flew away and in a few moments reappeared with quite a few of its friends. Each bee flew to Jesus's hand and placed a small drop of honey there. Faster than can be said, the large insects had left a pool of the golden liquid in the Master's palm.

"Now," Jesus said to Ember, "taste this!"

The girl touched her finger to the honey and placed it in her mouth. Immediately her eyes got wide, and she gasped in amazement. "Oh, my goodness!" the girl said in astonishment. "I have never tasted anything so good! How..."

But Jesus cut her off with a mischievous smile of His own. "*My* honey!" He turned her hand over and poured the rest of the delicious liquid into the girl's palm so that she could enjoy it. Ember was surprised to see it flow like water. None of it stuck to the Master's hand.

They walked on together through the trees until they came to a low hedge that was covered in lovely blue flowers. The shrubs grew almost to Ember's chest, and as she and Jesus walked up to them, the Lord said, "Now look there."

As she viewed the other side of the bushes, she saw a small, open meadow of fresh green grass, and lying a short distance from where they stood was a huge and very powerful-looking cat. He was golden tan with bands of rippling muscles all over. Large white teeth and a luxuriant collar of long, thick fur completed his appearance. The massive beast purred contentedly as he enjoyed the grass and the pleasant breeze.

"You've never seen a lion before, have you?" Jesus asked.

"A lion?" the girl questioned. "I thought it was a big cat."

"He is. His name is Amorius."

"He's over twice as big as any bear I have ever seen!" Ember exclaimed. "Is he one of your special animals?"

"All animals are special to Me," Jesus answered. "Don't you remember what I wrote in My book? All things were made by Me and for Me. All animals are mine, and I love them.

"But as far as lions are concerned, you have them in your world also. They live in Africa. But none are as big or as magnificent as Amorius."

"He looks terrifying!" Ember said with shudder.

"Oh, does he now?" Jesus returned with a smile. "Look a little closer."

As Ember leaned further over the shrubs, she saw something moving on the ground where the large lion lay. Just then a head popped out of the grass, then another. Ember started counting and saw six cute, furry bunnies playing in between the huge beast's massive legs.

"Oh my!" the girl exclaimed. "They aren't scared of him at all. Why doesn't he eat them?"

Now it was Jesus's turn to give Ember a sideways look.

"Oh," the girl gave an embarrassed response. "I forgot. They are *Your* bunnies, right?"

"In my home there is only peace and love," Jesus reminded her. "No one eats anyone else. That only happens in the world of shadows where you live."

As Ember looked back, she saw that two bunnies had climbed on the lion's back and were sliding down his chest.

"I brought you to this spot because I want you to meet my friends."

"I'd love to!" she returned with a smile.

Just then the hedge in front of them parted by itself and made an opening for them to pass through. Seeing the movement, Amorius turned and spotted the Lord and His guest. The lion's mouth opened, and a deep, rumbling sound came from the beast's throat. Immediately all six bunnies lined up to face the King, and Amorius rose to his feet.

Jesus leaned down and whispered in Ember's ear. "Hear them," He commanded.

In that instant, as the lion growled again, Ember instead heard words coming from his mouth. "Your Majesty," the great beast said with deep respect, bowing his shaggy head.

"Yoos Magessy," said six squeaky voices as the large-eyed, floppy-eared bunnies imitated their great friend and bowed as well.

"Oh, Jesus, they are so cute!" Ember gushed.

"Cute!" Amorius snorted indignantly.

"I'm sorry, Sir Lion!" Ember said sincerely. "I meant the bunnies are cute. You, sir, are magnificent!"

On hearing this, the great beast's head rose, and a smile began to form across his face.

"Amorius," Jesus said with just a hint of sternness.

"My Lord," the big cat said defensively, "You didn't give me time. I was going to respond meekly."

Jesus had the faintest of smiles on His face as He turned to Ember and gave her a wink.

The large cat cleared his throat and spoke, "My lady, I am indeed honored by your compliment, but my great humility..."

"Ahem," Jesus said.

Nervously the lion continued, "Er, umm, what I mean to say is that I am the King's lion, and all that you see is simply what the King has given me." When he finished, Amorius looked expectantly at Jesus, Who smiled and nodded in return.

"Amorius is very important to me," Jesus said as he walked over and laid His hand affectionately on the great beast's head. "He keeps an eye out for the smaller animals and helps them find their way back home if they get lost. As you can see, they all love him very much, and so do I."

"Your Majesty," the lion said respectfully and bowed again.

"Yoos Magessy," repeated the bowing bunnies.

Just then a large bear with silver fur came lumbering out of the nearby woods. Glaring straight at the line of bunnies, she did not look happy. She also saw Ember and the lion, but Amorius blocked her view of Jesus.

"I thought I'd find all of you here," the bear growled. "Your warren chief had no idea where you had gone, and now he's got the whole forest looking for you. What do you thoughtless bunnies have to say for yourselves?"

Twelve very wide, clueless eyes just stared at the bear and blinked.

"Little ones," Jesus said as He stepped around the lion to face the bunnies, "your chief didn't know you were coming this far from your warren?"

"Oh!" the bear said with surprise. "Your Majesty!"

"Yoos Magessy!" six tiny voices said in unison and bowed.

"It is good to see you, Ursinia," the Lord said sincerely to the silver she-bear. "I miss our walks together."

"Oh, so do I, my Lord!"

"You don't usually travel so far from the Golden Valley," Jesus remarked.

"That's true, my Lord," Ursinia answered, "but I knew the otters and the forest bears near the river love to eat fruit, and I wanted to invite them to enjoy my sunberries. When I got there to tell them, the word was sent out to look for the bunnies. I thought they might be here with Amorius. He's like a big brother to them."

"I always love to see my small friends," the great lion said defensively, "but I did not know they had come without talking to their chief."

"My good friends," Jesus said to all of them, "I want you to meet one of my dear sisters. Her name is Remember Warren, but she likes to be called Ember. She's My guest today."

"A pleasure to meet you," Amorius said graciously.

"Pleasoo to mee yoos," six small voices repeated.

"Very nice to meet you, dear," Ursinia added.

"A guest?" the she-bear questioned the Master. "She's not a citizen of the City of Light?"

"No," Jesus answered with a smile. "Not yet. I brought her here from the world of shadows for a short visit. I wanted her to meet all of you. But now we have a job for Ember."

"A job. . .for me?" the girl asked with a questioning look.

"Yes, dear one. You must decide what should be done with our furry little rascals here who did not inform their chief where they would be."

"Me?" Ember said with a shocked look on her face. "I have no business making decisions like that."

"Of course you do," Jesus said confidently. "Didn't you know that you and all of my followers will one day judge angels? So tell us, what should be done with them?"

Ember looked down at the six pairs of sad eyes gazing nervously up at her. After a moment's thought Ember gave her verdict. "Well, they should all go back to the warren this instant and apologize to the chief."

As she spoke her judgment, the shoulders drooped on all six of the guilty bunnies as they gave sighs of disappointment at having to return home.

"*And*," Ember continued, "they should try very hard to remember to report to the chief before they leave the warren again."

"A very wise decision," the she-bear agreed.

"Ver wiss decisoo," murmured the six bunnies.

"I will make sure that they find their way back home," Ursinia said as she lay down on the grass. "Come, little ones. Climb on my back, and I will give you a ride back to the warren."

The bunnies, now thinking only of this new adventure, scampered onto the bear's silver back. When they were all in place, Ursinia carefully stood up.

"Thank you for taking them back to the warren, Ursinia," Jesus said sincerely.

"Of course, my Lord," the she-bear said with a smile.

"Ursinia is such a treasure to Me," Jesus said to Ember as He gave the bear a big smile. "She is like a mother to all of the animals. By her actions she constantly reminds them all how much I love them."

"Oh, Your Majesty!" she said gratefully with a bow of her head.

"Yoos Magessy!" the bunnies repeated as they stood and bowed. Immediately they all lost their balance, and tumbled face-first into the grass below the bear.

Ember covered her mouth with her hands to hide her laugh. The large silver bear sighed and shook her head. Lying in the grass a second time, she encouraged her tiny riders to once again resume their place on her back.

"We're leaving now," she announced as she stood on her feet and without hesitation ambled toward the southeastern edge of the woods.

Chapter Nineteen

AN IMPORTANT JOB

"**W**here shall we go now?" Ember asked the Lord eagerly.

"Let's walk to the river," Jesus announced as He strolled toward the east woods.

"Amorius," the Master called over His shoulder, "would you care to join us?"

"Thank you, my Lord, but I have found an especially comfortable spot in the sweet grass that I think I will enjoy a bit longer. When I lay here very quietly, I can hear that wonderful song that the blades sing in the breeze."

"Then I shall give you a nice breeze," Jesus called back. "Enjoy the song, my friend."

"Thank you, my Lord," the great lion called back.

"Goodbye, Amorius," Ember said as she followed the Master. "It was so nice to meet you."

"I enjoyed meeting you as well," the large cat returned. "Next time you come, spend some time with me, and we shall have ourselves an adventure."

"Oh, yes! That would be wonderful!"

"So, do you like my friends?" Jesus asked the girl as they approached the edge of the forest.

"I love your friends!" Ember answered quickly. "And I love this place!

"Please, Lord," the girl pleaded, "can't I stay this time? There is nothing for me back there...in the shadows."

"Oh, dearest," the Master responded with a smile and a fiery look in His eyes, "you are so wonderfully mistaken! You are seeing your life back there with *your* eyes...shadow eyes. You are viewing everything through your hurt, loneliness, disappointment, and even some remaining bitterness."

"But, Lord," Ember exclaimed, expressing her anguish, "that's what's in my heart!"

"I know, dear one, but I am greater than your heart. Trust in Me, and I will be everything you need."

With a disappointed sigh Ember asked, "So what do You want me to do?"

"Susanna desperately needs to know that I love her."

"I've already tried to tell her about Your love," the girl snapped angrily, "but she wouldn't accept it.

She's mean, rude, and I know she's the one who hurt me! She and I were the only ones at the creek, and she was already mad at me. She had made up her mind to try to escape, and when I turned toward the cabin, she hit me with something...either a stick or a rock or the bucket."

"It was the bucket," Jesus volunteered.

"She hit me with the bucket?" Ember asked with a shocked expression. "She could have killed me!"

"I protected you," the Lord returned.

"I wish You hadn't," Ember muttered.

"Dearest," Jesus explained with feeling, "if you don't go back, Susanna will never hear about My love for her. She will never have a chance to believe in Me, and she will be lost forever. Look at her through *My* eyes."

"Lord, she is a wicked, evil girl!"

"Her sins are no worse than yours, Ember, or anyone else's for that matter."

"She doesn't deserve Your love!" the girl shot back.

"Neither did you," the Master said softly, "but I gave it to you willingly." As He said this, He extended His hands toward her and revealed the deep scars in both of His wrists.

When Ember saw the terrible marks, she gasped and began to cry.

"Not only did I suffer and die for you, dear one," Jesus said tenderly, "I gave my life for

Susanna as well. I am not willing that *any* should perish, but that *all* should come to repentance. After loving her so much on the cross, it would break My heart for her not to hear about it."

Ember raised her head and looked into the eyes of her King.

"Would you love her for Me?" Jesus asked.

Tears still streamed down the girl's face as she tried to answer. "I want to, Lord," Ember sobbed. "I really do. But after all the hurt she's caused me, I don't think I can."

"One of the things I love about you, dear one, is your honesty. You're right, your hurts are too deep and too fresh for you to love Susanna. To be honest with you, even without your hurts, you could not love her the way I want her loved. *I* will provide all the love that's needed. If you will trust Me enough to ask Me, *I* will love her through you.

"So, Ember," Jesus continued, "will you do this? Will you go back to the shadow world and let Me love Susanna through you?"

With a big sniff the girl blinked away her tears and looked at the One she knew loved her more than anyone. "Yes, Lord," she said, trying to smile. "You are my King. If You will go with me, then I will go anywhere for You."

"My sweet one," Jesus answered tenderly, "I am with you always, even to the end of the world. I have important things for you to do for Me."

"Important things?" Ember questioned. "Lord, I'm just a girl."

"No, you're not just a girl!" Jesus said firmly. "You are *My* girl, and I do great and eternal things with what is mine."

Those thoughts reminded her of Eliza's words when they were last together. "Then with all my heart," Ember returned worshipfully "I will be *Your* girl."

They walked out of the woods and found themselves standing on the bank of a very swift river of deep bluish-green water.

"So must I go back now?" Ember asked with obvious disappointment in her voice.

"Not yet," Jesus smiled down at her. "Let's cross the river first. There are two others I want you to meet. Here, come with Me."

As soon as she gripped her Master's hand, He drew her after Him off the bank. To her astonishment Ember discovered that she was actually standing on the water. Though the current above them and below them was very swift and wild, there was a calm, flat surface beneath their feet.

Ember started giggling. "It's kind of bouncy!" she laughed as they walked across the water's surface. "It reminds me of playing on my parent's big bed when I was little."

Suddenly geysers of water began to splash up on either side of their path. The happy bursts of water began to spin and shoot from their tips like liquid fireworks. At the same time Ember was aware of a lovely, exultant song coming from the river itself. "The river is worshiping You, isn't it?" she asked knowingly.

"It *is* My river," Jesus smiled back, and He lifted His arms to receive the praise of His creation.

Beneath her feet the mesmerized girl could see fish of all sizes cavorting together in patterns of what Ember could only guess were dances of delight at being so near their King.

They passed slowly across the fluid surface so that Jesus could enjoy and bless the adoration of His creation. As the Lord led her up onto the opposite back, they both turned to face the river again. Hundreds of geysers erupted from the surface of the river, all in unison, and the upper third of each bowed to the King in one final offering of worship.

"Be blessed, oh waters of life," Jesus pronounced over the river. "Flow with strength and power. Bring joy and refreshment to all of Mine."

As the Lord continued their walk, they passed through an open patch of trees with shiny, golden leaves. The ground rose slightly, and eventually they came to a low hill in the middle of the beautiful, radiant woods. Jesus stopped and turned to face His friend. "Now, dear one," Jesus began, "I know you sometimes feel small and weak, but I want you to know that My presence and My power are always with you. I want you to meet two of My servants whom I have asked to look after you.

"Come!" Jesus commanded.

Suddenly, in the blink of an eye, two beings appeared on either side of the Master. Both immediately drew massive swords that seemed to radiate and hum with power. With the handles laying in their left hands and the ends of the blades resting in their right, the two angelic warriors dropped to a knee and extended their weapons as an offering to their King.

The one on Jesus's right was the smaller of the two, but he still seemed huge to the stunned girl. He wore a green robe with a golden belt and appeared to have armor on his chest and legs. His hair was radiant white, his skin had a look of metallic silver, and his eyes glowed like fire.

The second warrior was massive. Even though he was kneeling before the Lord, he looked over twice as big as the other angel. A gold-colored robe with scarlet trim fell from the giant's shoulders. His belt and armor resembled that of the first but were much larger. Contrary to the other, this warrior's hair was jet black, and his skin was a dark bronze color. His eyes had the same fiery look.

"Rise, My faithful ones," Jesus directed. "Replace your swords."

The two intimidating beings stood and returned their weapons to their sheaths. With wide eyes

Ember swallowed hard as she viewed the two powerful-looking warriors towering over her.

"Dear one," Jesus said as He looked at the timid girl, "there have been others, but these are two of My servants whom I have charged with ministering to you during your time in the shadow world. The one on My right is called Silvan."

The angel with the glowing white hair and the silver skin struck his chest with his right fist and bowed slightly as he said in a strong voice, "My lady!"

"This big fellow on My left is Barcos," Jesus announced as he turned to the larger warrior.

With the same show of respect, the bronze giant said *my lady* with a voice so deep and powerful that Ember felt the vibration of it.

"Are they my guardian angels?" the girl asked in awe.

"Yes, you could call them that," Jesus returned. "They are always with you in the shadow world, and they minister to you on My behalf."

"This is wonderful!" Ember said excitedly. "Even though I will probably not be able to see you back on earth, it will be such a comfort to know that you are both with me. And since I know your names, I can ask you for help and send you with special messages to Jesus."

Both angels shifted uncomfortably at the girl's words. Silvan cut his eyes over to Jesus, Who gave a subtle nod to the angel's unasked request.

"My lady," Silvan began in his rich baritone voice, "Barcos and I are servants of our Lord, King Jesus. Do not pray or make requests to us. We answer to our King, and we serve Him only, as do you. Let your requests and prayers be made to God through Jesus Christ, and Barcos and I will do what He commands."

"I'm sorry, Lord," Ember said repentantly as she bowed before Jesus. "I spoke without thinking."

"It's all right, dear one," Jesus said with a smile. "You are not the first of my followers to do that. Just remember, *I* am your way, *I* am your truth, and *I* am your life. *I* am everything that you will ever need, both in the world of shadows and in the world of light. *I* am your everything.

"Now, before I send you back," Jesus continued, "I have one more gift that I want to give you."

"Barcos," Jesus called to the giant, "hold out your hand."

The massive angel extended his huge arm upward towards his Master. Jesus held His fingers over the large, open palm, and Ember saw an iridescent blue essence flow from the Lord and pool in the angel's hand. Ember couldn't tell whether it was a heavy vapor or some form of liquid, but it glowed and contained tiny flashes of light.

In a moment Jesus pulled back his hand and nodded at Barcos. Both angels drew their swords and stepped on either side of Ember.

The girl looked up at the two intimidating figures towering over her, then back at her King. "Am I going now?" she asked.

"Yes, dearest," Jesus smiled back. "It is time for you to return."

"I love you!" she said with sincerity.

"That I know for certain, dear one, and I love you too!"

As He spoke, Barcos placed the blue essence in the palm of his hand against the back of the girl's head. To Ember, the beautiful colors and light seemed to fade, and the dull ache of her injury grew. As her surroundings darkened, she opened her eyes and focused, seeing Rebecca's worried face leaning over her.

"You woke up!" the younger sister exclaimed. "Praise Jesus, you woke up!"

Chapter Twenty

THE TRUTH

"I don't think you should be sitting up," Rebecca said with concern as Ember moved to the edge of Prisha's bed, where she had been placed after her injury. "You looked terrible when we dragged you in. That was almost a day ago."

"I'm doing okay, Becca," Ember said, managing a smile. "The back of my head is sore, and I'm a little dizzy, but really, I'm doing fine. If you could dip me out a bowl of that feverfew tea I smell steaming in that pot by the fire, I think it would help."

As Rebecca went after the tea, Ember carefully made her way to a chair by the table. The injured girl had sipped almost half of the tea when suddenly the cabin door flew open, and a very dirty and disheveled Susanna was shoved through the opening. The crying young woman stumbled across the small room and cowered by the shelves on the opposite wall. Behind her walked the squaw, carrying a long, thick switch.

As soon as Prisha saw Ember sitting at the table, she gasped and rushed to her side. "PRAISE MONETO, YOU ALIVE!"

"Yes," Ember said with a little laugh. "Moneto and His Son Jesus are very good!"

"When I find you and saw that wicked girl had hit you with bucket," Prisha said anxiously, "I was sure you head broke and that you must die!"

"Jesus said that He wanted to give me a gift, and He had something put on the back of my head," Ember said her thoughts out loud. "Maybe my head was broken, and He healed me. Anyway, I am doing okay now, and my head only hurts a little."

"Emba, you see Jesus again?" Prisha asked. The girl smiled and nodded her head. "You must tell me," the squaw said with an eager look.

Just then the squaw detected a movement to her right and noticed Susanna inching toward the cabin door. As soon as the older girl saw that she had been spotted, she sprang for the entrance. Instantly Prisha whipped her long switch in front of Susanna and yelled, "HIYEE!"

With a scream of terror, the girl stopped and rushed whimpering back to cower by the wall. Ember saw red whelps all over Susanna's arms and legs that had come from Prisha's switch.

"I'm sorry you're having to go through this, Susanna," Ember said with sympathy, "but it didn't have to be this way. I tried to warn you."

"DON'T TALK TO ME, YOU TRAITOR!" the older girl screamed through her tears.

"You're the traitor!" Rebecca exclaimed. "Ember didn't do anything to you, and you hit her in the head with a bucket! You could have killed her! You'll be lucky if they don't do the same to you!"

In response Susanna pulled her knees up to her chin and sniveled as she rocked fearfully back and forth.

Prisha reached for a leather rope hanging from a peg on the wall. She said something to Susanna in Shawnee.

"She wants you to put your hands together in front of you," Ember interpreted.

"NO!" Susanna yelled defiantly. Prisha growled and drew back her switch. With wide-eyes, the rebellious girl quickly did as she'd been instructed and extended her arms to the squaw. Once they were securely bound, the squaw tied the other end of the rope to a corner of the bed.

Satisfied that the defiant captive could no longer get away, the medicine woman, with Rebecca's help, worked on supper. Other than Rebecca having gobbled two left over pieces of bread she had found, no one else had eaten for almost twenty-four hours. Prisha decided to make a big stew of deer meat, beans, corn, and squash. As she worked, Rebecca was told to grind corn for more flat bread.

When the meal was ready, the squaw filled three bowls and placed them on the table with the fresh bread.

"I want some!" whined Susanna when she saw Prisha and the other girls sit down to eat.

The squaw spat some angry words back at the girl and pointed to Ember to translate. "She's very angry at you, Susanna," Ember began. "She says that because of all the trouble you caused, you don't get to eat this evening."

"WHAT?" the girl exclaimed. "But I'm starving!"

"I'm sorry," Ember continued. "She says that if you do your chores tonight and tomorrow, she may feed you then."

When she heard this, the older girl began to wail loudly. Immediately the squaw jumped to her feet and grabbed her long, thick switch. Just as quickly the wailing stopped, and Susanna resolved to cry quietly.

Remarkably, Ember felt almost no dizziness after her big supper. Even so, the medicine woman sent her to bed while Rebecca cleaned the hearth. The dirty dishes were stacked and placed in Susanna's unbound hands. Prisha then picked up her switch and marched the girl to the creek to wash them.

When Prisha and Susanna, who carried the cleaned dishes, returned, the squaw had both sisters put everything away and sweep the cabin. Once satisfied, Prisha pointed at Rebecca and sent her up the ladder to sleep with Ember. With a smile the younger girl quickly climbed to the loft.

"Where am I supposed to sleep?" whined Susanna.

In response, Prisha threw down a buffalo robe and pointed to the area beside the hearth where Rebecca had been sleeping. The older girl dejectedly dropped onto the robe with a sad moan. "Hey! What are you doing?" Susanna snapped as the squaw dropped a loop of the leather rope around the girl's neck and secured it with a firm knot. The medicine woman then hooked the rope around the top of a large pot, on which she stacked several bowls. The rest of the rope Prisha looped around a sturdy leg of the heavy table. She brought the end back to the older girl and tied it snuggly around both of her captive's hands.

Susanna realized that, if she moved her head, she would pull over the pot with the dishes, and the taunt rope binding her hands to the heavy table prevented her from reaching up and untying the neck rope. "But I can't move! How can I sleep like this?"

Prisha just waved a dismissive hand at the girl and went to bed, keeping her switch close by.

The next day it was obvious that Susanna was not happy, but she kept quiet and did everything the squaw ordered her to do. As the rest of them ate their breakfast, the older sister cried silently as she swept the cabin. In spite of what she had done, Ember began to feel sorry for Susanna as the hungry girl's stomach growled loudly.

After breakfast the squaw had Rebecca and Susanna gather the dirty dishes to take to creek. She intended to go with them to guard the rebellious girl, but a woman from the Shawnee camp walked in and asked for medicine for a fever.

"I will go with the girls," Ember offered. "You stay and prepare the medicine."

"You feel okay?"

"Yes, Prisha, I feel fine."

The squaw shook her head in amazement and said, "Jesus very good to you." Ember just smiled in agreement.

Prisha quickly stood up and confronted the older sister with her switch. She gave Susanna an angry little speech as she shook to long stick in her face. Then she looked at Ember and pointed at the older girl.

"She says that she doesn't want you to hurt me again, and if you run off, it will not be good."

"I think she said more than that," Susanna returned.

Ember just shrugged and said, "She's still very angry with you."

Arriving at the creek, the sisters placed the dirty dishes on the bank and began to wash them.

"Here," said a voice behind Susanna. She looked back and saw Ember holding two rolled up pieces of flat bread containing a large amount of the nut, berry, and honey mix.

Without a word the hungry girl snatched the offering and ate greedily. When she stuffed the last piece of bread into her mouth, she turned to Ember and glared at her. "This means nothing!" she snapped. "If you think giving me food makes us friends now, you are as dumb as you look!"

"Susanna! Stop it!" Rebecca cried.

"If that's the way you feel about it," Susanna shot back at her sister, "then you can just have Miss Goodie Goodie and her friendly gestures!"

Suddenly Ember was in the resentful girl's face so fast that it startled Susanna. "Let's get one thing straight," Ember said firmly. "I didn't give you that bread because I think that deep down you're a good person. I don't think that at all. I think that deep down *and* on the surface, you're a terrible person, and I don't like you at all. The reason I brought you the food is because, as hard as it is for me to understand, Jesus loves you, and He wanted me to bring it to you. So I'm not looking for any thanks or friendship from you. Jesus wanted me to bring you something to eat, and I obeyed Him. If you've got some problem with that, then you can gripe to Him."

Ember turned and walked back toward the cabin. When she got half way, she sat down on a stump to keep an eye on the rebellious girl.

After several minutes the angry girl turned to her younger sister. "I can't do this, Becca! I can't!"

"What are you talking about?"

"I can't stay here and be an Indian's squaw! But I can't run away either, and I'm too afraid to kill myself!"

"Have you tried praying to God like Ember suggested?" the younger girl asked sincerely.

"THERE'S NO GOD HERE!" the older girl snapped.

"Sure there is," Rebecca answered confidently. "Ember found Him here, and she's also been teaching me about Him. By the gift of food He just gave you, I'd say He's reaching out to you too."

The older girl snorted and turned back to her washing.

Rebecca added, "Ember read me some of the Bible last night before we went to sleep. God promises that He will never fail or forsake His followers."

"That's a lie!" Susanna snapped. "He's already failed us!"

"Are you His follower, Susanna?" Rebecca asked.

The older girl gave a long sigh and shook her head.

"Then the promise isn't for you. It looks to me like you're the one who has failed and forsaken Him."

Chapter Twenty-One

GRADUATION

The next day was a busy one for all of them. Because so much time had been lost with Susanna's escape attempt, there was a backlog of chores. Right after breakfast, Prisha left Rebecca and Ember to thoroughly clean while she took Susanna to check the traps and snares.

Three hours later, as the two girls in the cabin were finishing, Prisha and the oldest sister returned carrying six fat rabbits between them. Rebecca was given the job of skinning, cleaning, and cutting up the meat while the squaw took the other two girls with her. With a basket on each arm, they traveled up the wooded hillside behind the cabin and looked for edible mushrooms and herbs.

In the middle of the afternoon they returned with their loaded baskets. They found the younger sister busy grinding corn for flatbread. Prisha gave a nod of approval when she looked into a nearby pot and saw the cleaned hunks of rabbit meat. Ember and Susanna were sent to the creek to wash the mushrooms while the squaw started an early supper and stored the herbs they had collected.

Susanna sullenly ignored her companion as they did their work. Ember, for her part, was glad to escape the older girl's bitter and caustic remarks.

A movement caught Ember's attention, and looking behind her, she saw a squaw hurrying to see the medicine woman. A few minutes later both girls had finished cleaning the mushrooms and were returning to the cabin. Suddenly Prisha and the squaw stepped outside, and the medicine woman beckoned anxiously for them to hurry. When they arrived, Prisha explained that the woman's young daughter was coughing badly and had a fever. Because the medicine woman was concerned that Susanna might try to escape again, Prisha wanted Ember to treat the girl.

"You're sending me?" the girl asked nervously.

"Yes, you go," Prisha said firmly. "Now tell me what herbs you will use and how you will use them."

Ember thought hard about what she had learned about treating these particular symptoms. She listed the herbs Prisha typically used and how the medicines were to be prepared and administered. When she finished, Prisha nodded her head in agreement.

"Wiikano," the medicine woman agreed. "It is good." Prisha slipped the strap of her leather medicine bag over her head and placed it around Ember's neck. "The herbs you need are in the bag. Go and treat the girl. When you are done, you can find your way back to the cabin, yes?"

"Yes, I can," Ember acknowledged and beckoned the squaw to lead her to the sick child. As they walked hurriedly along the path to the Shawnee village, Ember prayed to the Lord to help her remember all that she had learned about illnesses like this one. She asked for favor that she would be successful in understanding what needed to be done to treat the girl and that Jesus would bless the treatments with healing. "For Your praise and glory!" she added.

When Ember arrived at the squaw's hut, she found a little girl on a buffalo robe, sweating and moaning. Prisha had taught her to always do an exam to identify all of the problems. The girl felt hot to the touch. Obviously her fever was high. That was the biggest danger right now, Ember reasoned, and must be dealt with before she looked further. The squaw was an experienced mother and already had a pot of water steaming on the fire. Scooping up a bowl full, the girl crushed dried feverfew leaves into it and covered it to let the mixture steep for a few minutes while she continued her examination.

Ember put her ear to the girl's chest and heard dry, rough sounds but no congestion. Her heart sounded strong. After looking into the girl's eyes, Ember noticed a slight discharge coming from her patient's ears. One was worse than the other, but they both had an odor.

Uncovering the feverfew tea, Ember gave the girl sips of the warm liquid. Turning that job over to the girl's mother, the apprentice healer moved the pot of hot water directly onto the coals, and soon it was boiling. She quickly crumbled two small bundles of dried herbs into the hot water, and immediately a strong fragrance began to fill the small hut. Using deer skin pads, Ember moved the pot beside the sick girl's head to let her breathe the vapors. Within several minutes the patient's breathing was noticeably better. Ember reexamined the girl and noted that her skin did not feel as hot.

Now for those ears, Ember said to herself. She searched through the medicine bag to see what was available. In the bottom she saw a bunch of dried yellow root plants. She asked the squaw for hickory nut oil, and the squaw uncovered a bowl and pointed. Pouring a small amount into a pottery dish, she set it over the coals. As it heated, she crushed the leaves of the yellow root as finely as she could and dropped them into the warming oil.

After a few moments she tested the temperature against her own skin. She wanted it to be warm but not too hot. When it felt right, Ember set the bowl near to the sick girl and, using the tip of her finger, dripped five drops of the warm oil into the infected ears.

Even Ember was surprised when, a few minutes later, the miserable little girl relaxed and went to sleep. "Moneto is giving her rest," Ember told the relieved mother, and explained to the concerned woman how to use the herbs to continue treating her sick daughter.

A little over two hours after she had arrived at the Shawnee's hut, Ember walked out to head back to the cabin. She was relieved, excited, and full of thanksgiving for how the Lord had blessed her work on the little girl.

"I think she's going to be okay, Lord," Ember prayed as she walked, "thanks to You. I was so nervous when I arrived, but You were right there with me. I felt Your presence, and that gave me peace. You helped me remember everything that I needed to do. As nervous as I was when I started, it would have been so easy to have missed her ear infections, but You drew my attention to them. Thank you for that, Lord! You are so wonderful!"

Ember spent the rest of the trip back thinking about all that Jesus had done for her. Suddenly the girl's worshipful thoughts were interrupted by a crash and screaming. Looking up, she saw the cabin thirty yards in front of her. There was a strange horse walking untethered in the yard, and the door was open. She heard the deep, angry voice of a man yelling. Another crash sounded, then more screaming.

Hurry, dear one! They need you!

Racing to the cabin, Ember scanned the situation as she entered. Rebecca was screaming as she huddled against the far wall. Susanna was picking herself up from a pile of broken shelves and pots where she had been shoved. To her left Ember saw the back of Rayford as he leaned threateningly over Prisha, who was lying on the floor beside the hearth. A swelling was forming under one eye, and her mouth bled. Ember also spotted a shattered whisky jug in a puddle of alcohol on the floor behind the angry trapper.

"AH'M DONE WI' YOU!" Rayford roared in a drunken rage as Prisha threw up her arms to try to defend herself from the repeated blows of the bully. "AH'M GETTING' RID O' YOU! AH'LL TAKE THE GIRL FOR MY SQUAW!"

Susanna, not sure if the raging drunkard was talking about her, her sister, or Ember, angrily grabbed the ax and stepped up from behind to swing it at the trapper's head.

Stop her! A voice sounded urgently in Ember's mind.

Ember grabbed the ax and snatched it out of the older girl's hands just as she started her swing. As Susanna whirled around to see what had happened, Ember pushed her out of the way.

Now stop him! Ember flipped the ax around so that she was holding it near the ax head and swung the oak handle powerfully into the back of Rayford's skull. There was a loud, solid *WHACK,* and the trapper collapsed unconscious onto the floor.

"Prisha," Ember cried with concern as she dropped the ax and rushed over to her injured friend, "you hurt bad?"

With the girls' help the medicine woman stood shakily to her feet. She stared at the unconscious man at her feet. "He bad...very bad man," the terrified squaw panted. "He come in cabin drunk and mad. Big girl was in his way, and he throw her against the wall...hurt her. That make Prisha mad, so I hit his hand hard with spoon. He yell and drop jug on floor, and it break all to pieces. Howiise! He big mad then! If you not hit him, Emba, he kill Prisha this time!"

"When he wake up, you be safe?" the girl asked.

"No," the squaw said firmly. "If we still here when he wake up, this time he kill us all! Take girls and go! Run away!"

Prisha turned and grabbed one of Rayford's leather traveling pouches from a peg on the wall and immediately stuffed flat bread and dried pemmican into it. Snatching a leather belt with a sheathed knife from a peg on the wall, the medicine woman shoved it at Ember and told her to put it on. Lastly Prisha bent down and felt under her husband's prostrate form, yanking his tomahawk from his belt. She started to give it to Susanna but stopped herself and handed the weapon to Rebecca instead.

"What is going on?" Susanna snapped. "I don't know what she's jabbering about, but when he wakes up, he will kill us all."

"We know!" Ember returned. "She told me that we have to run away for our own safety. She's packing this sack for us."

"Where will we go?" Rebecca asked anxiously.

"Are you coming with us?" Ember asked the squaw in Shawnee.

"No," Prisha returned. "I am medicine woman of my tribe. I must stay to help my people. I go to my sister. Be safe with her."

"But we don't know where to go!" Ember said with concern.

Prisha stooped beside the hearth and pulled up the large flat stone in the center. Quickly she withdrew two objects and handed them to the girl. "This Rayford's map and north pointer," the squaw said. "You use. You find friends. Go quick. Rayford rode horse he stole in last raid and got back before others, but the war party is coming. Be here soon. You go now."

Ember held the hand-drawn map and the compass she had seen the trapper use before. The thought of what she and the other girls were about to do was overwhelming to her. *Oh Lord. . .* she prayed desperately in her heart.

The squaw handed the pouch to Susanna. "GO NOW!" Prisha said urgently. Then the medicine woman turned to gather what she needed to escape.

"We're leaving!" Ember announced to the other girls. "She gave us a map and a compass to help. Grab blankets to wrap up in at night.

"Prisha," Ember said, touching the squaw on the shoulder. She took off the squaw's medicine bag and handed it to her mistress. When she saw it, the medicine woman paused a moment, took it, and quickly stuffed it with herbs and medical supplies.

Ember hurriedly climbed the ladder and snatched her deer skin with all of her medicine notes. As she descended to the cabin floor, Prisha met the girl and shoved the medicine bag at her.

"This for you now," the squaw said with a smile.

"Oh, Prisha, thank you!" the girl exclaimed, hugging the bag.

"Because of you, Emba," Prisha began, "I know Jesus. He my Chief. I am now Prishanese, the Maker's Medicine Woman...and you are Emba, the Maker's Medicine Girl. We both heal for Him."

Ember threw her arms around the squaw's neck and hugged her. The stunned Shawnee patted the girl's back tenderly.

"COME ON!" Susanna demanded impatiently.

Reluctantly Ember withdrew her arms and, looking into her friend's eyes, said, "Thank you for all you have taught me. I will never forget you."

"Emba," the squaw said sincerely, "you promised to sit with Prisha at Chief Jesus's table."

"Yes, and I can't wait!" the girl answered excitedly as she snatched one of Rayford's stolen blankets off his bed and dashed out the door, following the sisters.

Chapter Twenty-Two

AN UNEXPECTED SURPRISE

With the blanket under her arm, Ember tucked the deer skin with all of her notes into the medicine bag that hung from her shoulder.

"Susanna's gonna catch the horse so we can ride on it," Rebecca announced.

Rayford had been so drunk that he hadn't tied the horse, and it was wandering around the yard. Every time the older girl approached the animal, it shied away from her.

Just then, the sound of drunken yelling was heard coming from the south woods.

"What's that?" Rebecca gasped.

"The war party's coming back," Ember answered with dread.

"Oh no!" the younger girl exclaimed. "They're coming right for us! What do we do?"

"Lord, we need Your help!" Ember said a quick, desperate prayer. Just then an idea popped into her mind.

"I'll be right back!" Ember said and raced to the cabin.

She met Prisha hurrying out as she reached the door. "Emba!" the squaw exclaimed. "You still here? You must run!"

"The war party's returning, but Jesus gave me an idea!"

"Ha!" the squaw nodded with confidence. "Jesus take care of you!"

As the medicine woman ran up the path that led to the village and her sister, Ember dashed into the cabin. She moved even quicker when she heard a moan from Rayford's prostrate form. Snatching up a clay bowl, the girl scooped red hot coals from the fire. She noticed that six pieces of flat bread were turning brown on the hot cooking stone. Taking a quick look back at the unconscious trapper, the girl made her decision.

We'll need all the food we can get, she said to herself as she whipped out the knife at her hip and scooped up the bread. She slipped them into her medicine bag, replaced her knife, grabbed the bowl of coals, and dashed back out the door.

Susanna was still desperately trying to catch the balking horse. "Forget the horse!" Ember called. "Follow me!" She grabbed Rebecca's hand and ran toward the creek.

Susanna heard the words and turned to argue that they needed the horse when she saw Ember and her sister race away. The drunken yells from the approaching war party were closer. Stubbornly she made one more grab for the horse, but the beast had tired of the game and dashed off to the west. In a panic the older girl turned and chased after the other two. "DON'T LEAVE ME!" she cried as she ran.

When she arrived at the creek, she saw Ember and Rebecca in the water wading upstream. Susanna ran along the bank to catch up with them.

Hearing the older girl tramping through the woods, Ember whirled around.

"YOU STOP RIGHT THERE!" she snapped firmly at the older girl. "Turn around and run back to where we got in and walk in the creek to join us."

"That's ridiculous!" Susanna shot back. "I'm not getting my feet wet! That water's cold!"

"Then the Shawnee will easily track and recapture you," Ember returned, "but I will not let you lead the Indians to Rebecca and me. If you're going to be foolish, then go find your own way." Ember bent down and picked up a rock and held it threateningly. "The only way I will let you come with us is if you agree to do everything I say."

The older girl stared hard at Ember, trying to decide what to do. At that moment the loud Shawnee warriors stumbled out of the woods. Terrified, Susanna ran back along the bank, staying behind the brush and trees, and without hesitation stepped into the frigid water and waded toward the other two girls.

When Susanna stood in front of her, Ember looked hard into the rebellious girl's eyes. Seeing nothing but fear, she dropped her rock and led them further upstream. They came to what appeared to be a wall of brush and limbs blocking their way. Ember moved the foliage and revealed the mouth of the cave.

"What is this place?" Rebecca asked timidly.

"I saw Rayford come up here one evening when I was washing dishes. I followed him until he entered, but he never saw me."

"WHAT?" Susanna shouted. "Rayford knows about this place, and you brought us here!"

"Keep your voice down," Ember said firmly, "or the Shawnee will know where we are.

"Yes, Rayford knows about it," the girl continued, "but he doesn't know *we* know about it. Now come on."

There was a strong breeze blowing into the mouth of the cave as they prepared to entered.

"But won't we get lost in there?" the younger girl asked.

"Do you feel that breeze, Becca?" Ember asked with a smile. "That means that there is another exit somewhere. All we have to do is follow the breeze, and we'll find it."

"But where does it lead?" Susanna wanted to know.

"I don't know," Ember answered honestly. "Hopefully it will be far away from the Shawnee. Once we get out, we'll use Rayford's map and compass to try to figure out where we are and where we need to go."

"But it's so dark in there," the younger girl countered. "How will we see to find our way?"

"Grab some dry leaves and grass, and I'll show you." Ember led the way into the cavern. Once inside, she searched for the ledge where Rayford had a hidden torch. She was delighted to find five long sticks cut from the sap-filled heart wood of pine trees.

"We will only light one at a time to make them last longer," Ember announced as she gathered dry leaves and grass and laid them on the hot coals she still carried in the bowl. When a flame caught, she had the girls pick up all the torches and follow her. Once Ember felt they were far enough that the light would not be seen from the outside, she used the flame in the bowl to ignite the sap on one of the sticks. Their surroundings were suddenly illuminated by the glowing torch.

"Hey, what's that?" Rebecca asked as she pointed curiously to a drawing on the wall beside them.

"It's Indian markings!" Susanna snapped. "Ember, you dummy, you brought us into a cave they use all the time! They'll find us for sure in here, all because of you!"

"What a minute," Ember said, cutting the older girl off. "I've seen that symbol before.

"Becca, hold the torch for me." As the younger girl took the light, Ember pulled Rayford's map out of her medicine bag and unfolded it.

"Look here!" she said pointing to the center of the drawings. "See, it's the same symbol. This little box must be the cabin, and just behind it is the symbol."

"It's probably some Indian curse thing or something," Susanna said impatiently. "Let's just get out of here before some of them remember this cave."

"I've been here a couple of years," Ember returned, "and I have never seen anyone in this cave but Rayford. The Shawnee have never used it while I have been here. I honestly don't think they know about it. I don't even think Prisha knows about it. So why would he come in here and go to the trouble of putting this mark on the wall and his map?"

"It's obviously important to him," Rebecca reasoned.

"Yes, it is!" Ember exclaimed as an idea suddenly came to her. "He's hiding something in here! Quick, look for a hole or a crevice or a ledge where something could be concealed."

Rebecca lifted the torch so the light would shine brightly all around them. As the girls searched the walls, Ember looked down and noticed a flat rock embedded in the floor just below the symbol. Using her knife to pry up the edges, she was able to lift the stone and move it to the side. Underneath was a rectangular opening.

"What's in it?" Susanna asked, suddenly curious.

Reaching in, Ember pulled out a leather sack. It clinked when she set it on the flat stone.

"There are several pouches in this hole," she answered. Opening the first, she poured its contents onto the stone.

"Oh, my!" Rebecca gasped. "Gold and silver coins!"

"There must be fifty of them!" the older girl added excitedly.

Ember reached back into the hole and drew out another pouch. She noticed it was lighter than the first one. Emptying its contents, they saw a collection of rings, necklaces, broaches, and bracelets.

"It's treasure!" Rebecca gasped.

Ember stared sadly at the pile of jewelry and said, "It's the loot Rayford took from all the people he killed."

"You don't know that," Rebecca said, hoping that it wasn't true.

Tears began to flow down Ember's cheeks. "Yes, I do," she answered sorrowfully as she picked up something from the small pile. "This is my mother's ring."

Sliding the cherished memento onto her finger, Ember searched through the other items and found a necklace and a brooch that she also recognized. Overcome with emotion, Ember walked away and sat against the wall crying.

Quickly the older sister took her place and pulled out the remaining two sacks and emptied them onto the stone.

"The rest of them contain jewelry," Susanna announced, "and most of it is made of gold!"

"Hey, there's Momma's wedding ring!" Rebecca shouted as she pointed at the pile.

"So it is," Susanna said as she quickly snatched it up. "I always loved that it had the big ruby and the two smaller diamonds."

"Can I hold it?" Rebecca asked pleadingly.

"As the oldest daughter, I'm sure mother would want me to have it," Susanna declared as she slid the ring onto her own finger. Looking back down, her eye fell on a golden bracelet that she quickly grabbed. "This is her favorite bracelet too." She placed it on her wrist and looked at the armlet and the ring admiringly. "Don't they make a lovely set?"

"I want something of Momma's!" the younger girl pleaded, beginning to cry.

Annoyed, the older girl scanned the pile of jewelry and lifted up a locket on a chain. "That's Momma's necklace!" Rebecca exclaimed through her tears. "Can I have that, please?"

"Hmmm," Susanna said as she studied the object, "It's just silver. I suppose you can."

Rebecca snatched the offered gift and clutched it near to her heart as her tears continued to flow.

After several minutes Susanna gathered all the treasure and placed it back in the sacks. "There's a lot of gold and jewelry here," she announced. "What are we going to do with it?"

"I don't care," Ember returned sadly. "I don't want any of it."

"Well," Susanna said with a smile, "we certainly aren't going to leave this treasure for that animal Rayford." As she spoke, the older girl loaded the sacks into her carrying bag. "We'll take it with us, Rebecca. We deserve it for the hardship we've been through."

Chapter Twenty-Three

THE DEVIL'S PETS

"**L**et's keep moving," Ember announced with a sigh as she stood and took the torch from Rebecca. The passage was about ten feet wide and had a ceiling tall enough to allow them to walk upright. An underground stream flowed toward the entrance along a shallow channel in the floor. *At least we'll have plenty of water to drink,* Ember thought as she hurried along, trying to avoid the shallow pools and the mud.

After following the monotonous passage for over a quarter of an hour, the three hiked into a larger, open area. The ceiling rose to over twenty feet above their heads, and they could hear water dripping from the walls on both sides of the cave.

"Wait!" Susanna called from behind. "What's that over there?" She pointed to their left where she spotted light from the torch flashing off the white surface of rocks protruding from the wall.

Her curiosity peeked, Ember led them over to the spot.

"Are those diamonds?" Rebecca asked in wonder.

Susanna reached out and rubbed her hand over the glistening white surface. "I'm pretty sure it's not diamonds," the older sister answered, "but it's some kind of crystals."

"The water dripping from the roof of the cave is carrying minerals that dried and formed on the rocks," Ember explained. "My father told my brother and me about it once."

"It's so wonderful!" Becca exclaimed in amazement.

"It is," Ember agreed. "The Lord makes beautiful things."

"Can we *please* not turn this into a sermon?" Susanna said with a tone of annoyance. "Let's just keep going."

Ember continued carefully through the large cavern. On two different occasions the girls spotted dark openings in the walls, but when explored, they turned out not to lead anywhere. The fugitives had to work their way around and sometimes over boulders that had fallen from the ceiling in the past. The further they traveled, the larger the room seemed to get. They could no longer see the roof of the cave, and the blackness loomed like a dome over their heads.

"Ember, can we rest?" Rebecca asked wearily from behind.

"I think that's a great idea," their leader answered cheerfully. "As near as I can guess, we must have been at this for over two hours. We can get a drink from the stream and sit for a while on the rocks up ahead.

"Susanna," Ember added, "pull out some of the food Prisha packed in your sack, and we'll eat."

Thirty minutes later, rested and fed, Ember decided it was time to renew their march.

"Your torch is about to burn out," Susanna observed. "Light up one of these I'm carrying, and I'll take yours until it finally dies."

After another half hour of difficult travel, Ember called a halt.

"Why are you stopping?" the older girl called from behind. "We'll never get out of this horrible place if you don't keep going!"

"We have a decision to make," Ember answered. The glow of their light revealed that the cavern seemed to end just ahead of them. "I can see two openings in the wall. The one on the left is taller and wider than the one on the right."

"Should we go left?" Rebecca asked as she stepped next to her friend and put a hand on her arm.

"I'm not sure," Ember answered. "Let's check them out."

The three girls walked cautiously to the opening on the left. "This way looks better," Susanna said after she had compared it with the low, narrow opening on the right.

"I don't know," Ember returned as she waved her torch slowly in front of the wide opening. "I can't detect any air moving through here."

"Maybe you're not doing it right!" the older girl snapped in frustration.

Leaving the first tunnel, Ember walked to the other passage. When she stepped in front of it, the flame of her torch bent sideways as the draft drew it into the opening. "The exit is this way," their leader declared.

"Are you sure?" Susanna questioned skeptically.

"That way looks awfully spooky, Ember," Rebecca agreed.

"I know it's a smaller passage, and I don't want to go in there either, but the air moving through proves that this is the way out. Come on; let's go." Ember took Rebecca's hand and started into the cave.

Just as the flame of the burning torch entered the passageway, thousands of high-pitched shrieks burst from the opening, and a furious explosion of wings and small black bodies shot from the cave mouth, terrifying the girls. Screaming, they leaped back and covered their heads as the angry storm of living creatures shot past them. The three cowered in terror until the last of the bats had gone.

Ember shakily reached for the torch she had dropped. She praised God that it had landed against some rocks and had not been quenched in one of the pools of water on the floor. She stood and again cautiously explored the opening with her light. "I think it's safe now," she finally said.

"You *think* it's safe!" Susanna snarled angrily, still breathing hard. "How would *you* know? I followed you in here because I thought you knew what you were doing. You obviously don't! There is no way I am following you into that...that hole!"

"All right then," Ember returned calmly. "I will light the unused torch you're carrying, and you can go back the way we came. If you hurry, you should be able to make it back to the entrance before your light burns out."

"Me?" Susanna stammered. "You're sending *me* back... ALONE?"

"Listen to me!" Ember said firmly. "The breeze moving through here tells me that it leads to an exit. Scary or not, that is the way I'm going. Rebecca can come with me or go with you. It's up to her..."

"I'm going with you," Becca said quickly, grabbing Ember's hand.

Before Susanna could respond, Ember reached over and let the flame from her torch ignite the one in the older girl's hand. Immediately their guide turned and led Rebecca into the smaller passageway.

"What if more bats are in there?" the older girl called after them. "Those things could kill us! They're the devil's pets!"

"In that case, they'll like you," she heard her sister's giggling voice call back.

Susanna stood outside the tunnel shaking, partly from fear, partly from anger. Finally, with a furious growl, she stomped her foot and followed the other two into the narrow tunnel.

The passage was low and narrow, causing them to slightly stoop and walk sideways. To all of their relief, no more bats were encountered. Suddenly the narrow, small tunnel opened into a room, but to Ember's terror, there was no floor. With great care she leaned over the edge and let her light shine into the pit. All she could see was blackness below.

"What is it?" she heard Susanna's worried voice from behind. "Why are we stopping?"

"Give me a minute!" Ember called back. Using her torch, the girl searched. She could see a very small ledge along the left side of the yawning hole. The narrow shelf was only four or five inches wide, but it led across to the other side where another opening invited them. Ember quickly explained their situation to the others.

"Let me cross first," she said encouragingly to Rebecca, "then I can help you."

Please be with us, Lord! Ember pleaded as she stepped onto the narrow ledge.

"I'm praying, Ember!" Becca said nervously.

"Me too!" the leader returned over her shoulder.

Holding the torch in front and with her back pressed against the cave wall, Ember inched her way cautiously along the narrow ledge. She carefully explored the tiny foot path with her left foot before taking each new step. Ember locked her eyes on the opening across the room, which was her goal, and refused to let herself look at the gapping pit below.

"WHAT'S TAKING SO LONG?" Susanna called irritably from the darkness behind Rebecca. The shout startled Ember, and she swayed briefly to regain her balance.

"Be quiet, Susanna!" the younger girl hissed.

Taking a deep breath, Ember once again started creeping across the narrow ledge of rocks. When finally reaching the other side, she and Rebecca gave huge sighs of relief.

After a brief rest Ember prepared to help Rebecca. Finding a place on the side of the rock wall with a large crack, the older girl tightly wedged the base of the torch into it. With both of her hands free to help Rebecca, Ember called to the younger girl to toss the two unlit torches she carried across the pit. Ember was able to catch the first one. The second flew directly at her head, and she had to duck to keep from getting hit. The stick smacked the rock wall behind where her head had been, bounced off, and tumbled into the pit, disappearing into the darkness. It was several seconds later before they heard it bouncing off rocks far below.

Ember looked at the younger girl, who threw her hands over her mouth and said, "Sorry!"

"It's okay," Ember returned. "Hopefully the ones we have left will be enough. Now, Rebecca, start with your left foot and slide out onto the ledge. Keep your back against the wall and look straight at me. Don't look down. I will help you cross."

Once she had started, Ember stepped carefully back along the ledge to meet her. As they got close to one another, the older girl reached for the younger and said, "Grab my hand, Becca."

Together the two inched their way to the other side. Once Rebecca was safe, Ember turned and called to the older sister. "It's your turn, Susanna. Toss your torch over here so your hands will be free."

As she observed the older girl, Ember could tell that Susanna wasn't sure how to throw the light. Finally she grabbed the handle of the torch with both hands and, closing her eyes, heaved it in Ember's direction. The flaming missile flipped wildly across the chasm, and once again Ember had to duck. Rebecca screamed and threw her arms up to protect herself as the spinning firebrand hit the wall above her head and clattered along the floor of the tunnel, hissing and sputtering in a shallow puddle of water.

"SUSANNA!" the younger sister screamed. "YOU ALMOST HIT ME!"

"It's not my fault," Susanna shot back flippantly. "She said to toss it, so I did."

"Start inching your way onto the ledge," Ember said, trying to be patient, "and I'll help you like I did Rebecca."

"I don't need your help," the older girl shot back. "Just stay out of my way." As Susanna began her dangerous journey across the ledge, she made the mistake of allowing the bag slung on her shoulder to slip behind her back. With the bulky sack between her and the wall, it was more difficult to keep her balance on the narrow walkway. About half way across Susanna reached a spot where the wall arched slightly forward, and before she realized the danger, she felt herself sliding toward the pit. Trying to regain her balance, her right foot slipped off the ledge, and the girl screamed and flailed wildly for the wall. Her fingers happened to catch a protruding edge of a rock, and she was able to keep from falling.

"HELP!" she yelled at Ember in panic. "PLEASE DON'T LET ME FALL!"

Praying as she went, Ember slid along the narrow ledge toward the terrified girl. Susanna was too scared to move and clung fiercely to the knob of rock she gripped.

"HURRY!" the older girl cried. "I CAN'T HOLD ON MUCH LONGER!"

As Ember got close, she knew she had to grab Susanna, but she didn't want the panicking girl to pull her off the ledge as well. Using her hands to feel the surface of the wall behind her, Ember's fingers landed on a crack in the rock. Shoving her left hand into it, she was able to get a firm grip. Leaning down, she reached for Susanna's hand that grasped the protruding rock. Gripping the girl's wrist tightly, Ember pulled with all of her might.

"I've got you!" Ember said. "Stand up!"

With much crying and grunting and Ember's help, the older sister managed to get both feet back on the ledge.

"Alright, come on!" Ember said, and while still gripping the trembling girl's wrist, led her along the ledge to safety.

Chapter Twenty-Four

A DEADLY VISITOR

All three girls were relieved to discover that the new tunnel was larger than the last. They followed their leader's dancing torch flame along the damp passageway for almost half an hour, at which point Ember came to a halt.

"What's wrong now?" Susanna snapped irritably from behind. "If you keep stopping like this, we are never going to get out of this awful place!"

"I think we're supposed to turn here," Ember answered thoughtfully.

Susanna looked past her sister and saw that the wide passage continued on, but Ember was looking at a small opening to her right.

"You can't be thinking of crawling in there!" the older girl growled angrily. "That's not a tunnel! It's just a crack in the wall!"

"But the flame is being sucked into it," Ember argued.

"So what?" Susanna shot back. "We could get stuck in that little crack and die! Is that what you want? We'd be fools to go in there!"

"I have asked the Lord to lead us out of here, and I believe He's doing it with this draft," the leader countered. "The fool is the person who asks for God's help and then refuses to use what He provides!" Ember swallowed hard and pushed herself into the narrow split in the wall. Rebecca took one quick look at her sister and hurried after her leader.

With another angry snort of frustration, Susanna stamped her foot again and followed the others. The tightness of the walls made the way much more difficult, which was also magnified by the grumbling and huffing coming from the older sister in the rear. Ember's voice suddenly called back to the others. "Cheer up! It's starting to get wider!"

Eventually they squeezed into a much larger passageway about twelve feet wide and ten feet tall. The floor was damp, and a trickle of water seeped from near the right edge of the rock ceiling, falling into a small, clear pool just below.

"Oh, the air is warmer here," Rebecca observed.

As they walked along the wider tunnel, the flame of the torch suddenly began to flap vigorously up and to their left.

"THERE'S AN OPENING!" Ember called excitedly when she saw where the flame pointed.

Nearly six feet up on the left side of the wall was a hole big enough for someone to crawl through.

"I can see stars!" an excited Rebecca said as they studied the small entrance.

"Well, what are we waiting for?" Susanna called impatiently. "Let's get out of here!"

"We need to know what's on the other side of that opening first," Ember warned. "Rebecca, you're the smallest. Susanna and I will lift you. Look out and tell us what you see. We could be a hundred feet above the ground for all we know."

Ember propped her burning torch against the wall, and with more grumbling and complaining from the older sister, the two bigger girls managed to lift Rebecca high enough for her to look out the hole.

"Well, what do you see?" Susanna demanded impatiently.

"This is good," the younger girl called back. "There's no cliff. There is only an easy slope below the..."

Suddenly there was a loud snarl and a piercing scream of pain from Rebecca as she threw herself back into the cave, knocking all three of them off balance and to the tunnel floor. Rebecca fell the farthest and landed hard on the gravel below. The younger girl continued to scream in pain as she grabbed her left arm while she writhed on the floor.

"BECCA, WHAT HAPPENED!" Ember called urgently as she sprang to her feet.

"MY ARM! MY ARM!"

Just then a threatening growl sounded from above them. Glancing quickly back at the hole, the three girls saw a large black head with savage eyes and a lot of sharp, white teeth staring at Rebecca. The old panther had not eaten in three days and was determined to have the smaller girl as its prey.

"IT'S COMING IN!" Rebecca screamed as she saw the great beast crawl to the edge of the opening.

"THROW ROCKS AT IT!" Ember yelled, quickly grabbing a stone at her feet and sending it flying toward the creature. Susanna also flung missiles as they both shouted at the cat.

"GET OUT OF HERE!

"GO AWAY!"

In their fear and extreme excitement, the girls' aims were not accurate, and none of the rocks hit the beast. Irritated at all the noise, the panther prepared to leap to claim its victim.

Instantly the cave was filled with the terrified screams of all of the girls, but Rebecca's was the loudest. The cat sprang for her, and with no time to stand up, the young girl scooted quickly backwards in an attempt to escape the terrible jaws. The determined panther landed at the feet of the retreating the girl. Angrily, the hunter swung its claws at Rebecca to drag her to him.

As soon as she saw the cat spring, Ember yanked out her knife and ran for Rebecca, arriving just as the panther sunk its claws into the younger girl's leg. Instantly Ember's knife pierced the beast's shoulder. With an ear-shattering scream of pain, the injured cat swung around like lightening and slashed at the source of its agony.

The powerful blow knocked Ember backwards, causing her to stumble and fall against the opposite wall. Three long tears had suddenly appeared in the upper sleeve of her dress, and blood began to flow through the rips.

When she fell, Ember had lost her grip on the knife, which was still embedded in the shoulder of the now enraged cat. Momentarily forgetting about its prey, the maddened creature only wanted to destroy the one who had hurt him. With its eyes now locked on Ember as she lay against the rock wall, the beast limped closer and closer.

Desperately searching for a way of escape, Ember suddenly heard a voice speak. *The torch*, it said. Looking to her left, she spotted the flaming stick where it was propped against the wall. Frantically she seized it and shoved the fire into the face of the cat. As the blaze seared its lips and tender nose, the startled beast threw itself backwards to escape and almost bumped into Susanna's legs. Seeing the terrible creature so close, the older girl looked anxiously around her for some kind of weapon. Spotting Rayford's tomahawk in her sister's belt, she snatched it and swung it hard into the back of the panther's neck, putting a permanent end to the battle.

Ember stumbled painfully to her feet and hurried to the still crying Rebecca. "It hurts really bad, Ember!" the young girl sobbed. She held her left hand over the deep scratches on her right forearm and tried to reach her wounded leg with her right hand.

"Let me look," the healer said firmly. After studying the wounds, she looked back at her anxious companion. "I'm sorry you got hurt, Becca. The scratches are deep, but I can help you."

"Am I going to die?"

"No, dear friend," Ember smiled reassuringly at the frightened girl. "But because the wounds were caused by this cat's nasty claws, they could turn foul if we don't treat them. I expect them to heal, but your arm and your leg are going to be very sore for a few days."

"No, no, NO!" Susanna yelled as she realized the severity of her sister's injuries. "We can't stay here! We've got to keep moving! Rebecca, you'll just have to keep going! "

"I CAN'T, SUSANNA! I'M HURT!"

"Well, it's your own fault!" the older girl snapped back. "You should have been more careful!"

"STOP IT!" Ember snapped as she stood and looked the older girl straight in the eyes. "That was NOT Rebecca's fault, and she's not going anywhere until I can treat her wounds and mine!"

"Fine," Susanna returned, "then you two stay here, and I'll go get help—since it looks like neither of you are going to be able to travel for a while."

"And how will you find your way?" Ember asked suspiciously.

"I can read a map as good as you can," the older sister answered confidently.

There was a pause before Ember answered. "No, that would be too dangerous. We need to stay together, and when Rebecca can travel, we will all go.

"Here's what we're going to do," Ember continued. "I need hot water to treat our wounds, so, Susanna, since you're in the best shape right now, I need you to crawl out of the cave and drag wood in here to build a fire. I know you're both hungry, so when I finish working on us, we'll cook up some panther steaks."

She saw both girls curl their noses up at that thought. With a smile, Ember shrugged and added, "Well, it *is* meat, and as hungry as we all are, I figure that, if we cook them well enough, they can't be too bad."

With an irritated growl of resignation, Susanna started moving rocks to the wall just below the opening. She had to build a pile of several large stones to make a step high enough to pull herself up to and out of the opening.

"Now," Ember said as she smiled at her young patient, "Let's see what we can do about our injuries."

Chapter Twenty-Five

TREACHERY

As they waited for Susanna to return with firewood, Ember gently washed Rebecca's wounds with water from the nearby pool. When she finished with Becca's, she cleaned her own.

It wasn't long before dead sticks and limbs were shoved through the opening. As quickly as they hit the floor, Ember broke them into shorter lengths. When she had enough, she applied the flame of the torch to the pile, and soon a cheery fire blazed.

Pulling the bowl from the medicine bag, Ember filled it with water from the trickle feeding the pool and set it on the coals to heat. Opening her sack again, she searched for anything that she thought would help with healing deep wounds. Of the herbs she chose, two were crumbled into the hot water. The others she left in a pile on a small flat rock near the fire.

As Susanna lowered herself back into the cave, dragging larger limbs with her, Ember took out her knife and cut a wide strip from the bottom of Rebecca's skirt all the way around, making two bandages. Crushing up the herbs on the rock, she placed a third of them on Rebecca's leg wounds and bandaged them in place. She did the same for the girl's arm wounds, then repeated the procedure for her own injuries, using a strip from her own skirt for a bandage. Next, she and Rebecca took turns sipping the herbal tea she had brewed.

Susanna was busy with the tomahawk. She chopped the larger limbs until they were the right length for firewood and fed them to the flames.

"Alright, let's get some real food," Ember announced as she pulled out her knife and worked on the dead panther. It took almost no time for the girl to cut three thick strips of meat from the large cat's haunches. Attaching them to long, sharpened sticks, she suspended them over the fire to cook.

Even Susanna had to admit that the roasted meat tasted pretty good. Few words were spoken between them as they ate.

"So, Ember," Susanna said as she swallowed her last bite, "do you know where we are right now?"

"No, I don't," the girl said thoughtfully, "but I think I can guess pretty close." Ember flipped open the top of her medicine bag and pulled out the leather map and compass. Spreading the chart on a flat rock, she held the compass over it in her left hand.

"Okay, north is marked on the map as being this way," she said as she pointed to the top of the drawn chart. "The compass says that actual north is behind me. These large dots on the map are villages. The ones Rayford marked an *X* through are probably the ones they raided, so the closest one to us that hasn't been attacked is this one."

The older girl leaned over to look at the dot Ember pointed to. "So how do we get there from here?" Susanna asked.

"I checked the compass as we came through the cave," Ember answered, "and I discovered that we basically traveled more or less east. I can't tell distances on this map, so I'm guessing as to how far we have actually traveled from the cabin to get to this spot. I think we should be about here." She pointed to a place on the map east of the box that represented the cabin. "If we travel southeast, we should get close to the village marked on the map. As we get closer to it, I'm hoping we will cross trails or wagon roads the settlers have cut, and maybe they will lead us to the settlement. But I can't tell from this map how far it is or how long it will take us to get there."

"Okay," Susanna said, "I just needed to know that you have some kind of a plan."

Ember wrapped up the compass in the leather map and stuck them both back into her bag.

Taking a glance at the night sky through the cave opening, Ember made another decision. "For now I think we should try to get some rest. When the sun comes up, we will see if Rebecca can use her injured leg. If not, then we can stay here another night or two eating steaks until she can walk."

The herbs in the tea made Ember and Rebecca especially drowsy, and after tossing more wood on the fire, all three girls found a comfortable place close to the warm blaze to rest.

It was Rebecca's moan that woke Ember. When she opened her eyes, she saw a bright sky showing through the opening.

"Where is she?" the younger girl called.

Ember raised up on her elbow and saw Rebecca looking at her. "Where's Susanna?"

Ember glanced about the cave but did not see the older girl. "She probably went to get more firewood," the leader answered.

"I think she left," the younger girl returned.

"She wouldn't go off by herself in the wilderness," Ember reasoned.

"Her bag with the food and the treasure is missing, and she took my tomahawk," Becca observed. "She left."

In fear Ember quickly whipped around to look at her medicine bag and saw that it was open. "OH, THAT RAT!" she yelled angrily as she searched the bag. "SHE STOLE THE MAP AND THE COMPASS!"

Looking quickly at the fire, Ember said her thoughts out loud. "The flames have not completely burned down, so we couldn't have slept for long. She may not have very big head start on us. Can you walk?"

"Help me up," the younger girl asked and extended her good arm.

When she was standing, Rebecca tried her leg. "It's sore, but not too bad. The herbs are helping a lot. I believe I can walk on it."

"That's my brave girl," Ember said, smiling. "Let's see if we can catch up to that crooked sister of yours."

It took some work on Ember's part to stand on Susanna's pile of rocks and boost Rebecca up to the opening. When she finally got the younger girl out of the cave, Ember had to rest her arms a moment before she made the climb.

"So which way do you think she went?" Rebecca asked.

"Well, based on what I remember of the map," Ember answered, "the nearest village to where we are is southeast of here."

"Which way is southeast?" Rebecca asked, looking around them.

"The sun comes up in the east," the leader prompted as she pointed at the glowing horizon.

With a giggle of embarrassment Rebecca smiled and said, "I knew that."

"Which means southeast is *that* way," Ember said as she pointed in the direction they needed to travel. "Let's take it easy at first until we see what your leg can handle."

Ember led them down the sloping hillside and through the brush and trees, always keeping an eye on the position of the sun. Eventually they came to a large meadow and stopped on the wooded edge of the grassy plain.

"It will be easier walking across there," Becca observed.

"Yes, it would," Ember answered thoughtfully, "but it will also be easier for enemies to spot us. Let's follow the edge of the woods around the meadow and keep our eyes and ears open for anything suspicious.

"Are you doing okay?" Ember asked after they had traipsed through the woods for half an hour.

"My leg's doing fine," Becca smiled back. "My arm actually hurts more than my leg."

"Do you think you can travel a little faster?"

"Sure," the younger girl agreed.

As Ember increased their pace, she was pleased to see Rebecca kept up with ease. They made their way along the edge of the meadow until they reached the other side. Suddenly the forest silence was broken by yelling coming from the wooded hillside to their left.

"That sounds like Susanna!" Rebecca whispered urgently to her companion.

"Yes, it does," Ember returned. "Something or someone made her yell, so let's try to get closer. Be careful! There are exposed rocks all through those woods. Let's walk on them to make less noise."

Using the moss-covered limestone as a walkway, the girls quietly made their way toward the source of the sounds. As they drew near, they heard other, more sinister voices and moved with even more vigilance. Ember and her companion followed the stones along the wooded ridge, drawing closer to the angry voices and sobbing. Suddenly they froze as the girls realized that the ones they sought were not twenty feet away. Ember turned and whispered into Becca's ear. "We are just above them. Don't move or make a sound. Our lives depend on it."

Rebecca nodded that she understood as she froze in place, listening to the angry conversation nearby.

Ember raised her head slightly, and through the brush and leaves, she could see the face of Rayford staring angrily at something or someone below him. Around him stood over fifteen Shawnee warriors.

"IT MUST HAVE BEEN YOU OR THAT SISTER OF YOURS WHO HIT ME!" trapper roared.

"No, no! I wasn't me!" Susanna's terrified voice exclaimed. "I promise! It wasn't me!"

"YOU HIT ME, AN' YOU STOLE MY TREASURE, MY MAP, MY FOOD, AN' MY TOMAHAWK!"

"No, please!" the scared girl pleaded. "I didn't!"

Just then Ember saw the angry trapper swing his arm hard. She heard a loud smack, and Susanna screamed and sobbed again. "It was that other girl...Ember!" Susanna's voice said desperately. "She hit you! She stole the stuff. She made us take your treasure and leave! I didn't want to, but she made us!"

"WHERE ARE THE OTHER TWO?" Rayford demanded as he drew back his arm again.

"PLEASE DON'T HIT ME!" Ember and Rebecca heard Susanna's voice scream her response. "I'LL TELL YOU! I'LL LEAD YOU TO THEM IF YOU DON'T HURT ME!"

"WHERE ARE THEY?" the trapper yelled again.

"They're nearby! They're in a cave across the meadow! They're still there...sleeping! I'll take you right to them, just don't hurt me!"

"Show us!" Rayford ordered threateningly.

Ember saw Susanna's head suddenly appear from below, and the trapper shoved her down the sloping woods toward the meadow. They were followed by the Shawnee war party.

Chapter Twenty-Six

ON THEIR OWN

When Rayford and the Indians left with Susanna, both Ember and Rebecca looked at each other and let out a silent collective sigh. The older girl put her finger to her lips and very carefully leaned forward to view the area where their enemies had just been. Convinced that none of the warriors remained, she nodded to her companion.

"Can you believe that?" Rebecca said angrily in a low voice. "She betrayed us to save her own skin...*and* she blamed everything on *you*! I know she's my sister, but she's a terrible person!"

"Try not to be too hard on her," Ember said calmly. "She doesn't have Jesus. In her messed up thinking, all she has is herself. When you live for yourself, it always ends badly because you have no peace and are never satisfied.

"I can't believe I'm saying this, Rebecca, but I actually feel sorry for her. Look at the mess she's gotten herself into...and we can't help her!"

"I know," Rebecca agreed sadly. "Only God can help her now, so what do we do?"

"Well, as far as your sister is concerned," Ember returned, "we need to pray. I know that Jesus loves her in spite of what she's done or how she acts. Maybe He can still reach her and will do something to help her. Oh, and remember, Becca, Jesus loves you too.

"But our plans haven't changed. We keep heading southeast just as quickly as we can. When they discover we've left the cave, I'm hoping it will take a while before they figure out which way we've gone, but eventually they will—probably a lot faster than we want them too. Our only hope is to get as far away as we can before they track us."

Ember spotted the sun through the canopy of branches over their heads. Then she let her eyes look back across the meadow through the woods below them. "The distant tree line across the way is where we were when we arrived at the meadow, and as we stood there, the sun was just to my left front. It's a little higher in the sky now, so southeast should be that way." As Ember spoke, she found herself pointing uphill.

"Alrightee then," Rebecca said with a smile and a salute, "lead on, o' great commander!"

"Okay, follow me," Ember said smiling back. "Let's stay on the rocks as much as we can to make fewer tracks, but we need to hurry."

"Right!" Becca returned eagerly as she followed. "Quick, but cautious! Cautiously quick! Quitiously caut!"

"What are you talking about?" a confused Ember asked over her shoulder.

"I...I don't know," Becca muttered.

Ember only stopped briefly during the morning. It was almost noon when they came to a small creek where they rested and took a long drink.

"How about something to eat?" Ember suggested as they sat beside the flowing water.

"I'd love it," Rebecca answered enthusiastically, "but Susanna stole our food, remember?"

"She didn't steal all of it," the older girl returned with a smile, reaching into her medicine bag and pulling out one of the flat bread cakes she had grabbed as she left the cabin. She handed half of it to her companion. "I do have a few more in my bag, but we have to make them last since we don't know how long we will be traveling."

"So eat it slow, right?" Becca said.

"That's right," Ember agreed. "If we make it last, maybe we can fool our stomachs into thinking that they aren't empty."

Once they felt rested enough to continue, Ember got them traveling again. She didn't push the pace hard because of Rebecca's leg injury, but she kept them moving. Distance between them and their enemies was their only hope.

By the middle of the afternoon, they made it to the top of a wooded hill where they stopped to get their breath. Rebecca was looking at her friend when she noticed the older girl cock her head like she was listening, then she began looking from side to side.

"Did you hear something?" the younger girl asked with concern.

"I think I heard Jesus," Ember answered hesitantly.

"What did He say?"

"I believe He wants us to turn east."

"But that's away from where the map said the village is!" Becca argued.

"I know! I know!" the older girl returned defensively.

"We can't, Ember! We can't turn away from where our closest help is!" When Rebecca looked to see if her friend agreed with her, she noticed that Ember was looking past her, back the way they had come. Turning, the younger girl could see the last hill they had crossed over a mile behind them. Rising from the opposite side of that hill and coming toward them was a large flock of screaming crows.

"Do you think Rayford and the Indians may have stirred them up?" the younger girl asked with concern.

"Yes," came the answer.

"Then let's do what Jesus said," Rebecca returned with decisiveness.

"I can see a creek just below us," Ember said as she scanned the slope ahead. "Follow me."

Racing down the wooded hillside, they came to the banks of a swiftly flowing, shallow stream. Ember hopped into the water and drew the younger girl in with her.

"Stand here a moment," Ember said as she climbed up the other side and ran a short way forward. Suddenly she stopped and began to walk backward to the creek. She even stepped down the bank and back into the water walking backward.

"Hopefully, if they find our tracks, they'll think we crossed here and kept going," Ember explained. "Now let's stay in the water and go upstream."

"It does flow from the east," observed Rebecca.

"Right," Ember returned. "If it starts leading us in a different direction, we'll get out."

The girls waded through the stream in silence for almost half an hour before Rebecca broke the quiet. "Ember, what are we gonna do if they catch us?"

"Well," the older girl began thoughtfully, "if they do, it's obvious that we can't outrun them. That means that we either give up or fight them."

"I don't want to give up," Becca returned, "but how can we fight them? They're warriors, and we're just two girls."

"We would have to be warriors too," Ember answered firmly. "Let's think. They outnumber us, and they're stronger and faster than we are."

"And they have rifles, knives, and tomahawks," Rebecca added.

"That's right," the leader agreed. "But they most likely won't use their weapons because they want us as slaves or squaws. We're no good to them dead or wounded."

"That means they have to get close and grab us," the younger girl reasoned. "How can we keep them from getting close to us?"

Ember thought on the problem as they walked. "Hmmm," she finally said, "we don't have rifles, and I don't know how to make bows and arrows. We wouldn't have time even if I did know. Becca, a friend of mine named Eliza taught me that you can always trust Jesus to take care of you. We need to ask Jesus for help. Let's both start praying and see what He gives us."

Twenty minutes later the creek made a sharp turn to the north in front of a tall, rocky ledge, and the girls decided to get out. Ember found rocks along the southern bank to walk on so they wouldn't leave tracks.

"That tall cliff is going to keep us from traveling east for now, so I guess we head south."

"Has Jesus given you any ideas for fighting Rayford and the Indians?" Rebecca asked with concern.

"No, I've gotten nothing. How about you?"

"Me either," Becca answered. "The only thoughts I keep having are about Bible stories."

"What stories?"

"I don't know. Mostly about David, I guess."

There was silence for almost a minute when suddenly Ember stopped. "WAIT!" Ember exclaimed. "David might be our answer!"

"I don't get it," the confused younger girl responded.

"Rebecca, what weapon was David famous for using?"

"A sling?"

"Yes, a sling!"

"But, Ember, we don't have any slings."

"That's right, but we can make them!"

"How?" the younger girl asked.

"Out of our skits," Ember returned as she whipped out her knife. "We'll each cut another three or four inch strip off the bottom of our skirts all the way around, and it should be long enough to make an effective sling. There are certainly plenty of rocks lying around. We'll just practice as we walk. Surely it can't be that hard to learn."

Making the slings was easy and quick. Learning to use them effectively was another matter altogether. The girls discovered that throwing a stone accurately with a sling was a skill that required patience, practice, and a good eye.

It took them nearly twenty stones apiece just to figure out when to release one end of the sling to make the rock fly in the general direction of their target. It took nearly a hundred more for the girls to consistently hit the tree trunks and rocks they aimed at. By late that afternoon, both of the fugitives felt much more confident in their skill with the ancient weapon.

As the sun began to set, Ember looked for a place to spend the night. She scanned the rocky ledge on their left and eventually spotted a small crevice about fifteen feet above the ground. The climb was difficult, but it wasn't long before both girls sat comfortably in the shallow, cave-like opening.

"At least we'll be protected from the weather if it rains," Ember observed.

"We shouldn't have to worry about wild animals getting to us up here either," Rebecca added.

"While we still have some daylight left," returned Ember, "let's undo our bandages and replace the herbs with fresh ones. That will also give me a chance to make sure the wounds are healing properly."

It was dark when they finished tending their injuries. They shared another piece of flat bread, then quickly fell into an exhausted sleep.

Chapter Twenty-Seven

COMPANY

The sun was already above the horizon when Ember struggled to wakefulness. She could have slept for hours more, but her dreams were troubling and eventually woke her. When she opened her eyes and saw the brightening sky, her foggy brain managed to remind her that enemies were near.

"Wake up, Becca," she yawned as she shook her companion.

"What?" the younger girl mumbled.

"It's morning, and we've got to get moving. Come on. Let's go."

"Can't we eat something first?" Rebecca pleaded.

"We can eat while we walk. We've got to go now."

Climbing out of their crevice and down the ledge resulted in a few minor scrapes, but they arrived safely on the ground and immediately headed south, following the rocky ledge on their left. As they traveled, Rebecca spotted several rocks that were a little smaller than her fist. She picked one up, placed it in her sling, and launched it at a tree about thirty feet away.

"OW!"

What's wrong?" Ember asked.

"My shoulder is very sore!"

"*He, he.* I guess we did hurl a lot of rocks yesterday," Ember chuckled.

"If you think it's so funny, let's see you throw one," Rebecca shot back.

With a smile Ember picked up a rock and flung it. "OW!"

"See!" Rebecca said, giggling.

"I hate to say this," the older girl inserted, "but if we have to use these slings to defend ourselves today, we've got to work the soreness out of our muscles."

"How do we do that?" Rebecca asked nervously.

"We throw more rocks...lots more."

For the next twenty minutes, the sound of rocks thudding solidly against the trunks of trees was accompanied by grunts and groans of pain.

"You know," Becca observed, "it's miserable doing this, *ouch,* but I think I'm getting more accurate. I'm hitting what I'm aiming at most of the time now. *Ouch!*"

Eventually the soreness diminished, and the girls slung their stones with little discomfort.

"I've been thinking, Rebecca. The bluff is getting smaller the further south we go. It might be a good idea for us to pick up a few good throwing rocks and stick them in our skirt pockets to have ready in case there aren't so many available as we travel further."

They stopped just long enough to gather ammunition for their slings. Suddenly Ember hissed a warning, "Someone's behind us!"

Rebecca started to turn, but the older girl grabbed her arm. "Don't look! Just keep moving and keep a rock handy!"

"What are we going to do, Ember?" the younger girl said in a panic.

"Let's go as fast as we can...and pray!"

They hurried through the woods, but after a quarter of an hour, nothing had happened.

"Are you sure you saw someone?" Rebecca asked skeptically.

"They were some distance away," the older girl answered, "but I'm positive I saw someone with a hat watching us. Just as I spotted him, he pulled his head behind a tree. But I know I saw at least one person."

"It had to be Rayford!" Rebecca cried. "How could he have found us so fast?"

"I don't know," Ember answered nervously. "I thought we had bought ourselves more time."

"Why hasn't he done anything?" Becca asked again, looking back.

"I don't know, but I do know that someone is back there! Let's just keep moving and be ready!"

"Oh Lord, please help us!" Ember prayed urgently.

As the two terrified girls rushed through the thick woods, the tall ridge of limestone that had been on their left gradually became nothing more than a low outcropping of moss-covered rocks.

"Quick, this way!" As Ember spoke, she grabbed her friend by the hand and yanked her up the outcropping to their left. "Be still and quiet! We'll let him get close, then I'll hit him with a rock!"

Placing a stone in her sling, Ember squatted down to wait. Several long minutes later the girls spotted a large figure in buckskins and a wide-brimmed hat creeping silently through the woods. His head was down, intently studying the tracks. He was very near when he stopped to examine the ground where the girls had climbed the rocks.

Ember quietly stood and, seeing no one else around, let fly her rock. With a solid *thunk* the missile struck the tracker in the back of the head, and he collapsed with a groan.

"Quick, let's go!" Ember hissed, and they raced through the woods to the east.

"Was it Rayford?" Becca asked as they ran.

"Don't know," Ember huffed back. "It was a big man...dressed like him. Keep running!"

After fifteen minutes both girls had to stop to catch their breath. "I've got to rest!" Rebecca wheezed with her hands on her knees.

"We'll have to rest on our feet," Ember wheezed back. "Keep walking while we get our wind back."

Several minutes later Rebecca asked, "Do you think we got away?"

"No, he's probably already back on his feet and after us. Our only hope is to keep moving and pray we find help. Becca, we don't know when our enemies will catch up to us, but I'm sure they will, so we've got to have our slings ready."

The younger girl reached into her pocket and pulled out a rock that she loaded in the middle of her make-shift weapon. She held the sling ends in her right hand and gripped the stone with her left. Ember did the same. They wanted to be able to defend themselves at a moment's notice.

The woods they traveled through opened up, and the girls found themselves walking into a small, grassy glade. Rather than take the time to go around it, Ember led them hurriedly across.

"WELL, HEY THERE!" a nasally voice called loudly from behind. Instantly the two frightened girls spun and slung their rocks.

"RUN!" Ember yelled and raced for the opposite side of the glade. They had almost reached it when a large Indian warrior dropped from a limb above and landed directly in front of them.

Both girls screamed and grabbed for each other. Ember remembered her knife and whipped it out threateningly. "STAY AWAY!" the older girl cried as she pulled Rebecca back from the warrior.

"Great land o' Goshen, ladies!" the nasally voice sounded from behind. "You 'bout took my poor ol' head clean off with them rocks o' yours!"

Ember took a quick glance back at the speaker and saw an older, very thin frontiersman with a scraggly beard. He was dressed in buckskins, wore a wide brimmed hat, and had a hunting knife at his side. A steel-headed tomahawk hung in his belt, and he held a Kentucky long rifle in his right hand.

"Jus' calm down, ladies," the older scout said. "Me an Grey Fox ain't gonna hurt you. It ain't natural, you two bein' out in the wilds all by your lonesome selves, so we figured you might need some help."

"We do need help," Ember answered, still waving her knife threateningly, "but how do we know we can trust you?"

"Well, I reckon you don't know," the scout returned. "But the truth be told, me an' ol' Grey Fox is about the trustworthiest folks a person can meet. Ain't that right, Grey Fox?"

"Grey Fox can be trusted," the Indian said in broken English, "but Dirt Girley not keep his word."

"Here I am tryin' to calm these poor girls, an' you're a'sayin' stuff like that!" the older scout snapped. "This is about that deer again, ain't it?"

"You say Grey Fox not shoot deer from long ways," the Indian began, "but Grey Fox did shoot 'em."

"That's right," the scout returned, "you did, an' it was a mighty fine shot. I said that."

"But you bet hat!" Grey Fox insisted.

"I told you, Grey Fox, I was just teasing."

"You no teasing," the Indian argued.

"Be reasonable!" the scout tried again. "This here's the only hat I got!"

"Maybe Dirt Girley should change his name to Lying Polecat."

"Oh, Bertha's bunions! Just take the stinkin' hat!" The scout whipped off his bonnet and tossed it to his friend, who immediately placed it on his head.

"Hmmm," the Indian said with a smile, "Grey Fox look pretty good."

"So where are you from?" Ember asked, feeling a little more at ease.

"Oh, we're from the town of Larkinboro," the hatless scout answered. "It's about three day's march to the southwest from here."

"I think that's where we were headed," the older girl returned. "Could you take us there?"

"Well, shore. That won't be no problem."

"So he's Grey Fox, and you must be Dirt Gurley?" Ember asked.

"Solomon Ambrose Gurley at your service," the scout said with a bow. "But my friends call me Dirt. We actually have another friend of ours out here with us, but...oh, here he comes now."

From across the small glade, a broad shouldered young frontiersman approached. When he had joined them, Dirt turned back to the two girls. "Ladies, I'd like to introduce you to Will Hackett."

"We've met," Will said and grimaced as he rubbed the back of his head.

Chapter Twenty-Eight

A LITTLE HELP

"That's a nice looking hat you've got there, Grey Fox," Will said with a smile as he cut his eyes at the annoyed Dirt.

The Miami warrior held up his head, smiled, and gave his friend a satisfied nod. Will turned and looked at the older scout.

"Don't even say it!" Dirt snapped.

"I told you he'd get it," Will returned, unable to stop himself.

"I said, 'Don't say it!'" Dirt growled. "It's gettin' so's a man cain't even do a little teasin' around here without gettin' stripped neked for it...Oh, beggin' your pardon, ladies."

"So who are you two?" William asked, addressing the girls. "And what are you doing way out here by yourselves?"

Ember slid her knife back into its sheath before she answered. "I'm Remember Warren, and this is my friend Rebecca Norris. We're running for our lives." Ember then briefly explained what had happened to them and how they had escaped.

"There were three of us," Rebecca added, "but Rayford and the Shawnee recaptured my sister yesterday morning."

"Now wait just a minute," Dirt cut in. "I think I've heared about that guy Rayford from other woodsmen who have passed through Larkinboro. They say he traps up here in the northern part of the territory. I never could figure out how he could collect pelts in Shawnee country and still keep his hair."

"I guess you know now," Will returned. "He's one of 'em. The thing that worries me is that I was talking with Captain Parks, that American military officer who came through the settlement with his militia a couple of weeks ago, and he mentioned that trapper. He even called him by name. He said that Rayford is supposed to be a scout for him and General Clark."

"Well, he don't sound like no scout to me," Dirt shot back. "From what the little ladies jus' said, it sounds like the word *renegade* is too nice a word for that weasel. I'd say he's a two-timin', lowlife, yellow-bellied marsh rat...if'n you ladies will pardon my language."

"Can we please just go?" Ember pleaded. "Rayford and about fifteen Shawnee have been after us for two days, and they have to be getting close!"

"Say no more, ladies!" Dirt said with an air of command. "We're movin' out!

"Will, I'll have Grey Fox lead us back to Larkinboro, but how about you scoutin' our back trail? An' if'n you spot that Rayford character an' his war party of bog weevils, see if you can slow 'em down a bit for us. "

"Right," Will agreed. "I'll do what I can.

"Grey Fox," Will called to his friend, "which way will you be taking to Larkinboro?"

"Southwest," the Miami answered. "We cross river at the fords. Best way."

"If I can, I will meet you there," Will informed his friends. "If not, don't wait on me. Keep going." The young frontiersman then hefted his rifle and hurried back the way he had come.

"All right, Grey Fox," the older scout said, "lead us back to the fort. An' we need to go as quickly as these ladies can travel."

The Miami nodded his understanding and turned to start the journey.

"And another thing," Dirt growled. "Be careful! I don't want my hat gettin' all dirty an' beat up!"

"Dirt Gurley no have hat," the Indian called back over his shoulder with an irritating smile. "He lose in bet. Grey Fox take care of his own hat."

"I'll take care of your hat, you scum suckin' marsh eel!" Dirt growled back.

"MR. DIRT!" Rebecca gasped.

"Oh!" the scout responded defensively. "*Uh*...of course, *uh*, I mean that in the nicest way possible."

The two girls fell in behind Grey Fox as he headed toward the fords. While they marched, Dirt Gurley, who was in the rear, reached forward and handed both girls a thick piece of jerked deer meat.

"Here, ladies. Chew on these whilst we walk. I figure you two ain't had a decent meal in a while, an' you could use some strength."

"Oh, thank you, Mister Dirt," Rebecca said with feeling as she took the offered food.

"Yes," Ember agreed, "thank you for the food and for your help."

"Don't even mention it," Dirt shot back. "Why, it ain't nothin' more'n what the Good Lord would want us to do."

"Oh, do you know Jesus?" Ember asked with smile.

"O' course we do!" the older scout answered. "Me an' King Jesus has been close for quite a spell. Why, even that ornery ol' rascal Grey Fox is a follower of the King."

"Really?" Rebecca asked the Miami.

The Indian turned and glanced back at the girls. "Grey Fox has made King Jesus his chief."

Rebecca leaned next to Ember and whispered, "The Lord led us to the right people."

"Jesus knew which way we needed to go," the older girl whispered back.

William Hackett moved rapidly, but he made little noise as he passed. The young man was a woodsman of no little ability. Born with a natural inclination for the forest, he had learned much from Jack Cobb and Dirt Gurley, the two scouts who had led his family and friends into the Kentucky Territory almost five years ago. Once while on a scouting trip, Will had been captured by a hunting party of Miami Indians and kept as a slave for nearly two years. The Lord had blessed the young man during his captivity and had given him repeated opportunities to help and serve his captors. The result was that the tribe had adopted the frontiersman and gave him the name Kajika or *Walks Without Sound.* Later, when William was able to return to his own people, his Miami friend Grey Fox came with him.

As William raced through the woods, all of his senses were on high alert. He followed the girls' tracks until he arrived at the creek. Having seen no signs of the pursuing Shawnee, the young scout turned west and ran along the south bank. It suddenly struck him that something wasn't right. The youthful woodsman was so aware and intimate with the normal sounds and smells of the forest that even subtle changes in his surroundings were noticeable to his trained senses.

William froze in his tracks. Something had alerted him, but he wasn't sure what it was. Then it struck him. Behind, to his right and his left, he could hear birds, the buzz of flying insects, and the distant barking of squirrels. Straight ahead there was only stillness.

Gripping his rifle with both hands, Will bent forward and moved toward the quietness in a curious swaying and twisting motion that allowed him to travel almost silently as his sharp eyes spotted the perfect place to put each foot. The young frontiersman was so skilled in this long-practiced technique that he could pass through the forest like a ghost at a pace faster than most people walked.

Once again the youth halted and remained motionless as he studied the woods in front of him. About two hundred feet ahead, he spotted the band of enemy warriors moving his way. He counted ten on his side of the creek and four on the opposite bank, all moving east toward him, searching for the place where the girls had left the water. The big trapper that the girls had mentioned was leading the larger group along the south bank. An idea suddenly came to William, and he quietly slipped back the way he had come.

He searched the trees along the bank, trying to identify the source of the buzzing sound he had heard earlier. When he spotted it, he smiled. He looked for a way to cross to the other side without being seen. Keeping low and staying behind thick shrubs, William waded to the opposite bank and moved a little further north of the stream. He found a spot behind a large water oak where he had an unobstructed view of the approaching Indians.

William was disappointed that he would only be able to use his plan against the four on his side of the creek, but it was the best he could do. He had hoped that he could infuriate the whole bunch of them enough to forget the girls and entice them to chase him.

As the warriors advanced, Will used his ramrod to shove a second ball down the barrel of his already loaded rifle in order to give himself a little extra help to be sure his plan would succeed. Leaning around the tree, young Hackett braced his rifle against the trunk and aimed up into the branches of the beach tree beside the water. Just as the four Shawnee on his side of the creek drew abreast of him, William squeezed his trigger.

When the Indians heard the shot, they all whipped around to identify the source of the blast. Just then a very large, papery grey hornet's nest crashed to the ground directly in front of them and exploded into a cloud of furious, stinging insects. With shrieks of terror and pain, the four unfortunate warriors dropped their rifles and ran in all directions, trying to fight off the thousands of enraged creatures.

Bedlam broke out among the enemy fighters on both sides of the creek. Will took the opportunity to reload his rifle. The Indians furious yells began to settle down as the young woodsman slid his ramrod back into place. Stepping around the trunk, he screamed his war cry and immediately jumped for the safety of the tree again as rifles erupted in his direction.

Will Hackett, still yelling his taunting challenge, sprinted north through the woods away from the creek. He could hear shouting behind him as he ran. After racing for thirty yards, he ducked behind a tree trunk and viewed his pursuers.

"Rattlesnakes!" he spat in frustration. Instead of all of the enemy fighters chasing him, Rayford had only sent the four Shawnee on the north bank. The rest continued after the girls. "Well, it can't be helped," he murmured. "At least their numbers will be thinned down a little."

Snapping off a quick shot, William dropped the warrior leading the group pursuing him, then screamed his war cry again and continued north. Three rifles fired from behind, and bullets zipped past his head. One tore a hole through the right sleeve of his shirt near his shoulder, creasing his arm. Will glanced back and saw the braves stop to reload their rifles, and he did the same.

After running up a low, wooded hill another hundred yards, William whipped around and took aim at the Shawnee in the rear. His bullet slammed into the Indian's shoulder like a hammer blow, knocking him to the ground. Not waiting for return fire, the young frontiersman raced on, dodging behind trees as he ran.

William found himself sprinting up another hill, but this one had numerous rocky outcroppings protruding from the forest floor. At the top a waist-high limestone boulder appeared in front of him. He placed his hand on it as he vaulted over. There was a four foot drop on the back side of the rock, and when Hackett landed, he slid to a stop and threw himself against the base of the boulder. Just then both Indians came leaping over the same obstacle. Jumping up, William swung his empty rifle like a club, hitting the nearest warrior solidly in the thigh. Screaming in pain, the injured Shawnee fell hard, landing face first on the ground.

Will immediately charged for the second fighter, who was trying to stop, spin around, and fire at his attacker. The young frontiersman was too quick and was in the Indian's face before the rifle could be aimed. Gripping his own gun with both hands, William drove his opponent's weapon into the air and shoved the warrior backwards and to the ground. A sharp rap with the butt of his rifle rendered the Indian unconscious.

Rushing back to the first warrior, still writhing in pain from his leg injury, Hackett snatched up the Indian's rifle and fired it into the air. Then swinging it hard against the boulder, he shattered the stock. After doing the same with the other warrior's gun,

William threw both of their knives and tomahawks as far as he could into the woods.

Reloading his weapon, William headed south to catch up with his friends.

Chapter Twenty-Nine

CHANGE IN PLANS

After William had shot the hornets' nest out of the tree and dropped it into the midst of the four warriors, the Shawnee with Rayford wanted to cross the creek and chase the attacker as well. Their desire for revenge got even stronger when they saw Will drop the first of the warriors chasing him.

"Stay here!" Rayford ordered the rest of the Shawnee with him. "The braves will take his scalp!"

"The girls we chase have found help," Kolapeka, the Shawnee chief, said to the trapper.

"Yeah," Rayford agreed angrily. "Hunters or scouts from a settlement most likely."

"We must go after them," the chief urged, pointing at the three Shawnee pursuing William. "They take girls north!"

"I don't think so," Rayford returned. "The guy that attacked us is running fast—too fast to have the girls with him. And he wouldn't lead us to them. That means he's trying to lead us away from them."

"We have searched for their tracks along the creek but have found none," a brave beside them shot back.

"Right," the trapper agreed "When they were here, they were probably still in the creek. But we know something now that we didn't know before. They're getting help from people who know what they're doing. Those scouts will try to get the girls to their settlement as fast as they can, and they'll know how to get there. All the settlements are south of here, which means they'll have to cross the river to reach them."

"Yes, that's right," Kolapeka responded with an understanding nod, "and the easiest place to cross is at the fords."

"Now you got it, Chief," Rayford said as a sinister smile crept over his face. "They'll have to take those girls across the river at the fords. Since we know what they'll do, we're gonna stop looking for their tracks and run straight for where they'll be. We may even get there before they do, and we can set an ambush for them.

"Kolapeka, pick two of your best trackers and send them to find where the girls left the creek and to follow their trail. Have your braves chase them and whoever is with them towards the river crossing where we will be waiting for them."

Suddenly an excited war whoop shot from the Shawnee chief's throat. It was quickly taken up by the other warriors. "WE KNOW WHERE THEY ARE GOING!" the chief cried to his braves. "WE WILL TAKE THEM AT THE FORDS! THE MEN WE SCALP! THE GIRLS WE BRING BACK TO JOIN THE OTHER ONE WE CAUGHT AND SENT BACK!"

Immediately the entire war party exploded into a savage celebration as the eager fighters danced and yelled in anticipation of their coming victory.

The chief got their attention again and explained Rayford's plan to them. Then he picked two of his braves to continue pursuing the girls east along the creek bank.

"TO THE FORDS...QUICK!" Rayford called loudly. "WE'LL HAVE THEM THIS TIME!" The determined trapper led the war party of savage fighters to the southeast in a long-distance trot.

"What in tarnation are you stoppin' for?" Dirt snapped at Grey Fox as the older scout hobbled up to join the Miami and the two girls. The three of them stood together in the woods waiting for the older scout to catch up.

"You getting left behind," Grey Fox said sternly. "Your leg wound slowing you down."

"My leg's just peachy," Dirt shot back. "Now go ahead on! We gots to keep movin'!"

"Your leg getting worse," the Indian insisted.

"Let me see it, Mr. Dirt," Ember said. "I'm a healer."

"I don't need no healer!"

"DIRT!" Grey Fox barked, "your leg needs help!"

"I'm tellin' you I'm okay! We need to keep moving!"

"I give you hat back if you let her look at wound," the Miami offered as he held out the longed for hat.

"Well, all rightee then!" the old scout exclaimed with a smile as he accepted the offering and tugged it onto his head. Sitting on a nearby log, Dirt tenderly pulled his pant leg up above his knee, revealing a deep, angry-looking wound in his right calf.

"Oh, my!" the older girl gasped. "This is not looking good. What happened?"

"I tripped a couple of days ago and ran a sharp stick into it."

"No wonder it's painful," Ember observed. "It's starting to turn foul."

"Oh, it ain't so bad," the scout said defensively. "I think it'll be all right."

"No, it won't! If I can't get the heat and disease out of it, we will have to sear it with a hot knife."

Suddenly Dirt's eyes flew wide as he realized the severity of his situation. "Are you serious? Great granny's garters! I've had that done before, an' it ain't fun! I really don't want to go through that again! What can we do to keep it from happening?"

"When you were hurt," Ember asked, "did you get all of the wood out?"

"I'm pretty sure I did," Dirt returned. "The stick came out clean, an' nothing appeared to be broken off."

"Good," the girl smiled back, "then I will just need to clean it and bandage it with some crushed cone flower seeds, golden seal, and fever few. I wish I had some honey to pour into it as well, but we'll have to substitute prayer instead and make do with what I've got."

"Grey Fox wish you had honey too," the Miami spoke up. "Grumpy Dirt be sweeter then. Big improvement!"

"Now jus' keep your snide Injun comments to yourself!" Dirt fired back. "At least I got my hat back. Just in time too. Looks like we're gonna get some rain."

"Big storm coming," Grey Fox agreed as he studied the heavy, dark clouds rolling across the sky.

The medicine girl laid the needed herbs from her bag on a small, flat rock. She also pulled out Prisha's rounded grinding stone. In a few minutes she had crushed the dried herbs and seeds into powder.

Ember had Dirt cut a wide leather strip off the tail of his hunting shirt for a bandage to hold the herbs against his wound. By the time she finished securing the makeshift dressing, the older scout was starting to smile.

"Say now, that sucker don't hurt near as bad as she did before!" Dirt reported. "That there's some mighty fine medicine!"

"The feverfew helps a lot with the pain," the girl agreed. "The other herbs should help fight the festerers."

"Dirt can walk now?" Grey Fox asked as large drops began to fall."

"Yessiree, bob!" Girley exclaimed as he stood to his feet. "The little missy's got me all fixed up!"

"Good," the Maimi said, reaching over and quickly snatching the hat from Dirt and placing it on his own head. "Starting to rain. Need hat back."

"Why, you Injun-givin' swamp rat!" Dirt exclaimed. "You said you were handin' it back to me."

"Grey Fox did hand it back," the warrior returned, "but you have hat long enough. Grey Fox want his hat back to keep rain off head."

"GIMME BACK MY HAT!"

"You no have hat," the Miami answered. "You lose in bet. We go now. Keep up this time."

Dirt growled as the girls giggled.

"Ember?" Rebecca called as they started out again. The medicine girl stood several paces behind and did not move as she stared into the distance. "EMBER! Are you okay?"

Dear one, Ember heard a familiar voice calling to her.

Yes, Lord, she answered in her heart.

There is danger ahead. You must go a different way.

On hearing Rebecca's call, both Dirt and Grey Fox turned to see what the problem was. "What's wrong, young one?" Dirt asked with concern when he saw the older girl staring into the distance.

Finally Ember blinked and turned to face the others. "Grey Fox, where did you say you were taking us to cross the river?"

"We go to fords," the Miami returned. "Best place to cross."

Ember hesitated for a moment and said, "I don't think Jesus wants us to go to the fords."

"Did the Lord speak to you again, Ember?" Rebecca asked.

The older girl answered with an affirmative nod.

"Meanin' no disrespect to what you think you heard, little missy," Dirt said, "but there ain't really no other safe place to cross the river but at the fords."

"Jesus says that there is danger ahead of us. That means the fords are not safe," Ember insisted.

"Well now, I ain't so sure about that," Dirt began skeptically.

Tell Grey Fox what I said, the Lord spoke again. *The Miami will listen.*

"Grey Fox," the medicine girl spoke firmly to the warrior, "Chief Jesus says we must not go to the fords."

The Indian looked hard at the girl, then to Dirt, and finally back at Ember. "Then we obey Chief Jesus and go to cliffs."

When he looked back at Dirt, the older scout gave a shrug of resignation. Grey Fox glanced at the sun to get his direction, then led them due south towards the dangerous rapids and cataracts at the cliffs.

"How in the name of Amos Bosworth does she know that stuff?" Dirt asked Rebecca as they began their journey again.

"Oh," the younger girl answered, "she talks to Jesus all the time."

"So do I," Dirt shot back.

"Well, I do too," Rebecca answered, "but Jesus speaks back to her."

Chapter Thirty

THE CLIFFS

As Will Hackett hurried back to the creek to try to find Rayford and his braves, he noticed that dark clouds overhead were rolling rapidly along, pushed by strong winds. Even as he studied the threatening sky, rain drops began to fall. The young scout reached into a pouch at his hip and searched for a roll of oiled deerskin leather. Wrapping the wide strip securely around the frizzen pan and lock of his rifle, Will tied it securely in place with a thin leather strap. He also pulled out a carved, wooden plug and stuck it firmly into the muzzle of his barrel. Once he was sure the powder in his rifle would stay dry in the rain, he continued his journey back to the creek where he had first found the Shawnee war party. He discovered that his enemies were gone. By studying the ground on the southern bank of the stream, Will quickly identified tracks that gave him bad news.

Oh no! Will thought in frustration when he saw the direction the Indians had taken. *They're headed straight to the fords! I've got to stop Grey Fox before he leads Dirt and the girls into a trap!*

Will knew where his friends were when he left them, so he began to race back the way he had come. He had only taken a few steps when something stopped him. Just in front of where he stood, a set of tracks could be clearly seen continuing along the bank of the creek. The more he studied them, the more convinced he was that at least two of the Shawnee were trailing his friends.

Will already knew where the girls had left the creek, so to gain time, he ran to the bluff where the stream turned north. As he drew near, a movement just ahead caught his attention, and he quickly hid behind a tree. It was the two Shawnee, and they had spotted the girls' tracks coming out of the water. After a brief discussion the warriors ran south in pursuit of the fugitives.

Will wanted to bypass them and get to his friends as quickly as he could, but he didn't want enemies behind them. Allowing the Shawnee to get a head start, the young scout sprang from his place of concealment and raced after them.

After half an hour the Indians suddenly stopped. They searched the ground briefly, then got into another animated discussion. Finally they made a decision. One of the Shawnee raced as fast as he could to the southwest towards the fords. The other one turned and disappeared into the woods following the tracks.

As soon as they were gone, William hurried to the spot and studied the tracks the two Shawnee had seen. The young scout was surprised at what he saw. "Why did they turn south?" the young scout exclaimed out loud. "I don't know how he knew, but Grey Fox must have figured the Shawnee had set a trap for them at the fords, so he's taking them to the cliffs. One of the warriors is still trailing them, and the other must be going to tell Rayford about the change in plans. I'm glad Grey Fox avoided the ambush, but even on a good day, the cliffs are dangerous. Now, with all this rain, they're going to be treacherous. Lord, help us all!"

After this brief prayer, Will Hackett hurried south after the Shawnee tracker and towards his friends.

"We ought to be getting' close!" Dirt yelled through the noise of the storm. "Can you tell where we are?"

"It just up ahead!" the Miami yelled back. "I hear big water!"

"I don't know how you can hear anything in all this pourin' rain and thunder!" the older scout shouted.

It wasn't long before, even above the heavy storm, the roar of the crashing cataracts alerted them all of their location. Grey Fox stopped at the edge of a steep, rocky slope that overlooked the raging river a short distance below.

Before them was a small ravine thirty feet deep and stretching over sixty feet across before reaching the ridge on the other side. Cutting down the middle of the gorge was a fierce and powerful river. The water entered the ravine to their right as thousands of gallons a minute cascaded over a hundred feet from a plateau, forming a powerful waterfall. At the bottom, all the raging water turned into rapids that rushed swiftly along the limestone slope, disappearing to their left.

The sides of the ravine were solid rock, formed by large stones and boulders resting on ridges and ledges of limestone. The waterfall itself was tall and impressive, but it wasn't a sheer drop. The vast wall of water careened off the top of the bluff at a steep angle, but all the way down it repeatedly crashed into large boulders lodged in the riverbed. Several giant rocks lay at the bottom of the falls where they had fallen years before.

As all four of the friends stood on the ridge surveying the fierce torrent, a since of dread filled each heart.

"Great smokin' polecats!" Dirt exclaimed. "This ain't gonna be no easy thing! There's more water pouring over them falls than I've seen in all my born days!

"Miss Ember," the scout asked, looking to the older girl, "are you sure King Jesus wants us to cross here?"

"Yes, I am," the older girl answered more confidently than she felt at the sight of the terrifying task before them.

With a shaky hand Ember reached over and grabbed Rebecca's for support. She then turned to the Miami and said, "Lead us down there, Grey Fox!"

The warrior nodded gravely and said, "Rocks wet and dangerous! Ver' big dangerous! Be much careful!"

Through the powerful storm the Miami guided them cautiously down the slick, wet stones toward the raging river below. Slowly and methodically they picked their way down the perilous slope.

"CAN WE GO ANY FASTER?" Ember yelled impatiently over the noise of the waterfall and the storm. "RAYFORD AND HIS INDIANS COULD BE HERE ANY MOMENT!"

"NO!" Grey Fox called back. "MUST BE CAREFUL! VER' DANGEROUS PLACE!"

Just then one of Rebecca's feet slipped on some wet moss, and she fell hard on the rocks. Fortunately, Ember still held her hand and kept her from hitting her head. After helping the bruised and hurting girl back to her feet, they continued the descent.

Once on the river's edge, Grey Fox turned upriver toward the powerful waterfall cascading over and around numerous boulders protruding from the churning water. When he arrived at the base of the powerful cataract, the deafening noise and the raw power of all the water was hard to comprehend.

Pausing for a moment to let the others rest, Grey Fox considered the best way across. Finally he made his decision and turned to face the others. "THIS WHERE WE CROSS!" the Miami yelled. "VER' DANGEROUS! MUST GO SLOW! I GO FIRST, THEN YOU!" He pointed to Rebecca. "DIRT COME LAST!"

The others nodded their understanding, and Grey Fox turned to face the river. He leaped from the rocks on which they stood onto the closest boulder in the river and began carefully working his way across. Powerful waves of water crashed continually against it, splashing the Miami and threatening to loosen his grip and footing as he inched forward.

The difficulty was magnified by the fact that the Indian had to make his way along the wet rocks carrying his rifle in one hand. Upon reaching the end of the boulder, Grey Fox faced a nearly three foot jump over a roaring channel of swift water. Standing upright on the slick, wet limestone, Grey Fox pushed off and landed unsteadily on the next rock.

From where he stood, the Miami was more than half way to the other side, and he could see that the rest of the way was not as difficult. He decided to stay where he was and assist Rebecca. Waving to the younger girl, he laid his rifle down and prepared to help her make the dangerous crossing.

Will Hackett was getting nervous. He had been trailing the Shawnee for almost an hour. The young scout was fairly certain that the other warrior would have reached the fords by now and would have Rayford and the war party racing to the cliffs. Will needed to reach Grey Fox and the others and help them over the river before their enemies arrived. He knew that if his fleeing friends had to face the Shawnee while still on this side of the water, they would have no hope of winning.

The Shawnee warrior he had been trailing suddenly stepped from behind a tree only a few steps in front of the young frontiersman. The Indian leveled his rifle at Will's chest and pulled the trigger. The ominous click emphasized the fact that the pouring rain had dampened the Indian's gunpowder. Instantly both fighters dropped their rifles, pulled their hand weapons, and threw themselves at each other.

William spotted the Shawnee's descending tomahawk and parried it with the blade of his knife held in his left hand, while swinging his own tomahawk with his right. Just as he did so the young scout's foot slipped in the mud, and he lost his balance. As soon as he hit the ground, the savvy scout rolled hard to his right. The sharp blade of the Indian's hatchet drove into the mud where the young frontiersman's head had been. Pushing himself to his knees, William swung his weapon hard at his enemy, causing the Shawnee to jump backwards. Regaining his feet, the scout faced his foe and prepared for the fierce battle ahead.

The savage screamed his war cry and advanced, swinging tomahawk and knife furiously back and forth. Will was forced to duck as the hatchet swished towards his head. He momentarily lost track of the Indian's knife just before the sharp blade slashed across his chest, slicing his hunting shirt and exposing a red trickle underneath. The Shawnee saw the blood and lunged for the kill. Dropping his hatchet, the powerful youth threw his whole body at the attacking warrior. As William slammed unexpectedly into his adversary, the Indian's tomahawk swung past the youth. The scout's momentum lifted the Indian, and both slammed hard into the ground. Instantly pain and stars exploded in the young frontiersman's head as blackness engulfed him.

Chapter Thirty-One

THE CROSSING

Rebecca saw Grey Fox yelling and waving at her from the boulder in the midst of the roaring river. The noise from the waterfall and the storm was so loud that she couldn't hear his words, but she knew what he wanted. Squeezing Ember's hand one last time, Rebecca moved timidly to the edge of the bank. With more encouragement from Grey Fox, the younger girl took a deep breath and jumped onto the boulder in the torrent. Carefully she worked her way across. Twice her feet slid on the wet, slanting rock as she made the treacherous trip, but fortunately she had a good grip on the top edge. Moving cautiously, Rebecca finally made it to the end of the large, slippery stone and was faced with the terrifying gap between the boulders.

"JUMP!" the Miami cried over the roar of the cataracts. "I HELP YOU!"

The rocky surface was so slippery that Rebecca was reluctant to let go and stand up.

"YOU MUST JUMP!" Grey Fox yelled again.

Knowing that she had to do something, the young girl shakily and slowly pushed herself to an unsteady standing position. She felt her feet beginning to slide as she measured the distance she had to jump. Suddenly she heard shrieks and yells behind her. Glancing back, Rebecca saw Ember and Dirt pointing at the top of the ridge above and behind them. There stood Rayford and the Shawnee, whooping and hollering as they danced victoriously on the rocks above. Immediately the savage warriors began clambering down the slick, wet slope to claim their victims. Two of the savages raised their rifles and tried to fire at Dirt and Grey Fox, but in the pouring rain, the weapons failed to discharge.

When Rebecca saw the fearsome attackers coming for them, she screamed. In that instant her foot slipped, and she plunged into the churning water below, disappearing instantly. Ember and Dirt heard her and turned just in time to see her fall into the foaming current.

"REBECCA!" Ember screamed.

Grey Fox took a quick glance at Dirt and jumped into the water after the girl.

"DON'T WORRY ABOUT HER!" Dirt yelled to Ember. "GREY FOX WILL SAVE HER. JUST GET ON OUT THERE! IF WE CAN

CROSS THIS BEFORE THEY GET TO US, WE MIGHT CAN HOLD 'EM OFF! NOW GO!"

Spurred by the urgency of their enemies' nearness, Ember jumped to the first boulder and began her crawl. Once she had started across, Dirt leaped after her. When the older girl reached the gap, Dirt slid close to her and said, "NOW HOLD ONTO MY HANDS AND STAND UP! WHEN YOU'RE READY, TURN LOOSE AN' JUMP!"

Ember knew better than to think about it. She locked her eyes on the other boulder, said a prayer, and jumped. She was picking herself up when Dirt landed beside her. The older scout helped the girl regain her feet and picked up Grey Fox's rifle. Both of them quickly hurtled across the remaining rocks to the limestone ledge that formed the southern bank. They looked back from where they had come. The river was in front of them and a twenty foot wall of rock was at their backs.

"ALL RIGHT, LITTLE MISSY, YOU SKEEDADDLE ON ALONG THAT LEDGE IN FRONT OF YOU UNTIL YOU GET TO WHERE YOU THINK YOU CAN CLIMB TO THE TOP, THEN HIDE! ONCE IT CLEARS ENOUGH FOR YOU TO TELL Y'ER DIRECTIONS, HEAD SOUTHWEST!"

"YOU'RE COMING WITH ME!" the girl yelled back.

"I GOTS TO STAY HERE AN' KEEP THESE VARMENTS FROM CROSSIN' THIS RIVER. THAT'LL GIVE YOU A CHANCE TO GET AWAY! NOW GO!"

Dirt knew that, in the pouring rain, neither his rifle nor Grey Fox's would fire, so he dropped one. He held the other by the barrel and prepared to use it like a club as he watched the eager savages rapidly approaching. There was only one way across the raging river at this point, and the older scout was determined to hold it for as long as he could.

When Grey Fox broke the surface of the churning waters, he quickly scanned the waves ahead for Rebecca. Not seeing her, he was starting to get anxious when suddenly her head shot up from a wave to his right front. He was swimming for her when he heard a shout from behind. Taking a quick look over his left shoulder, Grey Fox saw two Shawnee warriors sprinting along the north bank in pursuit. He knew that they intended to capture the girl, but they would surely kill him.

Driving his powerful arms through the rough water, Grey Fox sped after Rebecca. He treaded water and looked for her again. Once more he saw her head bounce above a wave. Encouraged that she was much closer, he marked the direction and churned the water again.

Grey Fox heard a gurgling scream as he topped another wave and saw Rebecca close by. He drove himself through the violent current to reach her. She saw him just as he got near. The terrified girl threw her arms around the Indian's strong neck, and he kicked and swam for the rocks on the right. A large boulder lay in the water, and the Miami was able to swim behind it to escape the swift current. Both of them stumbled repeatedly as they climbed the rocks onto the bank.

When Rayford and the Shawnee reached the first boulder, the trapper halted their attack and held a council. Suddenly Rayford turned and pointed toward Dirt. A warrior leaped onto the slick rock and, balancing himself on the top edge, began stepping methodically across it. He had almost reached the gap when a rock flew from his left front and landed solidly against his shoulder, spinning him. Instantly his feet slipped out from under him. He slammed hard into the slanted limestone slab and disappeared into the churning mass of water.

When Dirt saw what had happened, he looked back over his shoulder and saw Ember loading another rock into her sling. "JUMPIN' JEHOSAPHAT!" the wide-eyed scout exclaimed, "AH AIN'T NEVER BEEN SAVED BY A STONE SLINGIN' AMEEZON SHE-MALE

BEFORE! I APPRECIATE THE HELP, BUT YOU NEED TO RUN!"

The fear she felt was strong as her enemies raced towards her, but she could not let this good man give up his life for her without doing what she could to help. So instead of running, Ember stood her ground, gripped her loaded sling, and looked for a target.

Rayford also saw what the girl was doing and ordered two warriors to cross, one after the other. Ember bounced a rock off the head of the first, sending him into the river as well, but the second one made it to the gap before she could reload, and he leaped for Dirt.

The older scout swung his rifle and caught the attacking Shawnee in the side of the chest. The Indian landed hard on his knees beside Dirt. The warrior desperately grabbed the scout by the legs and tried to pull him down.

Ember had another stone in her sling and looked for a way to strike Dirt's adversary, but at that moment she saw Rayford charging across the boulders, leading the rest of the braves. She slung her rock hard at the trapper's head, but he was prepared. As he leaped across the boulders, he raised his left arm near his head for protection. Ember's stone struck painfully against the muscles of Rayford's arm but did him no damage.

Dirt finished the warrior he struggled with and looked up to see the big trapper hurtling straight for him. There was no time to avoid it. Before Dirt could lift his rifle, Rayford crashed into him, driving him backwards and slamming the scout hard into the cliff wall. Dazed by the blow, Dirt's rifle flew from his hands as he collapsed on the rocky ledge.

When the trapper lifted himself off Dirt, he turned and stared menacingly at Ember. Knowing the wicked woodsman meant to have her, the girl dropped her make-shift sling and rushed as quickly as she dared along the narrowing ledge located directly above the treacherous river.

"You okay?" Grey Fox asked as he and Rebecca sat on the rocks, breathing hard.

"I think so," the girl answered. "When I fell in, I thought I was dead. You saved my life, Grey Fox. Thank you! But why did you do it? You could have died yourself!"

"It what Chief Jesus want," the Miami shrugged.

At that moment they heard more shouting. Looking downriver, Grey Fox spotted the two Shawnee warriors fifty yards away, leaping from rock to rock, making their way across the river.

"Enemies come!" he announced to Rebecca. "Can you climb?" Grey Fox pointed to the top of the small cliff behind them.

The young girl looked at the nearly twelve foot rocky ledge, then back at the pursuing enemies. "I think I can," she answered, "but you might need to help me."

"Grey Fox help," the Indian said as he stood and rushed to the wall of rock. "Come, we start now."

There were numerous shallow ledges and projections protruding from the wall, and they were able to find plenty of hand and foot holds. It took some work, and Grey Fox did have to help, but soon they were both standing on top of the south ridge overlooking the river.

Rebecca felt a sense of relief as she realized that they had made it across. Just then the Miami yanked his tomahawk from his belt and turned quickly. Pulling themselves to the top of the ridge were the two Shawnee warriors. They spotted Grey Fox and the girl immediately and, screaming their war cries, drew their weapons and charged at them.

"RUN!" Grey Fox called and prepared to face the two attackers.

Rebecca untied her sling from around her waist. When she reached into her pocket, she suddenly realized that all of her rocks were gone and there were none nearby. Glancing over, she spotted Grey Fox's ammunition pouch hanging by a strap around his neck. Reaching into it, she pulled out a fifty caliber lead bullet. Loading it in her sling, she twirled it once and sent the missile streaking toward the charging attackers.

The slug hit the first warrior solid in the chest, breaking one of his ribs. With a grunt of pain, he collapsed to the ground in obvious agony. The second fighter kept coming, intent on killing Grey Fox and capturing the girl.

"RUN!" the Miami cried again, but Rebecca had her hand in his bullet pouch again. With her sling reloaded, the girl launched another slug at the attacking enemy. Because the Shawnee was closer, the young girl was able to aim more accurately. The speeding ball of lead struck the charging warrior in the middle of his forehead, snapping his head back and sending his feet flying straight out in front of him. He was unconscious before he hit the ground.

Grey Fox stared in amazement at the mayhem the little girl beside him had caused. Finally he lifted the strap of the ammunition pouch from around his neck and handed it to the girl. "Here...You keep."

Chapter Thirty-Two

A POWERFUL WEAPON

A groan escaped William Hackett's lips, and he stirred as cold rain drops ran down his head, face, and neck. Painfully he pushed himself up and discovered that, when he and the Shawnee had fallen, his head had slammed against one of the rocky outcroppings protruding through the forest floor. As he rose, he was startled to see his adversary lying beside him. The knife the young scout had in his hand when he threw himself at the warrior had permanently finished the Shawnee's murderous career.

Will stood unsteadily in the pouring rain and stumbled to where he had dropped his rifle. Seeing the plug and the oiled wrap still securely in place, Will tried to gather his groggy thoughts. He wasn't sure how long he had been out, but for his friends' sakes, he hoped it hadn't been long. The young scout rushed as fast as he was able to the sound of the waterfall until he stood on the edge of the bluff overlooking the river. He arrived in time to see Rayford slam into Dirt and drive him into the rocky wall on the other side of the ravine. Quickly Will yanked the plug from the end of his rifle barrel and untied the oil wrap around the lock.

After being driven against the limestone ledge, Dirt Gurley was still conscious, but just barely. When Rayford saw that the older scout was unable to get up, he left his victim for the Shawnee behind him to finish. Seeing Ember so close, he rose to claim his prize. *THAT GIRL IS MINE,* the trapper's evil mind raged.

While Rayford pursued Ember as she shuffled quickly along the tapering ledge above the river, Dirt's clouded mind screamed at him to do something, but his battered body wouldn't respond. Just then Kolapeka, the Shawnee Chief, stood over him with a demonic grin on his face and a long, sharp knife in his hand. The savage grabbed the older scout by his thin, stringy hair and lifted him off the ground. Dirt emitted a painful moan and tried to fight, but he had no strength. All he could do was watch as the warrior lifted his weapon to finish him.

Suddenly over the din of the waterfall and the storm barked the distant sound of a rifle shot. The savage jerked, dropped his victim, and collapsed.

Finding himself again prostrate on the limestone ledge, Dirt painfully opened his eyes and looked across the ravine, spotting a small cloud of smoke on the opposite ridge. As the heavy rain quickly cleared it, Will Hackett and his rifle came into view.

The four remaining Shawnee warriors were startled to hear a gunshot in the pouring rain. Seeing their chief fall, the savages whipped around to find the shooter. They spotted a lone frontiersman quickly descending the ridge on the opposite side. With savage yells and cries of vengeance, the four hurriedly retraced their steps to meet the new threat, each eager to be the warrior to take this foolish one's scalp.

William saw them coming and hopped quickly from rock to rock down the slope. When he reached the bank of the river, he rushed along it toward the waterfall as the Indians raced to confront him. The young frontiersman's only hope of victory against so many was to try to defeat them quickly one at a time, but they were coming close together. Knowing this would likely be his last fight, the loyal young scout determined to fight to the end and sell his life dearly.

Something to the right caught his eye, and he noticed a large ridge of limestone protruding from the boulder-strewn slope. Under it was a sheltered cave-like grotto just large enough for a man to stand.

Instantly the youth bounded up the boulders until he stood in the natural shelter. William yanked the plug from his rifle barrel, poured in powder, pushed in a ball and patch, and tamped them once with his rod. He pulled the oil skin away from the lock and trigger mechanism. Pouring a small amount of black powder into the pan, he snapped the frizzen shut and took aim at the approaching Indians.

As the Shawnee warriors hurried across the slick boulders below the waterfall, they heard a sharp bang, and the leading Indian grabbed his chest and fell into the raging current. The three remaining savages looked up and saw Will under the bluff quickly reloading his rifle.

Too late the braves realized their terrible mistake. In a panic the Shawnee began frantically scaling the stones and boulders that formed the waterfall. With a grim smile William watched the Indians attempt the dangerous climb. He had a clear shot at two of them, but he decided that, since they weren't trying to kill him, he would let the Lord decide if they made it or not.

With his rifle reloaded, wrapped, and plugged, the young frontiersman hurried to cross the river to see how badly Dirt was hurt. When he reached the gap between the boulders that he needed to jump, one of the Indians trying to climb the waterfall suddenly came tumbling down the rocks and bounced into the raging current. Will glanced up and saw the other two had almost reached the top. Satisfied that they would be no more trouble for now, the young scout leaped the gap and rushed to see about his injured friend.

When Ember saw Dirt go down, she thought that she might be able to hit the trapper in the head with a rock while his attention was on his victim. But Rayford didn't look at Dirt. He locked his eyes on Ember. The girl knew that, in the wicked trapper's mind, he owned her and he intended that nothing would stop him from getting her back. Rayford never took his eyes off her as he pushed himself to his feet.

The eight-foot-wide shelf of rock on which they stood had narrowed to a foot in width where Ember perched. The girl froze in terror as she watched her attacker stand. It was like his hate-filled eyes had already apprehended her. The fear paralyzed her as the sling dropped from her numbed fingers.

RUN, DEAR ONE! The urgent words in her head shook her into action. Ember searched quickly for a way of escape. The wall of the ravine was climbable, but she couldn't do it fast enough to get away from the determined trapper. She spun and took the only other option. Placing her back against the rock wall, she shuffled her feet as quickly as she could along the slick, narrowing ledge. With a determination born of evil, Rayford rushed after her.

When he got close to the girl, he leaned out to grab her hand that was trailing against the wall. Ember realized what he was doing and quickly pulled her arm out of his reach. With a snarl of anger, the trapper saw that the ledge where the girl was had rapidly narrowed and was now no more than three inches wide. Following the girl's example, Rayford pressed his back against the rock and began shuffling in pursuit.

"You runnin' is only gonna make it worse on you when I catch you!" the trapper spat angrily. "You're mine, girl! You'll *always* be mine! You ain't gettin' away!"

Lord! The girl cried desperately in her heart. *I know You're with me, but my friends and I are in real trouble, and I don't know what to do!*

As she continued inching along, she looked at the churning rapids almost twenty feet below her. Suddenly Rayford's huge hand slammed into hers and clawed to grip her fingers. Ember screamed and yanked her hand away again. As she did so her left foot slipped from the mossy ledge, but she kept her balance. She could see the trapper struggling to move closer to her.

Should I jump, Lord? She asked. *Zoe said you were with her in the fire, and it wasn't too bad. I'm okay with dying if you're with me, Lord. I will get to be with You and my family.*

Tell him about Me, the beautiful Voice answered.

"Lord?" the confused girl questioned out loud.

Instead of jumping, tell Rayford about Me, the Voice said again.

Ember looked at her pursuer and saw the wicked eyes glaring at her as he inched closer and closer.

"Do you know that Jesus loves you?" the girl called over the storm and swift water. Ember saw something change in the trapper's face. For an instant she saw something replace the hate and anger in Rayford's eyes.

It's fear, she heard Jesus say. *He has done so much evil in his life, he is terrified of the truth.*

"You don't have to be afraid of Jesus, Rayford," the girl called again.

"STOP!" the trapper roared in a rage. "DON'T SAY THAT NAME! I'LL KILL YOU IF YOU SAY IT AGAIN! I'LL KILL YOU!" To emphasize his words, he slammed his hand repeatedly against the wall behind him.

"But Jesus loves you," the girl tried again, "and He can save you if you trust in Him."

The trapper suddenly screamed a loud, agonizing howl of insane rage. Then he roared back at her, "THERE AIN'T NO JESUS! THERE AIN'T NO GOD! THERE AIN'T NO HELL! YA' HEAR ME? THERE AIN'T NO HELL..."

Ember was stunned at Rayford's violent response. She saw tears of fury and fear pouring down his face as he continued his rant.

The girl tried to get further away from her raging pursuer, but the narrow ledge suddenly ran out. She could go no further. Suddenly she heard a crash and felt pain in her left shoulder as Rayford slammed his tomahawk into the rock beside her, chopping through her dress and cutting a shallow slice in her arm.

Insane with rage, the possessed trapper now only wanted to kill the girl who represented the One he hated and feared the most. He saw that, in order to bury his tomahawk in the girl's chest, he had to extend his reach. Holding the hatchet by the very end of the handle, Rayford leaned as far toward the girl as he could. With a hate-filled cry, the trapper lunged forward and swung with all his might.

EMBER! She heard the Lord's voice in her right ear.

The medicine girl turned quickly toward the voice, and in that instant her right foot slipped, and she lurched away from her attacker. The girl's leading hand, sliding against the rock wall, suddenly caught on a small, rocky knob. Rayford's powerfully swung tomahawk slammed into the ledge where the girl had been. Off balance, his foot slipped and, with a scream of terror, he tumbled into the churning rapids below.

Even though her legs were weak from fear and her shoulder ached from the wound, Ember pushed herself onto the narrow shelf of rock and inched back the way she had come. The entire frightening ordeal had been overwhelming to her. She felt light headed and dizzy.

No, please, Lord! She prayed urgently as she looked at the waters of death rushing below her. *You saved me from Rayford, please don't let me faint now!*

She began to see dark spots that slowly started getting bigger. The medicine girl understood what was coming and willed herself to keep moving along the ledge. As the world around her began to slowly spin, she knew she would fall. *I love You, Lord,* were her last thoughts as she lost consciousness and stumbled forward.

As she slipped from the ledge, a strong hand reached out and gripped her wrist.

302

Chapter Thirty-Three

THE AFTERMATH

"Ember...Ember!" the distant voice called.

"Lord? Is that You?" the medicine girl answered weakly as she opened her eyes and tried to focus on the blurry face in front of her.

"No," giggled a voice that now sounded much closer. "It's me...Rebecca."

"Rebecca," Ember smiled as her eyes finally focused on her friend, "you're in heaven too? Isn't it beautiful?"

"Well, the truth be told," sounded a loud, nasally voice from nearby, "this here place is plum e't up with beautifulness, but it ain't heaven."

Ember raised her eyes to look at the speaker and saw Dirt propped against the ravine wall. The rain was still falling, but not as heavily.

Ember sat up and looked around in confusion. "The last thing I remember is that I was falling into the river," she finally said. "What happened?"

"Will saved you," Rebecca volunteered.

Just then a pile of long tree branches crashed onto the rock ledge between the girls and Dirt. Looking up, they saw Grey Fox twenty feet above them, standing on the rim of the ravine. He bent down and, grabbing another arm-load of cut limbs, tossed them down. Will walked up beside the Miami, dragging more branches. As he began tossing them down, he spotted Ember sitting up. "Are you all right?" he called to the older girl with concern.

"Yes, I am," she smiled back as she rose to her feet, "thanks to you, apparently."

"The big trapper was after you," Will explained. "I was trying to get there in time to help, but before I could do anything, Rayford lost his balance and fell. With the wound in your arm and all you went through, you must have fainted. I was able to grab your arm as you fell and swing you back onto the ledge. You landed hard. I was afraid I had hurt you."

"I'm a little sore," Ember returned. "It's the cut on my shoulder that hurts the worst. I'm just glad to be alive. Thank you for what you did."

Will gave a faint smile and a nod as he turned to go find more limbs.

"I wish I had seen him do it," Rebecca sighed as she wistfully watched the young scout disappear behind the rim. "I know he must have been amazing!"

"Wait a minute!" Ember exclaimed. "I know I saw you fall into the river. Why are you not dead?"

"Because Grey Fox saved me," the younger girl answered matter-of-factly.

"Then she save Grey Fox," the Miami called from the ledge above as he dropped more branches down. While the Indian carefully descended the rock wall to join them, Rebecca told Ember what had happened after she fell in the river.

"Two Shawnee come after us," the Miami added to the girl's story. "It seem to Grey Fox that he have to fight both at same time. Not look good." The Indian turned toward Rebecca, placed his hand on her head, and smiled. "Then little warrior grabbed two rifle balls and throw them at enemies. She take each one out!"

"Great honkin' geese!" Dirt exclaimed. "They's both Ameezon women! Miss Ember was doin' the same thing to the Shawnee tryin' to get me! While I was standing there waitin' for the Injuns as they come chargin' across the river, that girl was standin' there purdy as you please, slingin' rocks like David fightin' Go-liath."

"Glad they on our side," added Grey Fox.

"So, Ember," Rebecca asked eagerly, "when I fell in the river, does that count as being baptized?"

"Sorry, Becca," the older girl laughed, "that was an accident. You don't get baptized by accident. You just got wet."

"Well now," Dirt joined in enthusiastically, "if gettin' baptized was what you wanted to do, we could help you with that right now—if'n we weren't on the banks of the ragin' river of death. You'll see Jesus a whole lot sooner than you were plannin' to if you try to do it here. The river by Larkinboro is slow. Once we get you ladies back home, we'll take care of all that."

Soon William returned with more branches. As he tossed them down onto the pile, Grey Fox constructed a shelter by leaning the long limbs against the wall of the ravine.

"So we're staying here?" Rebecca asked as she realized what the men were doing.

"Dirt's hurting too badly right now to make the climb out," Will answered. "Grey Fox and I thought we'd camp for a few days to let him have a chance to recover."

"Mr. Dirt," Ember said as she walked over to where the older scout lay against the wall, "I'm so sorry! I should have been checking on you."

"Now don't you be frettin' over ol' Dirt," the older scout said. "I'll be all right. But you're arm's bleedin,' so let's get you bandaged up first."

At Dirt's insistence, Ember's arm was treated, then she spent several minutes examining her wounded friend. She concluded his head injury was going to take a few days and some herbal teas to get better. She was glad to determine that being slammed against the rocks had only bruised his ribs and not broken them.

As Grey Fox and Will finished the construction of their large lean-to over where Dirt was lying, Ember asked a question. "I know everything is wet and the rain is still falling, but is there any way we can build a fire? I need to brew some herbs that would really help Mr. Dirt."

"I don't think that's going to happen," Will answered skeptically, "at least not today. Everything is absolutely soaked from this storm."

"To be ab-so-tively factical, little missy," Dirt added, "it's gonna' be purt' near impossible to find something' dry enough to burn after all this rain."

The Miami snorted and then announced, "Grey Fox will start fire."

"WHAT?" Will shot back in disbelief. "You can't start a fire as wet as everything is!"

"Grey Fox will start fire."

"Now listen here, Grey Fox," Dirt persisted. "You're a mighty fine Injun. Best one I ever knowd. But you ain't no wizard. There's no way you're startin' a fire in all this wet!"

"Grey Fox will start fire."

Annoyed at his unrelenting friend, Dirt shot back, "I'll bet my hat you cain't start no fire today."

"Dirt no have hat," the Miami returned.

"Well, o' course I don't have a hat!" Dirt snapped. "You stole it from me an' then lost it when, like a yay-hoo, you jumped in the river with it on your head! Why didn't you leave it on the ledge before you dove in the water?"

"Because Dirt Gurley would steal it."

"Why, you ornery rascal!" Dirt growled. "If you hadn't a lost it, I'd a won it back 'CAUSE YOU AIN'T STARTIN NO FIRE TODAY!"

"Grey Fox will start fire," the Miami said firmly. With a snort he walked over to the ravine wall and quickly scaled it. The rain had stopped when he returned a few minutes later clutching something close to his body. Descending to the ledge, the Indian walked to where Dirt rested under the lean-to and dropped a small pile of dry wood bits into his lap.

"Hold this," the Indian barked, then began breaking up the smallest of the dead twigs and branches that he snapped off from the outside of the lean-to.

"Where'd you get this dry wood?" Dirt asked with surprise.

"Grey Fox chopped into underside of rotted log," came the answer.

"Well, I'll have to admit, that was pretty smart," Dirt returned. "But there's enough dampness in the air that you still ain't gonna get it to catch a spark, an' you sure ain't gonna get it to burn hot enough to catch the rest of your wet wood on fire."

"Grey Fox will start fire."

The Miami laid a row of small sticks side by side on the wet stone ledge. The dry chips Dirt held were placed on top. Small broken twigs covered them, then bigger sticks were added. Grey Fox took even larger wet sticks and laid them like a teepee around the rest.

"That's an awful purdy-lookin' stack of wood," Dirt teased. "Too bad we'll have to leave it for the next hunters that come through here."

When all was as he wanted it, Grey Fox stood up and loaded his rifle. He put in powder and a patch but no ball. Tamping them down firmly, he poured powder in the pan and closed the frizzen. The last thing he did was pour a large pile of black powder beside the dry chips at the bottom of his stacked wood.

"Hey, what are you doing?" Dirt barked as he watched his friend.

Without answering, the Miami placed the muzzle of his rifle beside the pile of black powder and pulled the trigger. As flame leaped from the muzzle, there was a sizzling roar as the black powder caught and flared into a white hot flame. Within seconds the super-hot fire ignited the rest of the wood.

"THAT'S CHEATIN'!" Dirt yelled as the rest of them laughed.

"Grey Fox no cheat," the Miami returned. "He start fire. Next hat you get belong to Grey Fox."

"I'm tellin' you, Will," Dirt said with a sigh, "that Injun's gonna be the death of me."

Chapter Thirty-Four

A NEW HOME

One week later Will Hackett and Grey Fox stood near the gates of the palisade surrounding Larkinboro. They talked with their friends Jack Cobb, Dirt Gurley, and Asa Whitlock. Jack and Dirt were the original scouts for the village, and Asa, who was a year younger than William, was one of his best friends.

"Any questions about what you two are supposed to get done?" Jack Cobb asked as he looked at Will and the Miami.

"No," the young frontiersman answered. "We're going to do the same thing that we were sent to do last week with Dirt but didn't get to finish. We scout the territory north of here and identify the locations of Indian tribes who are helping the British."

"Which is gonna be mostly the Shawnee and the Iroquois in the north," Dirt added. "I'm sorry I ain't gonna be goin' with you this time, but I'm still recoverin' from the beatin' I took on our last trip. I'd ask Jack to go with you, but he's takin' Jim Hart, and they're scoutin' the Cherokee tribes south of here."

"I thought the Cherokee were keeping to themselves," Will said.

"That's what we all thought," Jack answered, "until word came in earlier this week that British agents were down there courtin' 'em."

"Well, don't waste no time doin' your scoutin'," Dirt prompted. "That American captain who came by here said General Clark wants accurate information about the tribes as soon as he can get it."

Just then Asa elbowed William in the side. "Look! Look! Here comes Ember and Katherine!" he said in an excited, low voice.

As they watched the two young women approach, Will couldn't help but smile at how pretty Katherine looked in her red dress with her light brown curls falling around her shoulders. Equally as attractive was Ember Warren walking beside her. The freed captive wore a bright yellow dress and had her dark brown hair pinned on her head. Her medicine bag hung on her shoulder.

"Well, hello there!" Dirt called out as the girls approached. "It's mighty nice to see both of you lovely ladies on such a fine morning!"

Both girls smiled sweetly and gave a general greeting to everyone.

"Miss Ember," Dirt continued, "I ain't seen you or Miss Rebecca for several days. After all you've been through, I've been wonderin' how you two are adjustin' to your new lives here at Larkinboro."

"It's definitely been quite a change and is taking some getting used to," Ember answered, "but over all, it's been wonderful."

"Do you think you're gonna be able to put all that bad stuff behind you an' have a decent life?" Dirt asked with genuine concern.

"God has truly redeemed my captivity. When I lost my family and was suffering abuse, I didn't understand. I thought God had abandoned me. But He took what the devil designed to defeat me and trained me to be a healer. I have a new life now, one with purpose and value, one even better than before because Jesus is my friend. It is amazing. I should have trusted that God was working it all together for good even while it was happening!

"But to answer your question about Rebecca and I being here in Larkinboro, The Leavenworth family has taken Rebecca in. They treat her like she was their own daughter."

"Gardenia Leavenworth loves having a sister," Kate added. "My own sister Grace is close to Rebecca's age, and she, Rebecca, and Gardenia have become as thick as thieves."

"Katherine's family has been kind enough to let me stay with them," Ember added. "It's been a long time since I've had a home and a family."

"Seth, Grace, and I love having Ember as a sister," Kate said as she put her arm around her new friend. "She's been telling us the most wonderful things about heaven and Jesus."

"I've heard that everybody is excited to find out that you're a healer," said Will, addressing the medicine girl.

"Apparently I've been fully accepted," Ember returned. "I've treated someone almost every day since I've been here. This is my third house call today."

"I try to go with her when I can," Kate added. "She's teaching me to be a healer, although I'm not sure that I can do everything she has to do."

"You get used to it," Ember returned.

"But I don't want to," Kate answered with a giggle.

"So does Rebecca miss her sister?" William asked.

"Apparently they didn't have the best of relationships," Ember explained, "so she doesn't miss her in that way. But she is very sad that her sister is still a slave of the Shawnee. We pray for her daily."

"Er, um, Miss Warren," Asa said nervously, tightly gripping his hat, "I, uh, don't believe we've met yet. I'm, uh, Whit, uh, I mean, Asa...Asa Whitlock."

"Hello," Ember said with a smile, "Nice to meet you. I'm Remember Warren, but most people call me Ember."

"It's really nice to meet you too, Miss Ember!" Asa grinned back. "It sure is nice...uh, I mean...the day. You know...the weather? The weather's nice...today."

"I'm really glad you girls showed up," Will said, jumping in to save his friend any more embarrassment. "Grey Fox and I are just leaving for another scouting trip, and I was hoping to get to say goodbye."

"Oh, Will," Katherine said with disappointment in her voice, "you just got back, and are you going out again?"

"We have to, Kate," Will returned. "The last time we weren't able to complete our task."

"I believe that was my fault," Ember said, smiling and raising her hand.

"That couldn't be helped," Dirt shot back. "You girls was runnin' for your lives, an' getting' you to safety became most important. But I'm tellin' you, with the skill that you and Miss Rebecca have with slingin' rocks, it's clear that you two ladies weren't exactly helpless."

"Dirt was tellin' me about how you girls were defending your selves," Jack said with admiration.

"Hoo-wee!" Dirt shot back, "What you talkin' about, Jack? The way them two Ameezon women fling stones, they can part your hair at thirty yards, an' I don't mean maybe!"

"Well, anyway," William said, finishing his explanation, "Grey Fox and I need to get back out there and locate the northern Indian tribes for General Clark and his army."

"Just be careful," Katherine said sincerely as she placed her hand on the young scout's arm. "Is anyone going with you?"

"Dirt's still healing from his injuries, and Jack's taking Jim Hart and scouting south," William explained. "I thought I'd see if Asa wanted to go with us."

As all of them looked at Will's friend, Asa shifted nervously, cleared his throat, and said, "Well, uh, I don't think I'll be able to make it this time. I've got some things around here that I need to work on...but, uh, thanks for asking."

"Just be careful and come back safe," Katherine said sincerely.

"Yes," Ember added, "please be safe.

"Well, Katherine," Ember said to her friend, "I think we had better head to the cabin so I can see that sick little boy."

As the girls waved their goodbyes and started to turn, Asa spoke up. "Uh, excuse me, Miss Warren, but I could carry that heavy bag of yours for you. It would be no problem."

"Thanks all the same," Ember returned, "but I..." At that moment she felt Katherine bump her in the side. When she looked at Kate, her friend was looking at her intently and subtly nodding her head toward Asa.

Ember recognized Kate's prompt and turned to look more appraisingly at the young man her new friend seemed to think was worthy of attention. She saw an eager face, a bright smile, and a bird's nest of light brown hair piled on his head. *What do you think about this fellow, Lord?* Ember prayed as she looked into Asa's eyes.

Give him a chance, were the words that seemed to pop into her head.

With a nod Ember slid the strap of the medicine bag off her shoulder and handed it to Asa. "Okay," she smiled. "Thanks."

Asa eagerly took the large pouch and, as the girls walked away, he stepped up beside Ember. "You know, I almost got killed by a buffalo once..."

As he watched his friend leave with the girls, William reached up and scratched his head. "What's with him?" he asked with a confused look on his face.

Grey Fox only grunted.

Just then Dirt stepped up and put his arms around both of his young friends' shoulders. "Has anybody ever talked with you fellers about the birds and the bees?"

Suddenly Will's face turned red, and he mumbled some incoherent answer. Jack's eyes went wide, and he turned and quickly walked away.

"Well, let's jus' talk about the bee part," Dirt began with confidence. "It's like this: That Miss Ember is a beautiful flower, and Asa is the bee. Now bees is attracted to purdy flowers. So the bee starts buzzin' an' buzzin' around the flower like a nitwit, annoyin' the poor thing to death. When the bee finally wears her down, the flower gives up an' agrees to let the bee hang around. Then they gets married and has a bunch of kids. An' one day when the bee starts thinkin' straight again, he wonders how in the name of common sense he got hisself into such a fix."

When the older scout didn't say anything else, both Will and Grey Fox turned and looked at Dirt in confusion. The older scout just sighed and nodded knowingly.

Finally William said, "Well, uh, thanks Dirt. I'm glad we had this talk."

"Don't mention it," the older scout returned. "I'm jus' tryin' to help you fellers out by sharing some of my years of experience and wisdom."

As Dirt walked off, Grey Fox leaned next to Will and said, "What he talking about?"

Will shook his head slowly and answered, "I have no clue."

The End

Appendix A
Chapter Questions and Lessons

In writing this story, I not only wanted to create a fun and entertaining bonding experience for my family, but I wanted to teach some important character and spiritual lessons to my children as well. I have always told my children stories, especially the ones that I heard from my father, and there were occasionally some spiritual lessons stuck in them. I was impressed by the fact that those were the lessons that my children always remembered.

It struck me that one of the reasons Jesus used stories so much in His teaching was because they made the lessons so memorable. I researched and learned that, when teaching is placed within a gripping or engaging story, not only does the information reach the mind of the reader, but the teaching is also connected to the reader's emotions. Said another way, when the emotions are engaged, the lesson is remembered and the heart is taught, and that is where real life change occurs. Please understand, I do not believe that a teaching technique causes heart or life change. Only the Spirit of God at work in our hearts can do that. But when we follow Jesus's example of how to teach and combine it with fervent prayer, I believe that we are giving our children and students the best opportunity for the Holy Spirit to reach their hearts.

If it is your goal to use stories to reach the hearts of others, then I believe the most effective way to use my books is for parents to read them to their children or for teachers to read them to their classes. After completing a chapter, take time to talk about the spiritual and character lessons learned and give the listeners an opportunity to verbalize their discoveries. As a help, we have assembled this appendix with a collection of discussion questions and important lessons found in each chapter. Use any or all of these questions as a place to start, but be sensitive to the direction of the discussion, and add your own questions to accommodate what God is doing in the hearts of your listeners. Remember God's part in this whole process and always pray (if not audibly, at least to yourself) each time before reading, asking the Lord to use the story to teach His lessons to your listeners' hearts.

In His Service,

Alan W. Harris

Chapter One

Describe Ember's feelings after watching her family being killed and after being made a slave?

How did Jesus respond to sorrow in His life?

What does God do to reach Ember's bitter heart?

What are healthy ways to handle sorrow and grief?

What are some of the truths about God or promises of the Bible that would have comforted the girl?

Character Qualities to Identify:

Neither Rayford nor his squaw showed any **sensitivity** to Ember in her suffering.

Sensitivity: *the quality of being particularly aware of the hurts and feelings of others.*

This is in contrast with **callousness**: *being insensitive and having a cruel disregard for others.*

How did Jesus show sensitivity to others?

Chapter two

Describe Rayford. Identify some of his bad character qualities.

What effect did living with an angry man like Rayford have on the squaw?

What are some character qualities you can try to develop or things you can do to help you have a good attitude when faced with lots of hard work?

What bad character qualities did Ember display in response to her captivity?

Character Qualities to Identify:

Even though her attitudes were not good, Ember showed **obedience** when Prisha gave her commands.

Obedience: *respectfully submitting to another's authority.*

This is in contrast to **willfulness**: *deliberately and stubbornly refusing to obey, submit or give in to authorities.*

How did Jesus show obedience in His life?

____

Chapter Three

What happened to Ember that led her to believe her prayers were seemingly empty and useless?

Why is it important not to judge people by their appearance on first impressions?

What character qualities did Prisha and Ember have to use to effectively communicate to help the sick woman?

Explain the frustrations that Prisha and Ember felt toward each other.

How much are you worth to God?

Character Qualities to Identify:

In order for the medicine woman to effectively help the people she was called to treat, she needed to practice **thoroughness** in her examinations.

Thoroughness: *being extremely attentive to accuracy and detail in all you do.*

This is contrast to **incompleteness**: *inadequacy, lack, deficiency, shortcoming.*

How did Jesus show thoroughness?

____

Chapter Four

How did the squaw referred to as War Club show wisdom when they heard the wolves coming?

What character qualities did Ember use in the fight against the wolves?

How would you describe Prisha's response to Ember's snake bite?

What does this tell you about Prisha?

Character Qualities to Identify:

When her sisters were discouraging her, Prisha showed **determination** to save Ember's life.

Determination: *the act of making a firm and definite decision and carrying through with it.*

This is in contrast with **indifference:** *lack of interest, concern or sympathy.*

How did Jesus show determination?

Chapter Five

What do you think about Ember's experience in heaven?

What do you think heaven will be like?

How did Jesus show His deep love for Ember in this chapter?

Describe something you seen this chapter about Jesus that you love.

When Jesus told Ember that He was enough for her, what did He mean?

Character Qualities to Identify:

The main thing that Jesus expressed to Ember as He spent time with her was **love.**

Love: *lavishly giving to others without having the desire for any personal reward.*

This is in contrast with **selfishness**: *seeking one's own advantage, pleasure or well-being without regard for others.*

How did Jesus show love in His life on Earth?

Chapter Six

What character qualities and attributes did Prisha practice in her efforts to save Ember's life?

How was God working in Prisha as she cared for Ember?

How did Jesus define worship in this chapter? Do you agree with that?

What did God create you to do and be?

Based on Eliza's story, how can pain and heartache lead to good?

What did Eliza say Jesus did that finally won her heart?

Where does love for Jesus come from? (*I John 4:19*)

Character Qualities to Identify:

Ol' Sukie showed **Forgiveness** to Eliza by loving the girl in spite of the pain she caused Sukie.

Forgiveness: *willingly setting aside the wrongs others have done to me and allowing God to love them through me.*

This is in contrast to **rejection:** *dismissing another person and refusing to show kindness or compassion to them.*

How did Jesus show forgiveness in His life on Earth?

Chapter Seven

How did Zoe and her family overcome their fear of curses and persecution?

From Zoe's experience, what did she mean when she told Ember that Jesus is always faithful?

In order for Ember to get back to heaven, what did Jesus say was the only thing she needed to do?

What did Jesus say that He was going to do to get her back to heaven?

Why did Ember finally agree to return to her life as a slave?

How is saying *yes* to Jesus's will for your life true worship and true love?

Character Qualities to Identify:

When Ember determined to obey Jesus and go back to Earth, even though she wanted desperately to stay in heaven, she showed **meekness.**

Meekness: *willingly giving all of my rights, expectations, and desires to God.*

This is in contrast to **rebellion:** *defiant resistance to the authorities in your life.*

How did Jesus show meekness in His life on Earth?

Chapter Eight

How did meeting Jesus change Ember's view of her life?

Ember was bitten by a poisonous snake, and it almost killed her. How does Satan, the great serpent, "bite" us, and what effect does it have?

Describe Ember's new relationship with Jesus. How is it different from yours?

How did God direct Ember to become a medicine woman?

Ember had not been interested in learning the Shawnee language before. What motivated her to want to learn it now?

Character Qualities to Identify:

Empowered with a desire to live her life for Jesus, Ember now could do her work with **joyfulness.**

Joyfulness: *having a glad and delighted heart even in the face of difficult circumstances.*

This is in contrast with **resentment:** *bitter indignation at having been mistreated.*

How did Jesus show joyfulness?

Chapter Nine

How did God provide for Ember in her slavery?

What are some of the ways God revealed Himself to Ember and grew her faith?

In what ways is God revealing Himself to you and growing your faith?

When Ember realized that she was in a dangerous situation with Rayford, what was the most effective thing she did to protect herself?

What did Jesus say He would do for those who call on His name? *(Romans 10:12-14; Psalm 50:15)*

Character Qualities to Identify:

Rayford was living completely for himself and had no use for **temperance.**

Temperance: *voluntary restraint and moderation. Learning to say no to sin and things that are harmful.*

This in contrast to **indulgence:** *to satisfy a desire and to do what you want regardless of the consequences.*

How did Jesus show temperance?

____

Chapter Ten

What changes were manifested in Ember's life once she determined to live for Jesus?

What effect did Ember's growing relationship with Jesus have on the squaw?

What was the difference between the ways Ember and Jesus viewed Prisha.

How did Rayford react to seeing the Bible? Why do you think he responded that way?

How valuable was God's word to Ember?

Character Qualities to Identify:

In spite of her slavery, Ember was learning to do her work with **cheerfulness**.

Cheerfulness: *being noticeably happy and optimistic; an attitude that brings joy and good spirits to others.*

This is in contrast to being **sullen**: *being bad tempered, sulky and gloomy.*

How did Jesus show cheerfulness?

Chapter Eleven

Knowing what Rayford was truly like, and after seeing him interact with the American militia, what did you learn about his character?

Whom do you think Rayford worships?

When someone has attitudes like Rayford's, where do you think it will lead, and what kind of fruit will come from his life?

When Ember first arrived as a slave, what attitudes did she and Rayford share? What made the difference for Ember?

Character Qualities to Identify:

When Rayford talked with Captain Parks, he pretended to have **sincerity.**

Sincerity: *being eager to do the right things with transparent motives.*

This is in contrast to **hypocrisy**: *claiming to have moral standards and beliefs to which one's own behavior does not conform.*

How did Jesus show sincerity?

Chapter Twelve

How did Rayford deceive the militia, and what was his goal?

Why did Captain Parks believe Rayford?

What are some ways that Satan deceives us today?

Why do we believe Satan?

What eventually happens when you trust a deceiver?

Character Qualities to Identify:

With his constant lying and deceit, **truthfulness** had almost no place in Rayford's life.

Truthfulness: *honestly communicating with your words, actions, and attitudes that which is accurate, genuine, and correct.*

This is in contrast with **deception:** *misleading someone by concealing or misrepresenting the truth.*

How did Jesus show truthfulness?

Chapter Thirteen

Jesus worked in Ember to make her into a medicine woman, but what part did Ember have to play in order for Jesus to accomplish that?

As Ember read Isaiah to Prisha, what did the scripture say was God's attitude toward "bad people"? Who are "bad people"?

Why was it so important to Jesus that Prisha know that He loves her?

When a person fully understands how much Jesus loves them, what effect does that have?

In sharing the love of Christ with others, what is our part, and what is Jesus' part?

Character qualities to Identify:

By having Ember share His love with Prisha, Jesus taught the girl **empathy**.

Empathy: *the ability to understand and relate to the feelings and difficulties of others.*

This is in contrast to being **hard-hearted**: *unfeeling, lacking in sympathy and understanding.*

Name ways Jesus showed empathy?

____

Chapter Fourteen

Why did Ember kept praying in secret even though Rayford threatened to harm her if she did it?

What was Chief Kolapeka's response to the death of his friend?

How does Satan want us to handle tragedy and grief?

How does God want us to respond to tragedy and sorrow?

How can you tell that God was drawing Prisha to Himself? (*John 6:44*)

How can you tell God is drawing the people around you to Himself?

Character Qualities to Identify:

Even though Ember was threatened not to pray, she continued to do it, but with **cautiousness**.

Cautiousness: *being guarded, careful and using right timing to accomplish your goals.*

This is in contrast to **rashness**: *acting hastily without careful thought or consideration.*

How did Jesus show cautiousness?

Chapter Fifteen

How does Jesus want to be a shepherd to His followers?

How can you tell that Jesus was authoring faith in Prisha?

How was Jesus bearing fruit in Ember?

How did hatred and bitterness affect Kolapeka?

How would you describe the attitudes of the two sisters? Are their attitudes going to helpful to their situation?

Character Qualities to Identify:

Ember tried to use **persuasiveness** to encourage the girls to submit to their captors.

Persuasiveness: *using argument and entreaty to move a person to follow an undesirable course of action.*

This is in contrast to **contentiousness**: *quarrelsome, argumentative, tending toward strife.*

Name some ways in which Jesus showed persuasiveness?

____

Chapter Sixteen

Why did Prisha say that Susanna's future was going to be hard?

How do our attitudes affect our circumstances?

Joseph in the Bible was sold as a slave. How did his attitudes affect his circumstances?

How would you describe Rebecca's attitude about washing the clothes?

What did Ember teach the girl about accomplishing a hard task?

What was Ember's reason for helping the spoiled girl with her chore?

Character Qualities to Identify:

Ember had to show **forbearance** in order to help Rebecca.

Forbearance: *patient self-control, restraint and tolerance of others with whom you disagree.*

This is in contrast with **impatience**: *dislike of anything that causes delay or annoyance.*

How did Jesus show forbearance?

Chapter Seventeen

What good changes happened in Rebecca?

Why do you think these changes occurred in the younger sister?

How can you tell that God was drawing Rebecca to Himself?

As Ember explained to Rebecca how to face hardships like slavery, what did she say was her job and what was God's job?

What happens in our lives when we try to do God's job?

Character Qualities to Identify:

As Rebecca began trusting more in Jesus, she learned to face her troubles with **contentment**.

Contentment: *realizing that God has provided all that I need for that moment.*

This is in contrast with **consternation:** *being gripped by dread, fear, and anxiousness*

How did Jesus show contentment?

Chapter Eighteen

In your opinion, what will be the most wonderful thing about going to heaven?

What would heaven be like if Jesus was not there?

Why do you think Jesus refers to the earth as the "world of shadows"?

If a good judgment is to be given about a person or situation, what are some important things to consider before making a final decision?

Character Qualities to Identify:

Ember showed **justice** when she gave her verdict against the bunnies.

Justice: *a righteous concern for is right, peaceful, and respectful for all people.*

This is in contrast to **partiality** and **prejudice:** *preconceived opinions that disregard the value or others and their rights.*

How did Jesus show justice when He was on the Earth?

—

Chapter Nineteen

When Jesus asked Ember to look at life through His eyes instead of hers, what did He mean?

How can Jesus be everything we need?

Name some of the things in scripture that Jesus says He is for us? (*John 10:7, 11; John 11:25; John 14:6*)

How much does Jesus love us?

What did you learn in this chapter about what it means to belong to Jesus?

Character Qualities to Identify:

Ember showed **flexibility** by submitting to Jesus's desire for her to return to earth when she really wanted to stay in heaven.

Flexibility: *a willingness to change one's plans or ideas to benefit others.*

This is in contrast to **resistance**: *refusing to accept or comply with the desires of another.*

How did Jesus show flexibility?

Chapter Twenty

In this chapter, how would you describe Susanna's character?

How would you describe Rebecca's character?

How do you account for the difference between the two sisters?

What good qualities do you see Prisha showing?

Rebecca told her angry sister about one of the promises of Jesus to His followers. Can you think of other promises Jesus made to His disciples? (*Matthew 6:33; Matthew 7:7; Matthew 11:28-30*)

Character Qualities to Identify:

When Ember let Susanna know how she felt and why she gave the older sister the bread, Ember showed **transparency**.

Transparency: *honest openness, living a life that has no hidden agendas or motives.*

This is in contrast to being **questionable**: *having a suspicious character that is doubtful of honesty.*

How did Jesus show transparency?

Chapter Twenty-One

What does it say about Ember that Prisha sent her to treat the sick girl?

What do you think Ember had done to build that level of trust in Prisha?

What character qualities did Ember show in her examination of the sick girl?

How did Jesus show compassion for both Rayford and Susanna when He had Ember stop the older girl from hitting the trapper in the head with the ax?

Ember and Prisha showed genuine affection for each other as they parted. How do you explain this dramatic change in their relationship from when they first met?

Character Qualities to Identify:

Ember showed **alertness** when she examined the sick girl and found the infected ears.

Alertness: *a high degree of sensory awareness such as being watchful for danger and prompt to respond.*

This is in contrast to **carelessness**: *failure to give sufficient attention to avoid causing harm or errors.*

How did Jesus show alertness?

Chapter Twenty-Two

What good character qualities did Ember show as she tried to escape the Shawnee?

What poor qualities did Susanna show?

What do you think motivated Susanna to mistreat her sister so badly?

Where do bad attitudes, selfishness, and meanness come from?

What effect does having bad character qualities like Susanna's have on those people you are around?

Character Qualities to Identify:

Ember showed **perceptiveness** in coming up with a way to escape the Shawnee war party.

Perceptiveness: *keen insight and understanding; the ability to analyze a problem and arrive at a solution.*

This is in contrast to **obliviousness**: *a lack of awareness of what is happening around you, making it impossible to make wise decisions.*

How did Jesus show perceptiveness?

____

Chapter Twenty-Three

In what way did Ember use wisdom rather than her emotions to make decisions to find their way through the cave?

Why is it always better to make decisions based on wisdom and knowledge rather than how you feel about something?

Compare Susanna's character with Ember's character in this chapter.

What good qualities did Ember show when she risked her life to save Susanna?

When we have opportunities to help people who dislike or mistreat us, how does Jesus want us to view them? What does Jesus think they are worth?

Character Qualities to Identify:

Ember showed **tolerance** for Susanna when she risked her life to save the older girl.

Tolerance: *the* willingness *to endure unpleasantness for the purpose of accomplishing what is needed.*

This is in contrast to **prejudice**: *being biased against someone because of a preconceived opinion.*

How did Jesus show tolerance?

Chapter Twenty-Four

What did Ember mean when she said, "the fool is the person who asks for God's help and then refuses to use what He provides"? What spiritual attributes did Ember show here?

How did Jesus reveal Himself to Ember in this chapter?

What do you think Satan is trying to do through Susanna during the escape?

What should our response be when we see Satan at work against us?

What promises has Jesus made that will give us encouragement when facing the attacks and temptations of the enemy? (*I Corinthians 10:13; Hebrews 13:5; Psalm 50:15*)

Character Qualities to Identify:

Rebecca showed **steadfastness** in her friendship and loyalty to Ember.

Steadfastness: *unwavering loyalty and faithful allegiance.*

This is in contrast to **treachery**: *dishonesty and a betrayal of trust.*

How does Jesus show steadfastness?

Chapter Twenty-Five

What are some of the sins Susanna committed in betraying her sister and Ember?

Why is betrayal so hard on those who have been betrayed?

What does it say about you if you are willing to betray those who trust you?

Why is betrayal especially hard to forgive?

Jesus was betrayed by Judas and Peter. When confronted with their sin, how did these two men respond? How did Jesus respond to their betrayal?

Character Qualities to Identify:

Susanna showed no **self-control** when it came to getting what she wanted.

Self-Control: *applying discipline and restraint over your desires, emotions, and behaviors in order to accomplish what is good.*

This is in contrast to **indulgence**: *the unrestrained pursuit of your own selfish desires and wants.*

How did Jesus show self-control?

––––––––––––––––––––––––––

Chapter Twenty-Six

What are consequences of living for yourself?

What did Ember mean when she said, 'when you live for yourself, it always ends badly'? Do you agree?

How does seeing Jesus as He really is help us to get rid of our dependence on self?

In what ways did Ember show wisdom as she directed the escape?

How did Ember show wisdom in coming up with a creative way for Rebecca and her to defend themselves?

If you trust in Jesus, why should prayer always be your first response to trials and problems?

Character Qualities to Identify:

During the course of their escape, Ember grew in **leadership**.

Leadership: *using wisdom and experience to direct and manage others to most effectively achieve important goals.*

This is in contrast to **impotence**: *the inability to take effective action, helplessness.*

How did Jesus show Leadership?

Chapter Twenty-Seven

As the girls painfully worked the soreness out of their arms by slinging more rocks, what good character qualities did they show?

Ember demonstrated bravery when she opposed the hunter who was tracking them. Does being brave mean that you are not afraid?

How does God want us to respond to fear? (*Psalm 56:3; John 14:1; Isaiah 41:10*)

How did God answer the girls' prayers in this chapter?

Character Qualities to Identify:

When they realized the nearness of danger, the girls showed **preparedness** by having their weapons ready for instant use.

Preparedness: *being alert and ready to effectively meet what is to come.*

This is in contrast to **negligence**: *failure to use reasonable care or precaution resulting in damage or injury to another.*

In what ways did Jesus demonstrate preparedness?

Chapter Twenty-Eight

When a person like Rayford spends his or her life telling lies and being dishonest, what do you predict about that person's future?

When the temptation is strong to lie, what does it take to tell the truth?

How important is it to be known as a person who always tells the truth?

What are the consequences of being someone who is not trustworthy?

What good character qualities did Will Hackett use in his encounter with the Shawnee?

Character Qualities to Identify:

Dirt, Will, and Grey Fox showed **generosity** by sharing their food and time to help the girls.

Generosity: *realizing that God owns all that I possess and being willing to let Him use it as He chooses.*

This is in contrast to **stinginess**: *unwillingness to share, give or spend what you have on anyone but yourself.*

How did Jesus show generosity on Earth? Does Jesus show generosity now?

Chapter Twenty-Nine

Rayford is a smart man, but how did Satan use Rayford's intelligence?

How did Grey Fox show both compassion and persuasiveness to help Dirt's injured leg?

What character qualities did Ember show as she cared for Dirt's leg?

Both Grey Fox and Dirt Gurley were followers of Jesus. Why do you think Grey Fox listened to what Ember said about Jesus, but Dirt was reluctant to?

Do you know of a time when God tried to direct you and you wouldn't listen?

When we make mistakes, disregard God's will, or sin, how does that affect God's love for us? (*Lamentations 3:22-23; Romans 5:8; Ephesians 2:4*)

Character Qualities to Identify:

Grey Fox expressed **benevolence** by showing concern for Dirt's injury.

Benevolence: *expressing good will and kindness to those in need.*

This is in contrast to being **inconsiderate**: *thoughtlessly causing hurt or inconvenience to others.*

How did Jesus show benevolence?

Chapter Thirty

What character qualities did William Hackett show when he took time to protect his loaded rifle from the rain?

What was the first thing William did when he realized that his friends were headed for the dangerous cliffs?

What character qualities did Grey Fox use to get them down the dangerous climb to the waterfall?

How can a follower of Jesus have peace in his heart in the middle of a scary situation? From where does that kind of peace come. (*John 14:27; Philippians 4:6-7*)

Character Qualities to Identify:

Because his life depended on it, William fought his enemy with **tenaciousness**:

Tenaciousness: *the quality of being determined to do or achieve something; firmness of purpose.*

This is in contrast to **faintheartedness**: *fearful or timid in the face of a challenging situation.*

How did Jesus show tenaciousness?

Chapter Thirty-One

When you are in the middle of a dangerous and scary situation, what do you need to do in order to make good decisions? How can you avoid the crippling effects of fear?

What character qualities did Dirt and Grey Fox show as they risked their lives to save the girls?

Where does the courage to risk your life for someone else come from?

What kind of courage did it take for Jesus to go through the cross for us?

What did Grey Fox say was his reason for risking his life to save Rebecca?

What good character qualities did Rebecca show as she faced the Shawnee warriors charging to kill Grey fox and capture her?

Character Qualities to Identify:

Rebecca showed **acuity** when she used Grey Fox's bullets as ammunition for her sling.

Acuity: *the ability to think clearly enough to understand a situation and to come up with creative solutions.*

This is in contrast to **obtuseness**: *the lack of ability to understand, mentally dull.*

How did Jesus show acuity?

Chapter Thirty-Two

Why does a follower of Jesus not need to fear death?

What good character qualities did William show as he prepared to fight to the death to save Dirt?

How did Ember show that she was trusting in Jesus even as she was being pursued by Rayford?

Why do you suspect that Rayford was so scared of Jesus and the Bible?

How is the fear of death and judgment taken away when a person trusts in Jesus? (*I John 4:18; Romans 8:1; I John 1:5-2:2*)

Character Qualities to Identify:

William showed **mercifulness** when he refused to shoot at the escaping Shawnee.

Mercifulness: *being kind, lenient, or compassionate toward those who don't deserve it.*

This is in contrast to being **cruel**: *willfully causing pain or suffering to others with no concern for them.*

How did Jesus show mercifulness?

Chapter Thirty-Three

Why was it both wise and caring to stay a few days by the river before traveling to Larkinboro?

What does Rebecca's comment about baptism tell you about her commitment to Jesus?

What good character quality or qualities did Grey Fox show as he deflected Rebecca's praise for how he saved her and instead praised her for how Rebecca had saved him?

Why is harboring pride a harmful thing?

How does God feel about pride in us? (*James 4:6; I Peter 5:5-6; Proverbs 16:18*)

Character Qualities to Identify:

Grey Fox showed **assiduousness** by refusing to give up until he had started the fire.

Assiduousness: *the unrelenting commitment to accomplishing a goal.*

This is in contrast to being **idle**: *a lazy person who avoids difficult tasks.*

How did Jesus show assiduousness?

Chapter Thirty-Four

What are some of the character qualities Will and Grey Fox needed to scout the enemies' camps successfully?

After having their parents killed and their experience as Shawnee slaves, what kind of help might Ember and Rebecca need to learn to live a normal life?

How does God want us to feel toward and respond to those He puts in our lives who have experienced hardship and tragedy?

How are the Middlebrook and Leavenworth families treating Ember and Rebecca like Jesus would?

Character Qualities to Identify:

By inviting the orphaned girls to live with them, the Middlebrook and Leavenworth families showed **hospitality**.

Hospitality: *kindness and friendliness to guests, visitors, and strangers.*

This is in contrast to **aloofness**: *remoteness, indifference, or standoffishness.*

How did Jesus show hospitality?

About the Author

Alan Harris is a retired veterinarian living near Columbia, South Carolina, where he and Valerie, his wife of over forty years, make their home. They have six children whom they homeschooled for twenty-seven years, a growing host of beautiful grandchildren, whom they adore...and a pug.

Alan was motivated to write when he desired to share an exciting story with his children. He did not want to just entertain them, but to also teach them important character and spiritual lessons. It became clear that the tale needed to be very suspenseful, and the characters had to be engaging and fun, in order to keep his children interested. The results were *The Tales of Larkin* series, which has five books. You can find out more about them as well as how to use them to teach at **StoriesChangeHearts.com**.

In searching for other subjects about which to write, Alan came up with *The Flintlock Sagas* series. <u>The Maker's Medicine Girl</u> is the second book in that new series and is a story dedicated to girls who love God and an exciting story. As in all of Harris's stories, he included plenty of adventure, laugh-out loud humor, and abundant opportunities to learn character and spiritual lessons.

It is Alan's prayer that his new series, *The Flintlock Sagas*, and this second book in that series, <u>The Maker's Medicine Girl</u>, will not only entertain his readers, but also help them grow in godly character and draw them closer to God the Father and His Son, King Jesus.

Book 5 **Fiery Trials** - This picks up the continuing story of Hawthorn and his friends. Two years have passed since the end of book 3 and the jealous Shaman have an opportunity to finally destroy the followers of Jehesus. Devastating disease and an unimaginable disaster must be faces if the King's followers are to survive.

The Flintlock Sagas

Book 1 **The Young Frontiersman** - Young William Hackett is a part of a group of pioneers starting a new life in the wilderness of Kentucky in the 1770's. They share constant peril, as well as facing the threat of attack by savages stirred up by British agents. Set during the Revolutionary War the exciting story demonstrates God's faithfulness to us, whether the battles we face are against physical enemies or spiritual ones.

Keep up with Alan Harris, his future works in *The Flintlock Sagas*, and his first series, *The Tales of Larkin* at **www.StoriesChangeHearts.com**.

If you wish to contact Alan you can e-mail him at **StoriesChangeHearts@gmail.com**.